MAN HANDLE

ON A MANHUNT
BOOK 6

VANESSA VALE

Man Handle by Vanessa Vale

Copyright © 2023 by Bridger Media

Cover design: Sarah Hansen/Okay Creations

Cover graphic: Deposit Photos: dafnachka

What happened to my life? One minute I'm just a single dad and fire chief. The next, I'm Mr. January.

That's right, Georgia from Georgia's been hired to organize the annual fundraiser. The former pageant queen's not satisfied with a chili dinner. No. She came up with the crazy idea of a firefighter calendar. With puppies and kittens.

The department's gone crazy over the idea. And her. So has my six-year old because he thinks she's shown up to be his new mom. For that to happen, she has to be mine. Oh, I want her. She's gorgeous. Sassy. Smart. But Georgia is only here for a job and the only thing worse than you getting your heart broken? Is her breaking your kid's.

PREQUEL

MAC

"Have a good Christmas, bud?" I asked Andy, dropping down onto his bed beside him. It had been a long day, and I was ready for the couch, quiet, and the football game. Something hard poked me in the ass. I lifted to reach beneath the covers and found the action figure he'd gotten, then tossed it to the bottom of his bed.

"Hey! He's sleeping with me!" Andy said, offended by my disregard that only a six-year-old could muster.

I reached for the half human, half lizard and set it carefully on the pillow beside Andy's head.

"There." Pulling up the covers with dinosaurs on them, I tucked them beneath his pajama-clad arms. "So? Good holiday?"

He nodded, but didn't look me in the eye.

"I asked Santa for something, and it didn't come," he admitted in a soft voice.

I thought through the list he'd given me right after Thanksgiving, the one he'd sat at the kitchen table and diligently worked on, sounding out the words as he went. Bike, books, baseball mitt. All the B's it seemed. Only the baseball mitt came from Santa, not wanting him to ever think the big guy handed out expensive presents. But I thought his top wants had been met.

"Oh?" I asked.

"Yeah."

"I saw your list, bud, and I'd say you're one lucky kid. Plus, you're going with Grumpy to the big amusement park in California this spring."

He nodded, raised his hand to pick his nose, then eyed me quickly as he remembered he shouldn't and tucked it back under the covers.

"Yeah, that's going to be awesome!" He wiggled with excitement. "I can't wait to see Grumpy throw up on the saucer ride."

Out of all the things he could say about a weekend with his grandfather at an amusement park, this wasn't what I expected. My mouth tipped up imagining my father getting sick from too much spinning.

"No, Daddy. I asked Santa for a new mom."

My smile slipped.

Holy. Shit. This was a big deal. One of those I-need-a-child-psychologist moments. What did I say to a kid whose mother was my drug addicted sister who'd stayed clean long enough to have him–thank fuck–and linger for six weeks before dumping her newborn with me? She bailed on her baby so she could go off and do... I had no idea what.

"I don't think a new mom would fit down the chimney," I told him, hoping to make light of a serious situation. I couldn't get Tracy to get her shit together enough to want to stay, nor come back to Hunter Valley. Hell, after all this time, I wasn't sure if I wanted her to. Only if she was clean and sober.

Andy was mine now. On paper and in my heart. I might be his uncle, but he was my son.

As I hoped, Andy grinned. A bottom tooth was missing, and it was only a matter of time before he looked like a Jack O' Lantern. "That's silly. Moms come through the front door. And make cookies. And smell nice."

"Women do smell nice," I admitted. It'd been a long time since I got close enough to appreciate a woman's... cookie.

Andy turned to his side, pulling his woobie, his small blanket he always slept with, out from under the covers to tuck beneath his chin.

"Do you think he sent my new mom to some other boy or girl?" he asked, his small voice tinged with worry.

"You watched a bunch of holiday movies this month. Did you see Santa ever pack a person into his big bag?"

He shook his head. "No, only toys."

I had no idea what else to say. In order for Andy to get a mom, that meant I had to meet, find, fall in love and want to keep a woman.

A woman who smelled nice and whose cookie I wanted to eat for the rest of my life.

"So..." he began, breaking me from my naughty list thoughts. "Maybe Santa's just slow. Maybe sometimes it takes a while. Just like pooping."

I grinned, leaning down and kissing his forehead. "Yeah, bud. Sometimes it takes a while."

1

MAC

FOUR MONTHS later

ANDY RAN out of the secure area of the airport with the biggest grin on his face, his little backpack bobbing. "Dad!" he shouted.

My father followed him at a more sedate pace, smiling at the eager reunion.

I leaned down and scooped Andy up into my arms. "Hey, bud. Did you have fun? See Mickey?"

He nodded enthusiastically, then pointed to the hat on his head, the one with the big black ears. "I did. And Pluto and Goofy."

"Wow."

"We ate chicken nuggets shaped like Mickey, rode on an old train, a monotrain and a big boat."

"A monotrain?"

"Monorail," my dad corrected as he joined us.

"Yeah, that thing. It was really cool. There were fireworks and a parade and the haunted house which made Grumpy really scared but I held his hand in the spooky elevator and–"

I expected the excited recount, but he didn't even take a breath. "All that? Did Grumpy throw up on the teacup ride?"

"I didn't." Dad said with a puffed chest, but then looked a little sheepish. "*Barely.*"

I turned. "Come on, let's go see if your suitcase is here yet."

Andy wiggled in my hold and I put him down. "Not yet. We need to wait."

I frowned down at him. "Wait?"

"Yeah, we have to wait for her. She was sitting next to us and she's very nice." He came close, put his hands around his mouth and whispered. "She's pretty, too."

"You made a friend on the plane?"

I looked to Dad for guidance and he rolled his eyes, although he still smiled, which meant he was being indulgent.

"Yeah. Not just a friend. More than a friend." Andy

turned and looked down the hallway that brought incoming passengers from the secure side of the airport. "There. That's her!"

I looked up and... if I were a cartoon character, my eyeballs would pop out of my head. They'd turn into hearts and little birdies would be chirping. An anvil would fall next.

Andy's new friend wasn't a kid. She was *all* woman and holy shit, she was beautiful. Not girl-next-door pretty, but stunning. Everything about her was perfect. From the top of her carefully styled dark hair to her heeled boots. Dark eyes, a pert nose, high cheekbones, full lips. She was... breathtaking. Dressed casually in black pants, a white blouse and jean jacket didn't hide that she was soft and curvy. A hot pink scarf of the softest and fluffiest yarn was around her neck. Silver earrings dangled. She screamed high maintenance and definitely not a Hunter Valley local.

She just got off a plane, you dumbass!

"Miss Georgia!" Andy called and waved his little hand as if he was seeing Minnie Mouse in the theme park parade.

The woman's face lit up at the sight of Andy and she went right to him, wheeling her pale pink carry-on. Holy hell, that smile. I wanted that aimed at me.

"There's my friend," she said, her voice soft and kind.

"I knew I couldn't get lost in the big ol' airport if y'all were here."

He nodded, completely under her thrall. I could relate.

"The circle thing for the suitcases is over there." He pointed in the direction of baggage claim.

I couldn't stop staring, taking in every inch of her.

Dad cleared his throat.

I stared some more.

"Mac," he whispered. "Close your mouth."

I shook myself out of the female-induced haze I was in and snapped my mouth shut. Licked my lip because it was possible I drooled.

Dad chuckled as Andy and the woman he called Georgia approached.

"Dad, she sat beside me on the plane. She likes ginger ale and gave me her bag of peanuts."

I nodded and took in Georgia up close. Responding to medical emergencies as part of my job, I could size someone up quickly. My expert eye said she was in her thirties. Five-nine. A hundred sixty pounds. She wasn't a skinny little thing, but that worked for me. My friends were finding their women, and they were all tiny. Thin. To me, who was definitely rough around the edges, breakable.

I wanted a curvy woman I could hold onto. Sink into. Grab. Man handle.

Georgia? She didn't seem breakable and I definitely wanted to get my hands on her.

She wore makeup, but it was applied subtly. Her mouth was a soft, kissable pink and shiny. Her dark lashes were long and... fuck, I could smell her perfume. Something soft and flowery and feminine.

She didn't look like the kind of woman who perspired or changed her own oil or hiked up a mountain or got her hands dirty. I doubt she shoveled her walkway. Or even owned a shovel. From her pale pink nail polish to her glossy curls tumbling artfully over her shoulders, she screamed high maintenance.

In comparison, what was I? Low maintenance. Hell, I was *no* maintenance. I had on my sturdy leather boots, which I wore when on shift or running errands, jeans and black t-shirt. For once, the house had been quiet this weekend and earlier, I'd lounged on the couch and watched a basketball game on TV, although I fell asleep sometime during the second period.

Because of that surprise nap, I'd rushed out of the house to get to the airport. I sure as fuck wasn't prepared to meet a gorgeous woman. Hell, when was I?

I was a single dad. The Hunter Valley fire chief who lived as much at the station as I did at home. There was always grease or dirt under my nails. I had calluses on my palms. The disposal needed to be replaced in the kitchen. The wall I took down to the dining room patched and painted. I should've gone to the dentist six months ago. My hair was an inch past needing a trim. I skipped shaving this morning. And yesterday morning.

I wanted to run home, get cleaned up–if I had any clean clothes to change into because I only got one load into the washer this weekend–comb my hair and track down some flowers and come back and hand them to her. Then bend her over the hood of my car in short-term parking and muss her all up and get her to scream my name.

"Dad?"

I shook my head, realized I was staring even more, then offered her a smile. "Hey. I'm Mac, Andy's dad." *And the guy who was having very filthy thoughts about you.*

"Georgia Lee Gantry."

Her hand–with nails painted pale pink–was small in mine. Tiny. Soft. Warm. And I didn't want to let go.

"Thanks for sharing your peanuts with Andy," I replied.

She laughed, soft and light. Had I mentioned she appeared soft all over? Or what I could see. I wanted to strip off all those ironed and freshly laundered clothes and see if the rest of her was, too.

I'd bet two months of engine washing that she had on pretty lingerie that matched. Yellow lace. No. Lavender satin.

Fuck, me. Cool satin against those full tits and spank-able ass?

"Dad?" Andy asked again.

I looked down at him. When she tugged her hand, I realized I was still holding it. I let go, ran mine over my unruly hair.

I cleared my throat. "What, bud?"

"I was right. Sometimes it takes a while. And you were right. She doesn't come down the chimney, she comes on a plane."

"Yes, she came on your plane from Denver," I told him.

Andy shook his head and gave me an eye roll that I had a feeling was only going to get perfected as he got older. "Miss Georgia's it, Dad."

"It?" I asked. Me, Dad and Georgia eyed him. "Yeah. My new mom!"

2

GEORGIA

OH MY STARS. Those sweet, ruthless words.

"Honey–"

"What the–"

A deep bark of laughter.

All of it happened at once as all three of us grownups stared at Andy and reacted at once. The little boy was so eager. So earnest. His little face was lit from within with excitement and pure joy.

About me being his mom.

Me. His mom.

So bittersweet. So perfect. Yet, the little guy wasn't mine. No way. Some other woman had the privilege of being his mom. Of being the Tooth Fairy and slipping coins under his pillow... frequently lately since he didn't have any top teeth. Of trying to keep that little cowlick that popped up on the back of his head down for at least five minutes. Or answering all of his questions. I sat next to him and his grandfather–who'd introduced himself as Drew–on the flight up from Denver and I didn't think the little boy had stopped talking once. Not even when he ate the in-flight peanuts. It hadn't been bothersome; it had been adorable.

If I was his mom, I'd get little boy hugs. I'd take him to see Mickey. And be called *Mommy*.

And I'd be with his Dad...

Mac.

He was... wow. Like insanely good looking and I couldn't stop eyeing him. He was different than any man in Calhan–or the entire state of Georgia–I ever met. Completely different than Art, my ex, who wore seer-sucker suits like a Southern gentleman and spent more time at his private country club playing golf than he did in his office. Or the green *was* his office, making big deals and schmoozing clients on the back nine. Too focused on his career to make a family with me. The key words being... with me.

No. No thoughts about Art! That was why I was two time zones away at a new job I wasn't sure I was even qualified for with my cheeks hot with embarrassment at Andy's statement that I was his new mom.

"Son, no. This nice lady isn't your new mom," Mac said gently, setting his hand on Andy's little shoulder and ruffling his hair. "She's probably got a husband and a boy or girl of her own."

My smile slipped, but only briefly because those words were my biggest trigger. No husband. No boy or girl. So instead of wallowing, I turned my smile up to full wattage as trained. Mac wasn't trying to be hurtful. He didn't even know me.

"Nope. No family," I said, hoping they couldn't hear the wistfulness and hurt over the loudspeaker message about not leaving bags unattended.

"Course she's my new mom!" Andy said, undeterred. "She's just what I asked Santa for. She's nice and she listens to me, and she said she likes dogs and French fries."

I did like French fries. The size of my clothes and my mother were constant reminders of that. With ranch dressing.

"If liking French fries was all it takes to be your mom, you'd have half the women in town tucking you in," Mac replied.

Andy ignored him and came over and took my hand. Looked up at me. I couldn't miss the resemblance he had with his father now that they were side by side. Same dark hair. Same chocolate eyes. "Come on, Miss Georgia. I'll show you where you can get your suitcase. It spins round and round on the care-sell. But you can't sit on it no matter how much fun it looks, or you'll get in trouble."

I glanced at Mac. His intense eyes met mine, then roved over my face, settled on my lips.

God, he was handsome. I wasn't a small woman, but he still had a few inches on me. He was fit. Solid. Sturdy, based on the way his black t-shirt stretched across his muscular chest and biceps. Had it shrunk or did he buy them small to have a shrink-fit look? His dark hair was unruly and tousled. I had to wonder if he'd driven with his windows down or if he never combed it this morning.

And... he had a mustache. A mustache that would probably be soft against my skin when he kissed me. Lordy, it looked good on him along with the whiskers that covered his square jaw. This close I could see a few flecks of gray.

He looked like he was the kind of man who had more important things to do than primp in front of a mirror. From the two minutes I knew him, he seemed like the get up, shower and go kind of man. That he didn't take stock in appearances, that actions were what mattered.

I forced my eyes away from Mac because of Andy's tug on my hand.

"Such a gentleman," I praised Andy. "Show where to find my bag." I let him lead me over to the carousel, although the bags hadn't arrived yet. I squatted down in front of him. "I am so glad we met on the plane." With a soft smile, I continued, "I can't be your mom, sweetie, but I would really like to be your friend."

"Why can't you be my mom?" he asked, cocking his head to the side. He had a drink stain on his shirt and his shoelace was untied.

"Because you already have one," I countered.

Out of the corner of my eye, Mac and Drew worked their way around the other passengers toward us.

Andy shook his head. "No, I don't."

The carousel alarm blared once, then again, then the belt began to move. The suitcases started to appear.

"Oh." My gaze flicked to Mac.

He was single. A single dad. With bulging biceps, a slightly crooked nose and–

"Miss Georgia didn't fly here to be your new mom," Mac told him, as if knowing exactly what we'd been talking about.

I sighed, thankful he was taking over. I didn't want to hurt the little boy's feelings.

Drew laughed again. I glanced his way, and he seemed amused by this interaction. He and I hadn't spoken much on the plane since Andy had chattered away. But I learned the two of them were returning from California from a grandfather/grandson weekend trip and was probably thrilled to let Mac take over.

The boy seemed to have endless energy.

"That's right. I'm here for work," I added.

Mac studied me, then nodded.

"But–" Andy looked between me and his father, confusion in his eyes.

Mac shook his head and pointed. "Go watch for Grumpy's bag. Holler when you see it."

Grumpy. Andy had called his grandfather that a few times on the plane, but the older man was far from a grump.

"Ladies first, though," Andy said. "You always say I need to have shiv-ree and be a gentleman. To show girls how special they are by taking care of them. Except Mabel Drumphries." He scrunched up his face as if he smelled something bad. "She likes to cut in line on the way to recess and isn't getting any shiv-ree from me."

I bit my lip to not laugh.

"Chivalry," Mac corrected. "And yes, you can be a gentleman and help Georgia get her bag, too."

"What color do y'all think it is?" I asked him–Andy, not Mac.

His little brow furrowed as he studied me. "Pink! Like your other bag."

"That's right. Pink's my favorite color."

"After you help her with her suitcase and we get Grumpy's, then we will say goodbye to Georgia and let her go do her work."

Andy's little shoulders slumped. "Okay," he said,

drawing out the word for about three seconds, then ran over to the conveyor belt, although with a lot less enthusiasm than before.

"Sorry about that," Mac said, running a hand over his head, messing up his hair some more. "He's been a little obsessed with this mom thing for a while now."

I waved my hand. "It's–"

"Here's the pink suitcase!" Andy shouted, loud enough for everyone from the ticket kiosks to the rental car counters to hear.

Mac winced and Drew chuckled again.

We turned at the same time, saw Andy tugging on my bag as it moved down the conveyor belt.

"Oh no!" I cried, noticing immediately that the bag's zipper wasn't closed, and bits of clothes dangled out of the opening as if a baggage handler had flipped the top shut. It looked like an omelet where all the fillings spilled out the sides. Lord, was that a bra strap?

"Shit," Mac muttered, rushing beside me before Andy could–

Too late.

With all his little boy might, Andy tugged my huge suitcase off the carousel, and it dropped onto the hard floor, popping open, my clothes falling every which way.

I dropped to my knees in front of it and quickly grabbed my clothes that were now strewn about. Tops, sweaters, a boot. A purple bra.

"Are those girl's underpants?" Andy asked, pointing. "How come yours have all that lacy stuff? Don't you have any with fire trucks on them? Mine have fire trucks because I want to be a fireman like– Hey! You brought a toy. Is that a submarine for when you take a bath?"

Andy commented on my panties before I could stuff them away. And fuck me. He pointed out my big, purple, silicone vibrator. And yes, it was a toy, and I did use it when I took a bath.

3

MAC

I was right about the lavender, but she wore lace. Little scraps of lace that would barely cover those more-than-a-handful tits and plump ass.

And in case anyone in a fifteen-foot radius–or further with really good eyesight–didn't miss her huge vibrator, Andy's booming six-year-old voice let everyone know the gorgeous Georgia was packing.

Having my dick hard at the airport staring at this woman's belongings wasn't chivalrous. Or the least bit gentlemanly. At least she said she didn't have a family. That meant she was single, and I wasn't lusting after someone else's woman.

But I was a conscious, thirty-five-year-old man who

hadn't had sex in over a year. She was a woman who was thick enough not to break if I fucked her good and hard.

She quickly shoved her unmentionables back beneath a dark green sweater. She didn't need any help with that task, but the zipper on the suitcase was obviously broken and there was no way she could move the bag with it staying closed, so I undid my belt.

Georgia looked up at me with those dark eyes, now wide watching my hands on my belt buckle. Yeah, so much for not getting hard. The vision of her kneeling like this before me, me undoing my pants and getting my dick out for her to suck, was impossible not to imagine.

"Here," I said, pulling the leather from the loops with one tug.

4

GEORGIA

MAC WAS TAKING off his pants. TAKING. OFF. HIS. PANTS.

Yes, please. I needed to see that package! I wanted to see if he had fire trucks on his underwear and how big his submarine was. It had been too long. I hadn't had sex with Art in the last months of our marriage because he'd been *working too much*, also known as he'd been fucking Pam Buttermacher. And knocking her up.

Since then, I'd sworn off men, but that vow was now broken. My libido had returned with one slide of a belt from Mac's pants. Lord, I bet that biscuit was buttered and I wanted a taste.

"Okay," I said, my voice and brain not working in sync.

He held the long strap of leather up in front of me. His pants were still on. His thick bulge–yeah, long and blessedly thick–and muscular thighs remained hidden but couldn't be missed.

I licked my lips because I was hungry. Andy had eaten my bag of nuts. Speaking of nuts–

He cleared his throat. "My belt. Wrap it around your suitcase to keep it closed."

I blinked.

Oh. My suitcase. Shit.

MAC

"THAT WAS ONE HELL OF A WOMAN," Dad said from the passenger seat of my truck, the country music coming from the stereo was turned down to be background noise. We were halfway back to Hunter Valley.

Andy was conked out in the backseat, head tilted back, mouth open, Mickey hat crooked. He'd made it as far as the first stoplight after the airport before he fell asleep.

"Who?" I asked, adjusting the rearview mirror, which didn't really need it.

"Who?" he repeated. I could see out of the corner of my eye he was giving me a look. "Georgia. The pretty woman from the plane. I didn't miss the way you looked at her."

"She was pretty." Admitting anything else would be stupid.

He held up his hands. "Beautiful. *All* woman. None of that I-can-open-a-pickle-jar-on-my-own shit."

I laughed. "What?"

"You heard me."

"There's nothing wrong with a woman who opens her own pickle jar," I countered, defending women everywhere. For a second, I thought that was a euphemism for the vibrator in her suitcase and taking care of her own needs. But Dad actually meant opening a real pickle jar.

"Sure, they can. But why would they want to?" he asked.

Wait, maybe he was talking about the vibrator and self-pleasure after all.

"When Mom–"

Gah. No. No euphemism. NO.

"I know," I cut in, switching back to his original intent because I wasn't thinking about the memory of my mother and a vibrator at the same time. "Mom let you take care of her."

She died fifteen years ago. I missed the hell out of her. So did Dad, who'd spent his life taking care of her. Being a gentleman. Chivalrous. I couldn't help but smile that Andy had picked up on that and applied it to Georgia.

Mom had taken care of Dad in return, although he'd never say it. He hadn't even gone on a date since she passed, not interested in settling down again. Or, as he put it, never found a woman he liked to help with her pickle jar.

Me? I had a few serious relationships, but nothing that stuck. I wanted the love my parents had, but at my age, I was starting to wonder if it was ever going to happen. Sure, there were plenty of women in Hunter Valley who didn't mind a single dad. I had the baggage of a precocious first grader. And a dangerous job that took up a ton of my time. As fire chief, I was always on call and spent half my nights sleeping at the station. Andy wouldn't go without, but I wasn't rich. There was no retirement in my future or private jets at my disposal like some of my friends. What did I have to offer a woman besides my jar opening strength?

Hell, I couldn't even manage a trip to the barber lately.

"Exactly," Dad said, but I forgot what we were talking about. "You just need to find the right woman. You want someone who wants you. Needs you."

I turned my head, gave him a bored glance, then focused back on the road. "Of course, I want a woman who wants me."

"I don't mean your dick. I mean your heart."

I peeked in the rearview mirror at Andy, who was out cold.

"After the weekend we had, he won't wake up until morning."

The sun was just setting, which meant the end of another full day for the little guy, so Dad was probably right.

"I'm surprised you're still conscious." Dad wasn't all that old. Only sixty-five. He was spry. Liked to keep busy. Fit, too. But two days at Disney with a six-year-old plus travel could wear anyone out.

He laughed. "I'm going to bed as soon as you drop me off. But you're redirecting."

I shrugged. "There's no reason to redirect. The woman who sat next to you is a pretty woman. I helped her with her bag."

The missing belt around my waist was proof of that.

He didn't say anything, so I pushed on. I wasn't sure if I was telling this to him or to myself. "Ten minutes at the airport doesn't make a relationship. My heart didn't have time to get involved." Nor my dick.

I was stating a fact, but it was also a shame. I had no idea I had a thing for full-sized, high maintenance women with a southern twang.

I never considered that watching a woman fuck herself with a purple dildo was a thing. Had I, like the younger guys at the station liked to say, had a kink unlocked? It was just hot as hell. Would Georgia use it tonight in her hotel room? Of course, she would. Why else would she pack it if not to use it?

Dad sighed. I shifted in my seat because my dick was still fucking hard.

"What?" I asked, knowing that sound had lots of meaning behind it.

"You need to date. Meet women. Get laid."

I gritted my teeth. We didn't talk about sex all that much and I was way too old for the birds and bees discussion. "I have a kid. A job with a crazy work schedule and the fundraiser coming up. I just got the first reservation for the rental over the garage. Arriving tonight sometime. A little too hard to get laid when I'm busy."

"No smart man is too busy for sex," he said.

I frowned because he was right. "You saying I'm stupid?"

"I'm saying... hell, I don't know what I'm saying. Andy's right. He needs a mom. You're doing an amazing job, son. Between the two of us, that kid knows he's loved. But he needs a woman in his life. Her love, which is different than what either of us can give him. Besides, he needs one to practice that chiv-ree on."

What Dad didn't say hung heavy in the air between us. Andy had a mother. Tracy. My sister, his daughter.

But she was no mom. She got hooked on drugs in college and could never kick them. Miraculously, she'd stayed clean during her pregnancy, but chose drugs over her own son a week after he was born. Over her family. She'd left Hunter Valley, and we hadn't seen or heard from her since. Andy needed a woman who'd stick. Who'd put him first.

"You're right. He does. I'm working on it," I muttered, flicking my blinker.

I saw him arch a gray brow as I turned right at the intersection.

"I'm well aware of your crazy life and I'm proud of what you've accomplished," he said.

Raising a kid.

Being fire chief.

I wasn't broke, but extra income only helped. We came up with the idea to convert the unused space over my unattached garage into a short-term rental. Hunter Valley was a vacation destination, and I was ready to cash in on that. It wasn't the new James Inn, that was for sure, but having guests stay–and pay–would help with Andy's college fund.

"Thanks," I said, meaning it. My dad's praise held value. "I couldn't do it without you." Like giving Andy a trip to see Mickey Mouse and friends.

He waved me off. "We're family."

He had his own house around the corner, but stayed

over when I worked my twenty-four hour shifts at the fire station, taking Andy to and from school, doing the laundry, grocery shopping and cooking. He was my man nanny. My manny, although I wouldn't dare call him that to his face. He was just Grumpy, what Andy started calling him instead of Grampy when first learning to talk.

"Crazy life or not, you might need to work on it a little harder. You need to find time for a woman."

"The *right* woman," I clarified. I was too old to fuck around, no matter what my dick told me.

"Too bad it won't be Georgia," he said. "I really liked her, and Andy sure had his heart set on her."

I was quiet as I turned down Dad's street, worried that Andy's obsession with having a mom was unhealthy. "Yeah. Andy has good taste. Did you learn anything about her on the flight?"

He eyed me. "I thought you weren't interested."

"I didn't say I wasn't interested, I said I wouldn't see her again."

He laughed. "Andy didn't give her too much chance to talk."

I could imagine.

"She's from some small town outside of Atlanta."

"Georgia from Georgia?"

"Yup. In Montana for work. No kids. Divorced."

"Andy asked her *that?*" I pulled into his driveway, put

my truck in park. Patches of snow lingered on the front lawn. Neighbors' lights were on. Everyone was having dinner or settling in for the night.

He shrugged and the corner of his mouth turned up in a smile.

"Sure did. One hell of a woman. Even if she doesn't have superheroes on her underwear."

I couldn't help but grin. He grinned back.

I shook my head because even after a short meeting, I felt a pang of disappointment at not seeing Georgia again. "Superheroes or lavender lace, she was only a beautiful woman at the airport. Nothing more. I won't see her again."

6

MAC

FUCK, was I wrong about that. Two hours later, the beautiful Georgia from Georgia, stood on my front porch.

7

GEORGIA

"MAC?" I asked, blinking at the sexy man standing in the doorway. The delicious scent of hot dogs wafted out from behind him making my mouth water. Or was it Mac himself that was so enticing? He hadn't changed since I saw him at the airport not two hours earlier. Nor had the fact that he'd seen my underwear on the baggage claim floor as well as my vibrator.

My vibrator! I was confident enough in my sexuality to use one, to pack one to accompany me on a work trip. But it had been safely tucked in my suitcase in complete privacy. Why didn't the small box of tampons tip out instead? Sure, that had been mortifying, but Andy pretty much shouted about my toy submarine.

While my attraction to the single dad with the nice father and adorable son had been undeniable, I couldn't wait to flee the airport and never see him again out of embarrassment alone.

Yet, not even two hours later, it seemed I was in front of him once more.

What were the chances?

Mac's eyes were probably as wide as mine. "Georgia? What are you–"

"I'm sorry, I must be mistaken," I said quickly, glancing around trying to figure out where I messed up. "I'm looking for Andrew MacKenzie."

Out of habit, I reached up to touch my hair and quickly lowered my hand. My hair was fine. I checked in the car mirror after I parked at the curb. Reapplied my lipstick, too.

I looked at the house number beside the door, then back at him. Yes, this was the place. Then why was he, of all people, answering the door? Although, if he was the one-man welcoming committee for every step of my trip, I shouldn't complain.

Except... he knew what my sex toy looked like. He knew I liked them big, vibrating and made of silicone. If my mother ever heard about the baggage claim fiasco... well, I didn't even want to think about how she'd react. Worse than the time I had the back of my plaid skirt tucked into my tights when I was five or the first pageant disaster. Or the second. She had a list of times I'd embarrassed her. It was long and it went way back.

Awareness lit his dark eyes. "That's me. Andrew MacKenzie, but I go by Mac. Too many Andrews in the family."

It didn't take me long to figure it out. "Right. Your dad's–"

"Drew," he replied.

"–and Andy's–"

"Andrew MacKenzie II."

"Well, Mac, I'm here for the carriage house?"

"The carriage house, right." He ran a hand over the back of his neck. "Well, that's what's listed online to sound fancy, but it's the apartment over the garage. Out back."

He thumbed over his shoulder in that general direction but kept his gaze on me.

"Oh. Good." But I didn't want to be a complete klutz. Twice. "Well. Um, I'm your renter."

If it was possible, he looked even more surprised. "You?"

I nodded. "Yeah, small world, huh?" I gave a little laugh and offered him my patented Georgia Lee Gantry pageant smile. "I'm here in Hunter Valley with James Corp for a stretch, so they, well, Bradley, put me up here."

"James Corp? Figure they'd put you up at their inn."

I shook my head. "No room. That place is booked solid."

"Good for them. I know the James brothers, Theo especially."

"I've never met them. I just started with the company." I'd never even been in the James Corp office in Denver. Bradley was my cousin and told me about the contract PR job here in Hunter Valley. Eager to get the hell out of Calhan... I submitted my resume. Amazingly, I got the job and now I was here for a few weeks helping out on a short-term assignment.

James Corp had offered up a resource on a local fundraiser, hoping an expert might be able to take the event from having successful results to being amazing. Every time I thought about it, I got nervous because *I* was supposed to be the expert. But Bradley knew me, knew my background and thought I was the woman for the job. I didn't argue with Bradley, HR who hired me, or the fact that it got me here.

Realizing I was frowning, I smoothed out my face. Mac might know the personal contents of my suitcase, but I wasn't giving him the sad details of my life. Like the fact that being in Montana was practically saving my life. Well, that might be a little drastic. Saving my mental sanity definitely. I'd stuck with a loser for too many years. Went along with him when he'd said he wasn't ready for kids. Strung me along until it was too late.

Now, I was divorced with a barely-ticking biological clock while Art was remarried with a baby on the way.

Him. A baby.

I guess I just didn't want one with you, he'd said, emphasizing the "you."

How did the song go? Me. I was the problem. It was ME.

Because Art was back in Calhan with his pregnant new wife picking out a minivan and taking birthing classes. I was in small town Montana alone with my vibrator, so I didn't have to live–even temporarily–with my mother a second longer.

He stared.

I stared back.

"Right," he said finally, snapping out of it. He grabbed keys from a glass dish on a side table and stepped outside, closing the door behind him. "Let's get you settled."

I stepped out of the way, then followed him down the driveway that ran along the side of the house. Calhan in April was full-on spring. Leaves on the trees. Flowers blooming. Sundresses and sandals. Here? The air was clean and crisp. Cold. Really cold. I could see my breath. There was even snow on the ground in places. The rental car agent advised me to get an SUV since snow didn't stop until the end of May. It hadn't even snowed once in Calhan this winter.

Hopefully, I packed the right clothes. I only brought one suitcase, and my wheeled carry on, and my huge purse, which for me was going light.

Mac's house was in what appeared to be the older part of town, close to Main Street. The house was two stories, a mix of stone and, from what I could see in the dark, light wood siding. Motion sensors had exterior lights coming on, illuminating our way to an unattached garage at the back corner of the lot. A tire swing hung from a large tree that probably shaded the entire back-yard in the summer. A deck was bare except for a large, manly grill by the back door. A pergola extended over it. I imagined it was a perfect place to hang out in the summer.

Mac stopped and I almost bumped into him. "Where's your luggage?"

"In the rental car," I said, thumbing over my shoulder.

Back at the airport, after I shoved everything back in, Mac had quickly shut my suitcase and wrapped his belt around it, buckling it closed. At the same time, Andy and his grandfather's bag appeared on the conveyor. With bags claimed and no reason to linger, we said our good-byes and parted ways. Andy offered one last look back and a little wave before I was left to get my rental car, find some dinner and make my way to Hunter Valley. I was due to start the public relations job in the morning and wanted to settle in.

I never imagined it would be over Mac's garage.

"Right."

I followed him up the outside staircase that was on the yard side of the garage, which had me enjoying the view of his very toned, very round butt on the way up.

Even though it was about forty degrees out, I wasn't cold. Who needed a coat to stay warm with that view?

He unlocked the door, pushed it open, reached in and flipped on the light switch.

"Go ahead in. I'll get your bags from your car."

He turned, squeezed past me on the narrow steps. I could feel the heat from his body and the lingering scent of soap or man or aftershave or... *him.* Yeah, not cold at all.

I stepped inside, took in the space. It was one large room with sloping ceiling on both sides. A king-sized bed took up most of the space. Across from it was a TV, set on a stand with an electric fireplace built in. An oak dresser was tucked in a corner and an overstuffed reading chair by the window that overlooked the backyard. A small kitchenette was by the door with a mini-fridge, sink, electric kettle and a microwave. There was a door that led to the bathroom. I could see the pedestal sink and a night light plugged in beside the mirror.

I doubted Mac was the decorator–because he didn't seem the type to put up a framed landscape photograph– but the room's colors were soft tans and navy. Masculine, but the small space was cozy and warm. It was really nice.

Mac's heavy footsteps signaled his way up the steps. My bags bumped into the doorframe as he came in, and he set them down off to the side.

He sighed, ran a hand over his hair. Caught his breath. "I'm not much of a welcoming committee. I admit, I'm new to this whole rental thing. You're my first guest, in fact. Towels are on the rack above the toilet. Thermostat is by the door. Oh, here's the switch for the fireplace."

He flipped it on the wall and the fake flames kicked on.

"That should heat this space better than the furnace if you need to make it warmer, but it's not too cold out now so I'm not sure if you'll use it."

The fireplace glowed in all its fake glory, but I could already feel the warmth the little fan was putting out and it didn't need any logs or cleanup. On, off. My kind of fire.

"This isn't *too cold*?" I questioned.

He grinned and my pussy clenched. Cold night, cozy room, huge bed. Fire. Hot man.

"Welcome to Montana."

Right. I was his guest, not his lover. I glanced around, then looked to him. "This is lovely. Thank you."

"The fireplace was Dad's idea," he said, as if trying to come up with something to say. "This was all boxes and junk, but we figured it might be a great way for some extra income."

"Smart."

"Yeah. As long as the guests aren't assholes." He winced, rubbed his neck. "Shit, not that you are."

I smirked. "No, not an asshole."

We were alone. No Andy. No father. Mac wasn't a huge man, but he made the place seem small. *I* felt small and we were making ridiculous small talk. It was him, me, a room with a big bed.

I mentally slapped myself because why would Mac want to carry me to the bed, press me into the soft bedding and make me shout Hallelujah and praise Jesus more than a Southern Baptist on a Sunday morning. If I lost a few pounds or hadn't shown him that I was so lonely and desperate for dick that I carried around a vibrator, maybe, just *maybe,* he'd have naughty thoughts about me.

"I'll, um, unpack and be sure to get your belt back to you," I said, finally looking away.

He grinned and just like that, my nipples hardened. He stepped closer.

Wait. Was he going to kiss me? Oh my stars in heaven.

Another step. I swallowed hard.

His gaze dropped to my mouth.

Lord, another step.

I licked my lips.

He raised his hand to cup my neck.

No, not to cup my neck. To dangle a keychain between us.

Oh. My pussy wept with shame and disappointment.

"Your key," he said, his voice gruff. "Unless you need help with anything else."

My mind went into the gutter. Yes, I had many things he could *help* with. Me out of my clothes, for one. Me with a man-made orgasm was another. He'd already seen the vibrator, so he knew my expectations when it came to dick size.

I was thirty-five. I wasn't sacrificing again after Art. No small dicks. No selfishness. I had to hope one of Mac's rules for being a gentleman was *ladies first*. Then he could give up being nice.

Sometimes a girl wanted a good pounding. Right? Hard. Rough.

His dark eyes held mine, then dropped to my mouth, eyeing it as if he wanted to kiss the lipstick right off. Lord have mercy, he was intense.

I swallowed. Hard. My panties were wet, and I couldn't help but squirm.

Maybe I took too long to reply. Maybe he wasn't referring to the different ways he could sexually satisfy me. Maybe he actually wanted to know if I needed help with anything else in the garage apartment.

Whichever option it was, I took too long because he said, "I go to work early so my dad will be here with Andy. He'll get him ready for school then drop him off. When Andy finds out in the morning you're staying here, be prepared. He'll probably want you to be his show-and-tell at school instead of the Mickey Mouse hat."

I wasn't worried about a six-year-old. Andy was sweet and bright and filled up the huge hole I had in my heart for a child of my own. It was his father who I thought was definite trouble.

Big, burly trouble.

8

GEORGIA

AFTER MAC LEFT and I got my hormones under control... okay, not under control at all, but at least I was away from that intense gaze and his potent pheromones, I unpacked, hanging up my clothes. There were only five hangers in the small closet, so it didn't take that long, but I had to lay everything else across every available surface so any wrinkles from the hasty repacking after the bag explosion at the airport would come out. I didn't find an iron, so I'd have to ask Mac sometime if he had one. Or buy one because it was my new goal to avoid him for the entire time I was in town. The only thing worse than having my hot new landlord/innkeeper see my panties and vibrator was if... well, I couldn't think of anything.

Then I went through my skin care routine, brushed my teeth, flossed, put in my night guard and climbed under the thick down comforter. I was plugging in my cell to recharge and saw Keely's text.

> Are you there yet? Did you get eaten by a bear? If so, as your BFF can I have your fake leopard fur jacket?

She dropped me at the airport this morning, so she must've been waiting for the right excuse–death by hungry wildlife–to inherit that coat.

> I'm here and in one piece.

Eaten by a bear? How about eaten out by Mac. I rolled my eyes at my naughty thoughts. The man was F. I. N. E. Fine. And I was a horny, single woman in the middle of a dry spell.

> I saw your momma at the Piggly Wiggly when I ran out to get more queso dip fixins.

I rolled my eyes and all sexy thoughts went away.

> What did she say?

> Nothing, I ducked into the feminine hygiene aisle. Figured since she's menopausal she might not head that way.

> Smart thinking.

> Sassy was with her. How does she get those curls so perfect?

Keely was referring to Sassy's hair. It was naturally curly but every day she straightened it, then went at it with a curling wand so instead of pretty, natural ringlets she had beach waves past her shoulders. It took her an hour. Every day.

> I'm fixin' to get you the hot iron for your birthday.

> Tommy and Sally Ann were with them. I swear they just came from a fashion shoot. Or church.

My nephew and niece were three and five. They always wore shirts with a collar. Sneakers were only for exercise and per my mother, dirt sullied their countenance, especially if a morning with the Lord was involved. Their presence at church wasn't about faith but about being seen.

Unlike me. I had my hair up in a sloppy bun, no makeup, I was wearing Johnny's hoodie and there was Cheetos dust on it.

Keely and I met at the Little Miss Calhan pageant when we were six. I got runner up and Keely fell off the stage during her talent performance. The only thing besides my weight and inability to baton twirl that my mother blamed for my perpetually poor pageant showing was Keely's influence. Which meant we became best friends and stayed that way, much to my mother's discontent. Looking back, she'd pretty much saved me.

So you looked normal.

Keely liked to look nice, but she didn't base her life around her looks, especially since she had three wild, dirt-smudged boys who took up most of her time. If Keely needed more queso, she wasn't going to do her hair and makeup to go get it. If she wanted melted cheesy goodness, nothing was going to stop her.

Exactly. You know how much your mother and sister hate to look normal.

They never looked normal. They always looked perfect, and I never once saw them eat chips and queso. Yes, I definitely took after them, dressing nicely and looking as presentable as possible. After three decades of constantly being told a woman never left the house without her face on, her hair done, and her clothes representing how much pride she had in herself, I felt naked without makeup and shoes without heels were uncomfortable.

I might be indoctrinated but I didn't drink the Kool-Aid.

> Gotta go. Nookie night.

I sighed, wishing nookie night for me meant more than my vibrator. And, God, thoughts of Mac sliding the belt out of his pants.

> Lucky bitch. Tell Johnnie hey.

> Will do. Knock their socks off tomorrow!

I set my cell on the small bedside table and turned off the light. Tomorrow. *Fundraiser liaison for James Corporation.* I could do this. I had to.

9

MAC

I SLEPT LIKE SHIT. Well, I hadn't slept from all the tossing and turning and thinking of Georgia and the way she looked as I'd approached her with the key to the garage apartment. Her eyes had widened. Her head had tipped back to keep my gaze. Her pulse had thrummed in her long neck. Her tongue... fuck, had flicked out to lick those glossy lips.

I'd wanted to kiss her. Press her into the bed. Hell, press her against the wall and give her a very personal and thorough welcome to Montana.

But no. I controlled myself. I'd had to rein in my interest since I caught my first glimpse of her as she walked through the airport.

How the hell had the woman who sat beside Andy and Dad on the plane turned out to be my tenant in the garage apartment? Why did she have to be so fucking pretty? How come I had to see her sexy underwear and know she liked delicate lace to cover her pussy? Why did I have to imagine she probably fucked herself to sleep thirty feet away with that big purple vibrator?

Those thoughts only got me hard, then harder until I couldn't take it any longer and had to rub one out for some relief.

Then I fell asleep but dreamed about a red lipstick stain around the base of my dick.

That, of course, meant when I got up I had to jerk off again. No way could I leave the house like that. Showing up at the station with a hard on would only get me looked over by the medics for priapism–a.k.a. perpetually hard dick.

Thankfully I left before Andy woke up, but I'd had to tell Dad about Georgia. He showed up at six-thirty, as usual, on the days I went on shift. I got right to it, not only because I didn't have tons of time, but because I didn't want to think too hard about why she was messing with my head.

"Georgia's the tenant in the apartment," I said, shutting the front door behind him. I tipped my head toward the garage.

He hung up his coat on one of the pegs on the wall,

and looked my way as he pulled his hat off. His gray hair stuck up every which way.

He cut to the kitchen to grab some coffee. "Georgia? The woman from the plane?"

I nodded and followed. "Showed up last night. Turns out, she works for James Corp, and they put her up here for her stay."

He laughed as he filled a mug he pulled from the cabinet. "Just last night you said you'd never see her again."

I glared, grabbed my fire department walkie talkie from the counter and left. The sound of his laughter followed. I also thought he said, "This is going to be fun."

Ten minutes later, I entered the station.

"Morning, Chief."

I waved and headed straight for the coffee for my second round. A regular coffee maker was too small, so we had a restaurant-sized brewer that kept us in constant supply of hot, fresh Steaming Hotties brew. Eve generously donated the beans to keep up with our caffeine needs.

"Had a strange car in front of your house last night," Noah Flowers said. He was one of the fire lieutenants. Close to my age. Three kids. Receding hairline. Tattoo of Sponge Bob on his right bicep he told us he got in college when he lost a bet. Nice guy, but unfortunately lived down the street and was really fucking nosey.

"Finally got the space over my garage rented," I told him.

He grinned, bumping me out of the way to refill his mug.

"Oh yeah? It's mud season. Not a skier. Not a hiker."

Was he a firefighter or a detective? "A woman who works for James Corp."

His bushy eyebrows went up. "Oh yeah? Pretty?"

I leaned against the counter and crossed my arms over my chest as I watched him pour way too much sugar into his coffee.

"Shouldn't you be asking if she's smart?"

He frowned. "Huh?"

"Yeah, Pansy," Maria Grasu told him, using his nickname. "I bet if it was a guy who was staying in Mac's place you wouldn't ask if he was pretty."

"Course not," Flowers said, offended. "All I meant was that you said Andy's been vocal about wanting a mom. Marissa said he mentioned it in class one day."

Marissa was his oldest and in the same class at school as Andy.

Maria's look changed from annoyed to curious. "In that case, yeah, Mac, is she pretty?"

I sighed. We were a close-knit group and sometimes I wished we didn't know each other's shit.

I ran a hand over the back of my neck. "Yeah, she's pretty."

Pretty was an understatement. She was fucking gorgeous.

They looked at each other and made funny kissy sounds like they were in fourth grade.

"Who's pretty?" Marcus Van Routen asked, coming from the gym and wiping his face with a small towel.

"Mac's guest in his new vacation rental."

"The space over the garage?"

I nodded.

"Andy know about her?" Flowers asked.

"She arrived last night after he went to bed." No way was I telling them she was with them on the plane.

"Good thing," Van Routen said, slapping me on the shoulder on the way to the sink to refill his water bottle. "Otherwise, he'd be planning your wedding before school."

I frowned. "I'm not marrying her."

"You could do worse," Flowers said, putting his spoon into the dishwasher. "She's pretty. On your property."

"You don't even know if she's eighty or single."

Maria shook her head. "No way an eighty-year-old gets up and down those steps. How old is she?"

A crew from the station came and helped me move some furniture from Dad's house and into the space last month. He had plenty of extra pieces after living there for over thirty years, although I did order a brand-new mattress.

Again, these guys knew too much.

I shrugged. "Thirties. I'm not looking for a mom for Andy," I said, running a hand through my hair. That was way too much pressure. I hadn't even had sex with a woman in a year, so the chances of marrying one were pretty fucking slim.

"I'm talking about a woman for you," Van Routen said, pointing at me.

"Yeah, you need a woman," Maria said.

"A wife? Same thing," I countered.

Van Routen shook his head. "A *date*. Hell, maybe a one-night-stand."

I shifted the fire department walkie talkie on my belt, not interested in talking about either my dating history or sex life with them.

That made me remember I gave my other belt to Georgia. When she was on her knees looking up at me. And–

NO! Stop thinking of her sucking your dick!

"I won't bring a woman into Andy's life and have her leave."

"Already happened, right?" Flowers reminded. "What was her name? The blonde?" He turned, leaned against the counter and took a sip of his coffee.

"Carrie," Maria tossed out there.

"Teri," I corrected. "Andy was two when I was with her. It'd be worse now."

Teri was the last woman I'd been serious about. An insurance agent. We'd dated for three months. She was nice. Pretty. Liked Andy, but in the end, didn't want someone else's kid. Hell, she hadn't been sure she wanted one of her own. Andy had cried for a few days missing her, but since he'd been so young, quickly forgot her. Last I heard, she'd moved to Helena. She was another reminder that women didn't stick.

"He doesn't have to know," Van Routen offered.

I shook my head and laughed. "She's staying over the garage. He'll know."

He'd probably think Santa had set this whole thing up.

"Your dad had sex with your mother for twenty years without you knowing."

I frowned and my dick was absolutely, positively, not hard any longer. "Jesus, Flowers. What the hell?"

He held up a hand. "You think people with kids never have sex? You have to get creative. *Helping Mom with the laundry. Looking for something in the basement.* How do you think people have more than one kid?" He waggled his eyebrows. "I have three."

Me, Maria and Van Routen all rolled our eyes pretty much in sync.

"All I'm saying is that there's nothing wrong with

scratching an itch," he continued. "She doesn't have to be Andy's new mom."

"She's temporary," I growled because the crew I trusted with my life in a fire was annoying the shit out of me.

Flowers put his mug down, went to the cabinet and pulled down a box of cereal. Since we were on shift for twenty-four hours, we ate our meals at the station. "Exactly. She knows she's not staying. You know it. Have some fun."

I sighed, looked down at my worn boots and set my hands on my hips. I wanted to have some *fun* with Georgia. I had a long list of things we could do. *Long.*

Van Routen took a big swig of water then wiped his mouth with the back of his hand. "What's the trouble, Chief? That's not the look a man should have when thinking sexy-times thoughts about a pretty woman."

"I'm all about having *fun*," I replied. "But with Georgia over the garage and Andy obsessed with getting a new mom? That's dangerous. Hell, *she's* dangerous."

He considered, then nodded. "Right. Stay away from her then."

The alarm went off indicating an emergency call. We dropped everything and ran for the bay, our gear and the engine.

10

MAC

TURNED OUT, there'd been a grease fire in one of the Hunter Valley ski resort buildings' kitchens. The fire suppression system had kicked on automatically and doused the flames just like it was supposed to, but we'd had to ensure there were no hot spots and treat a few minor burns.

This had me arriving an hour late for the fundraiser meeting. Since saving property and lives was my top priority, everyone knew I could be late, or a no-show. As chief, I was responsible for personnel, paperwork and outreach projects like charity events. This year, the fundraiser plan was to have a chili dinner instead of a pancake breakfast like last year. The money raised would go toward the kids' club that was being added on to the community center. It was going to be a place dedicated to supporting children with a safe place before or after school as well as breaks, tutoring help, mentorship programs, job assistance for teens and more.

We had the fire truck back in the station and the crew was getting on their morning chores of vehicle washing, hose rolling and whatever else needed to be done between calls. I veered toward one of the multipurpose rooms used for anything from trainings to meetings. Hopefully being late meant I missed creating the volunteer schedule, although hopefully I wasn't on shopping duty. I hated going to the mega-box store for ingredients like fifty pounds of kidney beans.

I pushed through the door. "Sorry I'm late. Kitchen fire and–"

"–this option will have the most bang for the–"

I froze. Holy shit.

It was Georgia.

Georgia from the plane. From my garage apartment. And now in my fire station standing in front of the fundraiser committee. Her words tapered off and her mouth hung open as she stared at me. I didn't miss the way her cheeks flushed. I'd interrupted her, then surprised her.

She surprised the hell out of me in return.

I took her in from bottom to top. Shiny red shoes.

High heels. Wide legged black pants. White turtleneck sweater. Silver hoop earrings. Hair in some half down, half up style that highlighted her round face. Her lips were painted the same red as her shoes. Her cheeks were flushed and her eyes were dark and fringed by long lashes.

I'd jerked off twice since I saw her the night before and both times, I hadn't downplayed in my mind just how pretty she was. I was definitely adding her wearing those high heels and nothing else in the future.

Like the day before, she was dressed up. While she was in pants, she was fancy for a Monday morning chili dinner fundraiser meeting.

Around the rectangular table was the rest of the fundraising committee: Patrick from B Shift, the mayor and Maverick James. I ignored them all.

"Georgia." I frowned. "What are you doing here?"

She blushed and her smile grew. "Mac. You're... um, a firefighter."

Her gaze raked up and down my body, took in my uniform. I was single but I wasn't a priest, and I knew when a woman was scoping and liked what she saw.

"Fire chief, actually."

"Chief?" she whispered.

"What are you doing here?" I asked, looking around. "This is the fundraiser meeting, right?"

Maybe I was in the wrong place. Was it supposed to be at City Hall? No, the mayor was here.

"This is it," Mav said. He leaned across the table, hand out for me to shake as way of hello. I hadn't seen him in a few weeks since we'd tossed cabers in Daniel Pearson's back yard. "You two know each other?"

I nodded.

"I'm staying in his vacation rental," Georgia shared, her hands folded in front of her.

Mav's gaze shifted from her to me and took a moment to consider. "Bradley arranged it?"

She nodded.

"He's my assistant," Mav clarified for those who didn't know, including me. "My brother's, too. Hell, he pretty much runs James Corp."

"It's really nice," Georgia praised. She was generous to say that since it was Maverick's company who was paying me the nightly fee. That was life in a small town. A lot of overlapping lives.

"Good to see you," Mav offered. "Thanks for housing my latest employee."

"I guess I should've charged more," I joked. Everyone knew James Corp was a billion-dollar business.

Mav settled back in his seat. "Theo told me about the fundraiser and the plans for the kids' club."

Theo was Mav's brother and of the four Jameses, he was the one I knew the best. He was one of the doctors in town, but he participated in the fire trainings. He was a good friend, too.

He continued. "While there's nothing wrong with a good old-fashioned chili dinner, Bridget has been driving James Corp into local philanthropic efforts and thinks we have untapped potential. She did the math and well, you know whatever she came up with is correct."

I knew Bridget Beckett and knew how smart she was. I went to school with her older sister, Lindy, who was, coincidentally, married to Mav's brother, Dex. Bridget and Maverick got together last summer when he came to town to keep the James Inn construction on schedule. Now, the inn was open for business and Mav was now a permanent resident of Hunter Valley. I wouldn't be surprised if he and Bridget got married in the not-too-distant future.

"Okay," I said, pulling out a chair and dropping into it.

"We hired Georgia because we're offering the town her expertise to make this fundraiser as successful as possible. We were just listening to some of her great ideas."

"About a chili dinner?" I asked, flicking my gaze to her. "We already have the vegetarian option planned and of course we can always add Fritos."

I was hungry and the thought of some corn chips

made my mouth water.

Georgia still stood at the end of the table. Her poise was that of a politician. No, a royal trained to stand just right.

"No. About other fundraising possibilities," she said. "The committee, while y'all were dealing with the kitchen fire, has decided on a different one."

The committee was me, the mayor, Patrick and Maverick. Now Georgia as well.

I frowned. "You're... donating one of your employee's time for the next few weeks to work on the event?" Looking to Georgia, I asked, "That's why you're here?"

"Yes."

Mav grinned.

"Georgia is here to make it happen, along with a sizeable James Corp donation to the Kids' Club. That will get the program up and running so there's a place for children to go once school is out for the summer," the mayor chimed in. She seemed thrilled about the hefty donation. Mary Morris had been mayor for a little over a year and was well liked. If she was able to get James Corp and their big purse involved, that said quite a bit. "Camps, drivers ed. Bridget and Mallory are going to spearhead educational catch-up programs."

Bridget was a Physics teacher at the high school and a math whiz while Mallory was Andy's first grade teacher.

"That's great," I said. "So if not chili, then... back to pancakes?"

"Not exactly," Patrick said, then bit his lip. Why was he trying not to smile?

"Georgia had an amazing idea instead of a chili dinner," the mayor said, grinning. "Something that will support the animal shelter, too. They're always eager for exposure and funding."

If I didn't have to buy canned beans, I was all ears.

Georgia took a step forward. "A chili dinner is a one-time event. The expense to profit margin is good, but with food prices these days, the money raised will be diminished. So we need something that has little over-head. That will also be exciting locally but can collect donations from places across Montana. Maybe even further."

I sat forward, rested my forearms on the conference table. "Okay, what's the plan?"

"Since we weren't sure if y'all were going to be done with the call, we made a decision without you. Instead of a firefighter chili dinner, we're going to have a firefighter calendar."

I blinked. Processed. Did she say– "A firefighter calendar?"

She nodded.

"You mean take pictures of the fire trucks? Fires? Trainings? I can't imagine that raising much money.

Other than maybe the Pearson guys who run the mechanic shop, who wants a picture of an ambulance or brush truck on their wall?"

Mav shook his head. Patrick started laughing. The mayor blushed.

Why was the mayor blushing?

Georgia shook her head. "No. Pictures of *firefighters*."

"Standing in front of the new engine," the mayor commented.

"Dressed only in bunker pants," Patrick said while waggling his eyebrows.

"Holding puppies," Maverick added.

What? *What?* WHAT?

Georgia raised her arms out to her sides as if she was a game show hostess. "As fire chief, you'll be Mr. January."

11

GEORGIA

"Mr. January," Mac repeated. "I'm an hour late for a meeting and now I'm *Mr. January?*"

Oh my goodness, Mac was the fire chief. FIRE. CHIEF. He just got hotter and hotter.

I'd laugh at my pun about him setting my panties on fire, but he didn't look too receptive to the idea of putting them out. When the committee said the chief would be late because he was on a call, they never used Mac's name. Not once. Patrick, who also worked on the department, called him Chief.

I hadn't known him very long, perhaps interacted with him a total of fifteen minutes or so between the airport and over the little apartment over his garage. In that short time, I took him to be a calm, levelheaded sort. Not one quick to temper or overreaction. Not with a six-year-old at home and being the fire chief. Or letting strangers stay on his property.

Maverick nodded at Mac in confirmation. I held my breath. Since he'd missed the beginning of the meeting and me introducing my crazy idea of the calendar, Mac needed to catch up. Especially since he was the chief, the one who was officially in charge of the fire department that was doing the fundraiser. And, since it was his buff body I imagined first when I thought of the calendar. I wasn't going to tell him this, but he was my inspiration for the project.

Mac, no shirt, in bunker pants and only red suspenders over his washboard abs and broad chest, his biceps bulging as he held up a puppy from the animal shelter.

I'd *throw* my money at that calendar. I'd get one for my girlfriends. Hell, I might even get one for my mother.

Of course, I didn't know officially if he had washboard abs, but a girl could imagine. And hope. No, yesterday's black tee and today's fire department uniform shirt clearly outlined sculpted pecs, broad shoulders, fabric-stretching biceps and a narrow waist. I bet he even had that V thingy at his hips.

And he, nor any of the other firefighter models,

would be shirtless like Patrick teased. The project was family friendly.

"*Mr. January?*"

I blinked. Oh yes, he would definitely be Mr. January. Maybe even the cover guy, although I had yet to meet the other months' options.

"You can be July if you want. I hear that's your birthday month," Maverick stated. The corner of his mouth twitched and his eyes pretty much sparkled with amusement. He was definitely having fun watching his friend squirm.

Maverick James might be even calmer than Mac. He did run a billion-dollar corporation, and signed my paychecks, so I wasn't going to say a word bad about him. He was also the size of small car, so there was that, too.

"How is a calendar 'getting the community involved and in on it'?"

"Because we'll do a contest when the calendar is out and let everyone donate for their favorite hero or cutest animal."

His mouth fell open slightly. If we were eating something, it would have fallen into his lap.

"You're a bunch of smart, sane, educated professionals. Where on earth did you come up with an idea like that?" Mac asked, pretty much shifting his glare around the table.

I cleared my throat. "That would be me."

Whenever his dark gaze turned and settled on me, I got butterflies in my stomach and hard nipples. This look? Intense, and not in a good way. In a way that said he wanted to drive me back to the airport and put me on a plane back to... anywhere.

He pretty much implied that I wasn't smart, sane, or educated. I had no issue with being in a calendar with puppies and kittens, but I grew up in southern pageant life. Mac, I doubted, hadn't.

"You're here in Hunter Valley again, why?" Mac asked me, his question pointed.

My smile slipped for a moment, but I was used to being judged, to being doubted. To feeling like shit for not being perfect or pretty enough or, well... valued.

I hadn't been valued for my looks on the pageant circuit. No, I had, and was found lacking. I hadn't been valued as a daughter, not like Sassy, my sister, the true pageant queen. Well, her real name was Sue Ann, but everyone called her Sassy. I hadn't been valued by Art as worthy of being his wife or the mother of his child.

Out of the blue a few weeks ago, Bradley called me about this job, thought I'd be perfect for it. As Maverick's personal assistant, he knew what the job entailed, and he knew me. I was here because *he* valued me and my expertise. Sure, I'd never done a fire department fundraiser, but pageants were all about supporting the community. Being the pretty, smiling face of it.

So was the idea a little far-fetched? It wasn't like I invented the concept. It had been used for fire department fundraisers for years. The Hunter Valley one might not be as good as some of the Australian ones I'd seen since they had single, hot firemen with koalas. I couldn't compete with koalas. And the shirts stayed on.

Still, I was here and I made a solid, cost-effective suggestion so I turned the volume of my smile back up. The others on the committee liked it and approved.

But Mac–

"Mac," the mayor–Mary–scolded.

I tipped my chin up, pretended he was a judge asking me a pageant interview question.

"I was hired to reinvigorate the fundraiser into one that supports and is supported by Hunter Valley with an increased bottom line and reach," I said slowly and clearly, as if I was on stage.

Before I left Calhan, I practiced and refined that before my mother quizzed me on why I was crazy enough to take a temp job in "freezing cold, boring, desolate Montana." Those were her words. I would agree that it was cold, but so far it didn't seem like the place was boring and the little town of Hunter Valley was far from desolate. In fact, it seemed like there was more happening here than in my small town of Calhan, Georgia.

Mac leaned back, crossed his arms over his

formidable chest. Frowned. "Sorry, I don't mean to be rude. It's just... who doesn't want chili? That and the pancake breakfast have been a fundraising staple for HVFD for years."

"Patrick shared a list of other fundraisers that have been done in the past," I said, turning to what I wrote on the white board earlier. "Carnival, car wash, birthday parties. All great options."

I gave Mac my big smile, hoping to hide my growing nerves at the look on his face that wasn't going away. The others on the committee were in, but it was crucial Mac was, too. While the donations would go to the kids' club and I was here as full-time support from James Corp, this was a fire department fundraiser and he was the chief.

"Look, Mac," Maverick began. "It's not the fundraiser that's changed but the charity being supported. The kids' club is what's different this year. In the past, the charities supported were small and the donations collected were enough. We're all thinking bigger this year. The kids' club involves building an addition onto the community center. Funding a full-time employee to be on staff. Part-timers as well. There're monthly expenses."

Mac held up his hand. "I'm aware of what's involved."

"If you take the donations earned from last year's pancake breakfast, it will only get us one tenth of the way to the needed goal to get the kids' club up and running." He tipped his head down to look right at Mac so he'd hopefully get the point. "In five years. This fundraising idea's projected income potential is substantial for less overhead and less effort." Mac stated a number but slid the projection sheet I'd made late last night after I came up with the idea across the table. I'd outlined rough numbers for a photographer, graphic designer and anticipated time commitments. It wasn't exact, but I was confident in the estimates. They were positioned besides Bridget Beckett's numbers for running the kids' club. "Plus, the process can be duplicated every year."

Mac's eyebrows went up. Just like they had the day before when Andy had said I was his new mom. "Bridget's math?"

"Bridget's math," Mav repeated. "And Georgia's estimated fundraising costs."

"That's... impressive." He looked at the list. "Calendars need to be printed. Where's that expense?"

"Calendars are like paperback books," I explained, setting my hands on the back of one of the chairs. "They are sold online and printed on demand. This means they're only printed when someone buys one. There's no overhead because the cost is taken by the production company with each sale."

"So the fundraiser is just on a website and people buy the calendar and have it delivered to their house?"

I nodded. "That's one option to get it. We'll have

calendars on hand to sell at a community event on the day and time when the chili dinner was scheduled."

"And get autographs," Patrick added, messing with Mac. From my perspective, he wasn't being helpful, but I knew they worked together and were probably friends outside of this meeting and he was having a little fun.

"I'll ask local businesses if they would stock and sell copies as well. The ski resort and other places tourists visit." Hopefully, that would help sway him.

Mac frowned. In fact, he looked downright constipated. "I don't like it."

"Is it because you're Mr. January?" Maverick asked.

"Of course it is!" Mac tossed his hands up, then looked to Mayor Mary. "It's not Georgia or the idea that's at issue here, but me? Why me?"

That was his problem? That he had to be in the calendar? He had no idea how attractive he was. If he was on the cover, they'd make a killing. I thought of all the women who'd be ogling Mac and I was suddenly a tad possessive.

"You're the fire chief," I said. "This is a fire department fundraiser."

"Aren't you worried about sexual harassment or an issue with it being demeaning or debasing? We'd be perpetuating that people are valued for their bodies and how they look."

I could so relate. Coming from a pageant lifestyle, I

knew all about the haters, those who thought women should be quiet and pretty. That they're judged for their poise, how they looked in an evening gown and swimsuit. But pageants were more than that. Sure, I wasn't up for sexualizing little girls who did them, but this wasn't the same thing at all.

"What are people going to tell their kids?" he asked.

"That the fire department is full of healthy men and women who take care of their bodies through exercise, skill and knowledge," I said. "That the fire department and those who work for it, are safe, friendly and approachable. That they care for animals."

Mary nodded. "First off, it's not just men," she explained. "It'll be women, too. Liz on B Team already said she was in. Anyone else who wishes to participate can, but this committee will decide the final photos that end up in the calendar instead of the website."

"Website?" The little vein in Mac's temple was throbbing.

"Patrick may have been messing with you when you'd only wear your bunker pants," Mary continued. "This is a family fundraiser. If you're that shy, or uncomfortable then–"

"Yeah, Chief. If you don't think you have the body to be Mr. January, then we'll go with Smutters." Patrick's words had Mac spinning to face him.

The vein in his temple throbbed. "Smutters? Are you serious right now?"

I didn't know who Smutters was or even if that person was a man or a woman. Or a dog. It sounded like a dog's name.

Mac raised his hand. "Wait. If I'm stuck doing this, then Smutters is fucking in. And you." Mac rolled his wrist and pointed at Patrick. "You're doing this, too."

Patrick raised his left hand, showed off his wedding band. "Sorry, no can do. I'm married."

"So?" Mac stood. "Your wife is going to flaunt that calendar to all your friends, showing off how she's got Mr. March or whatever in her bed. She'll buy ten copies."

Mary snickered and Patrick's humor slipped away.

"We're going to make the calendar be of bachelor and bachelorettes," Maverick said. "Singles."

"Singles," Mac repeated. "As in on the market? You want to peddle us as *available?*" Mac asked Mary, his voice finally rising. Clearly, he thought the mayor had a little more discretion.

She blushed some more. "Not everyone who's single is as grumpy as you," Mary countered, making it clear her stance on discretion. "Others are looking for someone."

"You're saying I need to be in a calendar to find a date?" He ran a hand over his neck in blatant frustration.

"How about this? If you're off the market, you don't have to be Mr. January," Maverick said.

"No way. If I'm in, then Patrick can be in, too. Relationship status should be irrelevant."

An electronic siren came through a speaker I didn't know was on the wall. I jumped. It went off again, followed by a voice giving an address. Oh, an emergency call.

Mac stood abruptly and headed for the door. He stopped, turned around and looked my way long enough to say, "I'm in, but we have to talk. I know exactly where to find you."

12

GEORGIA

I WAITED until I was sitting in my rental before I called my cousin. "What are you up to?" I asked.

"Why are you whispering?" Bradley asked.

I frowned because I had no idea. I was alone.

The fire station was at the south end of Main Street. Parked in the front lot, I stared out across the street at Steaming Hotties. Through the coffee shop window, I saw Mav sitting at a high-top table across from a woman with her hair pulled back in a bun and glasses perched on her cute face. The way he was smiling at her, I assumed she was the math-smart Bridget.

"Why did I get this job?" I asked Bradley, adjusting the vents so the heat, when it finally kicked in, would blow right on me. The sun was out but it was freezing. My coat didn't do much against the cold.

"Because you're talented," he said immediately. No hesitation. Not because I was pretty or because I'd represent the company well. That my face was what was important, nothing more.

"I'm a former pageant queen," I reminded. He was well aware of my past.

"Yes, you are."

"Former, as in I never got beyond Little Miss Calhan," I clarified. No Miss Georgia for me, like Sassy.

"I'm well aware. Aunt June points that out every chance she gets. You think you'd be better qualified for this job with your sister's pageant record?"

Bradley was my mother's brother's son. Uncle Dan married a woman from Colorado and settled there. Bradley lived in Denver and had worked at James Corp for close to a decade. While he and I only saw each other once or twice a year, we talked all the time. Out of all my relatives, including my mother and sister, I was closest with Bradley. We weren't just cousins, but close friends and knew all about my mother's obsession of success via tiaras and sashes.

"I get it every time I talk to my mother." I pursed my lips. "And no, having Miss Georgia on my resume wouldn't make a difference in this job."

"Exactly. Your momma loves you in her own warped

way, but don't listen to her. Or your sister. They've breathed in way too much hair spray."

That got a smile out of me, at least for a moment.

"It's hard not to when I'm living with her. She and Sassy gang up on me." I was definitely bitter by the constant reminder that I was never good enough. Like Sassy. Perfect. *She* got the Miss Georgia tiara. Not me. I was too clumsy. Too fat. Too... Just too much. Or too little.

I was too old to live with my mother again, but without realizing, I set myself up for it. My assistant job at the PR company hadn't been well paying, but when Art and I had been married, it hadn't mattered. Divorced, though, it didn't cover my rent. I'd trusted in my marriage, that together we were financially secure and preparing for a family.

But that went away and so did my job when I quit. So back home to Momma I'd gone.

Temporarily. Now I was in Hunter Valley. A reprieve I had Bradley to thank.

"That's why you're in Montana. Everyone is a former something, GG. I did wrestling in middle school. I can safely say I am a former wrestler."

Absently, I pushed the hazard button on and off.

"Fine. But what does my background have to do with a fire department fundraiser in Montana?"

"You have the PR background."

"I was an assistant," I reminded.

He ignored me. "You're open, a strong leader–"

I laughed at that. "Strong leader? Are you serious? A leader is the mayor of this town. Mac as fire chief. Maverick as CEO of a billion-dollar company. You remember him. Your boss?"

"Yes, and that's why you're in Montana."

"Is it? Because I'm starting to think my presence here has nothing to do with this job."

"You wanted out of Calhan and this opportunity came up. So yes, you're there because you wanted an escape. I pointed out the opening, knew you'd be perfect for it, but you got the job all on your own."

I sighed. "Thank you for that. Truly. Besides my mother, it feels so good not to have to worry about running into Art at the grocery store or see him at a restaurant with Pam."

"Art's an asshole. Be thankful you're rid of him. And I know how much you wanted kids, but you really don't want one with him."

"I want a baby, B," I admitted wistfully. The heat was finally coming from the vents, and I relaxed my shoulders.

"I know you do," he replied, his voice soft. "But not with Art. Not with a man who didn't respect you. You deserve it all."

"And you think that's with Mac?"

He was quiet for a moment. "Mac, the fire chief? Why would you say that?"

"Oh, I don't know. Flying with his son? Staying in his vacation rental? Him being the chief of the department that is having the fundraiser I'm here to organize?"

"You flew with his son?"

I rolled my eyes. "I don't know how you did it, but yes."

"I'm good, but not that good."

I doubted it. Somehow, he got into the FAA computers or the airlines seating chart and put me on the same flight and in the same row as Mac's father and son.

Hmmm... okay, maybe he wasn't that skilled.

"Look, you're there because Maverick wants to see Hunter Valley thrive and that a chili dinner won't show off how tight knit the community is. Donating a talented resource to the project is him helping."

"The chili dinner is out," I corrected.

"Oh? What's in its place?"

"A firefighter calendar."

He was quiet for a moment, then laughed. "Excellent idea. I assume you came up with it."

"Yes."

"Plus, puppies and kittens from the animal shelter for cross charity support?"

"Yes."

"Perfect."

"If you came up with that yourself in two seconds, why aren't you doing this?" I asked.

"I already have a job."

I winced. "Ouch."

He was pointing out that I'd quit when I couldn't stand seeing Art all the time. Another thing I should have considered, because looking back, it was a big red flag. But when one was young and in love, working for the same company was romantic. Driving to and from work together. Sneaking into the copy room for a quick kiss...

Yeah, not the same thing as when it's him, you and his secretary he fucked. To escape, the only option was to quit, which I did before they married and got pregnant.

To make ends meet, I took up pageant coaching again and moved in with my mother. The ultimate double whammy of misery. All my mother could see was that I couldn't satisfy and keep my husband happy and that the only job I would be good for was back in pageants, as a coach for little girls on how to walk, how to smile. How to answer questions and be poised and confident.

Not fun at all. None of it.

I'd needed a new job so badly that I hadn't thought twice about it being in Montana. Bradley had come through. An epic rescue–income and a different state. At least in the very short term. When the fundraiser was done, I'd be back in Calhan because the job was a contractor position only. If I did a good enough job, maybe I'd be hired on full time in Denver. That had been tossed out as a possibility from HR and I glommed onto it with every hope in my body. New state, solid job, near my favorite family member?

But that was a tomorrow problem. I had a different one today.

Mac.

My new innkeeper? Landlord? Top billing on my flick-the-bean list? Yeah, I used that vibrator thinking of him last night. I'd brought the thing and been totally mortified over it spilling out of my suitcase onto the airport floor in front of him. I was definitely using it.

"You came up with the calendar idea," Bradley said, breaking through my thoughts about Mac being featured in my self-pleasure fantasies. "The puppies, too. It shows you know your stuff. *That's* why you're there."

Except I had a very cranky calendar cover model. And landlord. If he hadn't gotten an emergency call, what would he have done? I had to sway him to the idea. The success of the fundraiser depended on it. Same with my new divorced life.

13

MAC

THE NEXT MORNING after my shift, I went in the house and headed straight for the kitchen. I could smell the coffee my dad had brewed.

On nights I worked, Dad stayed in the guest room, which was pretty much half the time. He liked to wake up early and have his coffee and read the paper before Andy stirred and the craziness of getting a first grader out the door for school began.

"Morning," I said, unclipping my walkie talkie and setting it on the charger on the counter.

"Quiet night?" Dad asked. The paper was open and on the kitchen table, but his coffee mug was on the counter beside him. He was putting together Andy's lunch. A half a peanut butter and jelly sandwich, apple slices and cheese puffs were in plastic baggies. A fruit roll-up was beside it along with a juice box.

"Chest pains around eleven," I shared. "Carbon monoxide alarm at three. Everyone's fine."

"Good."

I ran a hand over my eyes. Even though we had bunk rooms where we slept during the night, even simple calls took time and paperwork so I clocked about four hours of rest. I was ready for bed. I'd get about six hours before I had to do afternoon school pickup.

"Where's Andy?"

They were leaving for school in about ten minutes. Dad would drop him off and then go on about his day, returning tomorrow morning when I was back on shift.

"Brushing his teeth. Or at least wetting his toothbrush."

Andy's cereal bowl was by the sink, but his orange juice cup got missed when he cleared his dishes from the table.

As if perfect timing, I couldn't miss Andy's little feet overhead as he moved from the bathroom into his bedroom.

"Be prepared," Dad advised.

I glanced at him over the rim of my mug. "For what?"

It seemed Dad couldn't help but smile and chuckle. "He knows about Georgia staying here."

I closed my eyes, took a deep breath. "Great."

Andy clomped down the stairs.

"Dad!" he shouted, running to me and wrapping my legs in a hug. I set my hand on his head, his hair damp.

"Did you comb your hair?" I asked, surprised. Getting him to use toothpaste, soap or a comb were difficult tasks. Him using one of those voluntarily?

He looked up at me and nodded. "Miss Georgia's coming for dinner tonight and I want to look my best."

I turned my head toward Dad, who was tucking the lunch items into the Ironman lunchbox, a grin on his face.

"She's coming for dinner?"

"Mhm," he replied.

Andy let me go and hopped up and down. "I asked her to come last night because she's our guest, but she said she couldn't. Then I asked her to come to dinner tonight and she said yes!"

"Go get your coat on," Dad told Andy.

"See ya later!" he said, not giving me a backward glance as he ran into the living room to grab his coat from the peg on the wall.

"Your six-year-old son has a hot date tonight," Dad said, zipping the lunchbox closed. "He has more game than you. Is that how you say it?"

Georgia had my son combing his hair. She had Mav and Mary and Patrick wrapped around her little finger.

Coming in here and getting Andy to think she was his new mom and coming up with the fundraiser concept from hell.

Starring me.

"That woman is a menace," I said.

Since the fundraiser meeting yesterday morning, I'd thought about the calendar idea. And Georgia. So I washed Engine 1 with a little more vigor than necessary, but I'd had to work off the frustration–mental and physical–at being in Georgia's presence. Everywhere. At work, at home, in my fantasies.

I was equally turned on and annoyed. Just shaking hands with her at the airport and I wanted to touch her more. I wanted to find out if she dabbed her sweet scent at her neck or between those lush tits. I wanted to see what color panties she wore. How she looked with her legs parted, knees bent and that vibrator between them. No, me between them, my head lowering, and–

"Georgia?" Dad asked. "What's she done now?"

I cleared my throat, got my head back on why I wanted to strangle her, not jump her curvy body, and make her forget her name and cry out mine.

"The fundraiser's changed to one of her brilliant ideas," I growled. "It's now a firefighter calendar. I'm Mr. January."

Dad's eyes widened, then widened some more, as if I

told him we were going to raise funds by selling kidneys we harvested from emergency calls.

Then he laughed, completely at my expense. When he finally stopped, he said, "Spaghetti and meatballs for dinner. Andy's sure it's Georgia's favorite."

Dad usually got groceries for us and planned dinners since I was either working or sleeping off my shift during the day. When he told me the menu, I wasn't surprised. Since the Italian dish was Andy's favorite, we had it frequently.

"Grumpy, let's go!" Andy shouted from the other room. "Simon got a pet snake and he's going to sneak it into his backpack. I want to see it."

For a second, I panicked about there being a snake roaming the school, but I was off-duty and that was someone else's problem. Specifically, Simon's mom or dad.

"Set a place for me," Dad said. "I'm not missing this."

14

MAC

THE DOORBELL WOKE ME. I ignored it, thinking maybe Dad ordered a package and it was delivered. But it rang again.

Climbing from bed, I stomped downstairs and pulled open the door. If I had to sign for something, I could do it in my boxers.

It wasn't a delivery driver.

It was Georgia. In a thick furry robe and slippers. Her hair was back in a ponytail, and she didn't have any makeup on. She looked different, but still amazing. And that wasn't a good thing in only boxers.

"Um, sorry to wake you," she said to my chest. "But I have no hot water."

The cold air was coming in, which stirred my brain. Which meant I was thinking, and my thoughts were on whether she had anything on under that robe.

Yeah, my boxers weren't going to contain my dick for long.

I stepped back.

Got my head out of my underwear.

"Shit, you must be cold." Of course, she was. I left her standing out there long enough for her to have to ring twice. "Come in."

She scurried inside.

"Probably the pilot light's out."

"Right, well, I don't want to bother you since you're trying to sleep." She was still talking to my chest. Because it was bare. And I was only in my boxers. If she looked any lower, she was going to get more of an eyeful than she bargained for.

"Georgia."

"Hmm?"

"Up here," I said, waving my finger toward my face.

She whipped her head up and blushed.

"Why don't you take a shower here and I'll look at your hot water heater later. If it's okay with you, I'll go in while you're working and check it out."

She nodded, clutching the front of her robe closed. "Fine. That works for me."

I pointed up the stairs. "First door on the right.

Towels are on the shelf above the toilet. Oh, um, there's only Andy's shampoo in there."

She held up a bag I missed before. "Got everything I need in here."

"Good."

She eyed me a little more, then blinked and scurried upstairs.

"Georgia," I called.

She turned around on the top step.

"Hope you have your toy submarine."

Fuck, it was fun making her blush. And glare. Yeah, payback was so sweet.

The bathroom door slammed and I made my way to bed, tipping over face first. I may have thought my little teasing was a good idea, but I barely slept because all I could think about was Georgia down the hall, naked, wet and using that purple vibrator.

15

MAC

GEORGIA SPENT forty-five minutes in the bathroom. I knew because I watched the clock. If I hadn't heard a hair dryer go on, I'd have wondered if she had stomach problems. I might have been single, but I knew better than to question what a woman did in the bathroom. But forty-five minutes?

When I heard the front door close behind her, I finally, FINALLY, slept for a few more hours. Stirring, I grabbed my cell from the charger on the nightstand. I had a shit ton of texts and messages. Dropping back onto the side of the bed, I started to scroll through them.

Theo texted first thing, probably right after he got to

the clinic and his office manager, Verna, filled him in on all the local gossip.

> Heard about the calendar. If you're going to be a cover model, you might need to start waxing now. I've heard that shit is painful. No one likes to see a hairy bikini line.

"What the fuck?" I said aloud, scratching my balls through my boxers. Why the fuck would I need to wax anything? My hand slid up and over my chest. So I had some hair, but I wasn't Sasquatch. No woman yet had run away screaming or tried to French braid it. "Asshole."

Delete.

The next was from Smutters. He was the captain on C shift. While I couldn't fault Pete on his skill as a fire-fighter or paramedic, the guy had the biggest chip on his shoulder. Sure, he was considered handsome by the ladies and–per him–didn't lack for bed partners, he was annoying as fuck. The only ladder he could climb at the station was one in a fire, not from captain to chief. That was my job. I didn't plan to go anywhere but I knew if given a chance, he'd be putting in for it.

"Asshole," I said again. What did he want now?

> Meeting w Georgia to talk about the calendar and who should be on the front. Got anything you want me to add?

I pictured the two of them together. Pretty boy Smutters sitting across from Georgia having a cup of coffee. He might talk with her about the fundraiser, but he wanted in her pants. She was, to him, fresh pussy.

"Not fucking happening," I growled, feeling very possessive.

I scrolled down and saw he texted again a few minutes later when I didn't respond.

> Didn't think so. Don't worry, I'll take good care of her.

I clenched my teeth and was ready to throw my phone against the wall. He thought he was getting the calendar cover over me! Not that I wanted it, hell no, but there was no fucking way Smutters was representing HVFD on the front. I could handle Smutters. Always had. But him and Georgia? That was next level shit. Him taking good care of her by bringing her back to the garage apartment? No fucking way. I'd have to burn the mattress at the next training.

The next text was from Dad.

> Take the loaf of garlic bread out of the freezer to thaw.

That shouldn't have riled me up, but it did. We usually ate garlic toast, just slices of sandwich bread with butter and garlic and seasonings. Never a fancy loaf.

Except Georgia was coming for dinner. I'd have to see her and wonder if she got it on with Smutters and wished it was me.

Fuck, my dick got hard thinking about being with her again over the garage. That big bed. Her in just the purple lace. The vibrator. Reaching into my boxers, I gripped my dick, gave it a pump.

That was the last of the texts but there was one voice-mail. I hit play.

> Hey Mac, it's Mallory. Just wanted you to know that Andy just told the class his new mother is coming over for dinner. I... um, didn't know you were dating anyone, but congrats. I'm sure I'll see you and this mystery woman around.

"Fuck!" I shouted.

Special bread. Smutters, the not-so-subtle man slut. Andy and his new mom obsession. Me with my hand around my dick. Hot water heater pilot light. All of that had one thing in common.

Georgia. *Georgia.* GEORGIA!

16

GEORGIA

THE PROJECT WAS GOING WELL, although it had only been a short time. Since the fundraiser meeting the day before, Mayor Mary had connected with two local photographers and a graphic designer, all interested in working on the calendar. They'd donate their time because of the exposure the calendar would bring to their services and were available right away.

I'd made a signup sheet for Noah to share at the station for firefighters who might want to participate and their availability. I met with Peter Smutters, the firefighter mentioned during the committee meeting. The one Mac didn't seem to like. He'd volunteered to help me in any capacity I needed. The way he winked I had a feeling he wanted to help me out of my clothes. He was harmless because his cinnamon roll charm wasn't anything I was into.

This morning, I went to the animal shelter and met the very friendly, very eager director, Kennedy. She said she'd have adoptable animals brought for the photo shoots, no problem.

It had only been a day, but it was slowly coming together, and I was pleased. And surprised. I expected some resistance, but I have only been met with excitement and encouragement. Except for Mac.

He gave me the grumpy face. The look. Oh, and the, *we need to talk* line. Which meant he didn't like me, my ideas or how he was stuck being in the calendar he didn't even want. I recognized he had to save face by being in it, especially after meeting Peter Smutters. Mac would never live it down. But he was probably thinking he'd never live it down if he was *in* the calendar either.

I didn't know what he imagined, his body slick with oil, only wearing bunker pants with one suspender off his shoulder as if he'd been caught getting dressed.

Oops, I forgot my shirt! Oh, and here's a puppy you should adopt!

I could see his point.

But he was attractive. Boy, was he. I saw him in only his boxers this morning. I hadn't expected that when I rang his doorbell. My shower in the little apartment had turned out to be nothing but cold water, so I'd had no choice but to throw on my robe and ask for help. I agreed with Mac that it was probably a blown-out pilot light, but I had no idea how to fix that. I'd burn the place down or blow it up and that would make Mac look even worse if the fire chief's garage exploded.

On the doorstep, I'd ogled him like a nun who'd never seen a man in boxers before. He was F.I.T. Crazy fit. With a smattering of hair on his chest. And the tattoo. And abs. And sturdy thighs and... yeah, I'd have to fan myself if I thought about what was beneath those boxers that had pizza slices on them. Yeah, that hadn't diminished his sexiness at all.

So, back to Mac and the calendar. He was attractive. Skilled.

The photos of him–everyone–would be tasteful. Fun. I knew what it was like to be shown off like a prized chicken. Forced to preen and smile and do a shoulder thrust so small boobs appeared larger. To be ogled and valued for outward appearance and the ability to sing or dance or twirl a baton. This was different. Better. It was for a good cause, and it got the community involved.

Sure, Mac was sexy but in the photo I'd show his strength and friendliness–ha!–over the need to count his abs. We'd told him that, but his surliness was a good indicator that he didn't believe me.

Now, I was going to have dinner with him. He

couldn't yell at me too much since we'd be chaperoned. Right?

Sure, the calendar had been my idea, but the committee had agreed. I hadn't strong-armed them. With the feedback and interest I received since then, it was a good idea.

Trying to organize photo shoots, I learned that firefighter schedules were complicated and the chief's was even worse. While he worked full twenty-four-hour shifts with a crew, he was also an administrator, so he worked regular day shifts as well. Plus, being on call for any extreme emergency. So there was never a good time for him because there was always a chance he wouldn't be able to show up.

Maybe I shouldn't have turned down Andy's and Drew's dinner offer the night before when Mac worked. I was a guest on their property, but I hadn't wanted them to feel obligated to feed me. Or entertain. I'd felt bad and declined. Except I couldn't keep saying no to Andy for the next week or two, so I'd agreed for tonight instead. He hooked me with spaghetti and meatballs. It was my favorite, although I didn't have it very much with all the carbs and heavy meat and cheese. A calorie bomb.

But I wasn't staying with my mother and if I wanted pasta, I was having pasta.

But I was having it with Mac, the perfect female snack.

Yeah, I thought of that rhyme. My mouth watered and it wasn't for pasta.

Before dinner, I spent thirty minutes deciding on an outfit and ultimately decided on black jeans and an angora sweater. Casual, but nice. Coming down the apartment-over-the-garage stairs, I wondered if I should ring the bell at the front or knock on the back door. Andy must've been watching for me out the kitchen window because he came flying out of the house and onto the deck.

"Miss Georgia! We're having garlic bread and the snake got taken away and the napkins go under the forks and they have to be folded."

He met me at the edge of the bare deck, practically rocking back and forth with excitement. His hair was neatly combed, his shirt was tucked in, and he didn't have any stains on him. At least for the moment. Keely's boys would be mussed and stained within five minutes.

I held up my hand and didn't make a move to get closer to their house. "Y'all have a snake in your house?"

He shook his head. "No, Simon has one. He took it to school, but it got taken away before I could hold it and—"

"Andy, let Georgia come inside. It's freezing out there," Mac shouted through the open back door.

Andy spun on his sneakered feet and made for the door but skidded to a halt.

I followed because there wasn't a reptile in his house.

If he said they had one, I would have reconsidered the dinner offer. I didn't like snakes one bit.

"Women first," Andy said.

"Thank you," I said, entering the kitchen before him.

He shut the door and the scent of Italian filled the air. Leaning down, I passed to Andy the champagne-looking bottle of sparkling apple juice I bought at the store earlier.

His eyes widened as he took it. "For me?"

I nodded. "Guests bring a little gift as thank you for being invited to dinner. Since you did the asking, the gift is for you."

He spun around and held up the bottle for Mac and Drew to see. "I gots a gift! Can we drink it? What is it?"

I met Mac's gaze across the set kitchen table and counter.

Drew told Andy what it was and that we could have it with dinner, but he had to wash his hands first. Andy ran somewhere in the house, most likely to a powder room. But I stared at Mac.

Because Mac was staring at me.

He was in an ovary-exploding flannel shirt and jeans. His hair, too, was combed.

"And this is for you," I said, holding his belt in my other hand. I'd folded it in half, then let the tail end drop. He didn't step closer so I set it on the counter by the house phone, bucket of pens, pencils and scissors, and sticky notes.

"Hello, Georgia," Drew said, a bright smile on his face. "Good to see you again. Heard you had a little problem with your hot water heater."

I glanced at Mac. "Um, yes."

"It was the pilot light. You should be good to go," Mac said.

I blinked, turned my attention to him. "Thanks for that, and for inviting me. I, um... heard there was garlic bread."

Drew smiled. "That's right. In fact, I need to pull it from the oven." He turned and grabbed oven mitts. It seemed he was just as at home in Mac's house as Mac was. In fact, I didn't even know if Mac could cook.

Andy ran back into the room, flapping his hands as if he were air drying them. "Miss Georgia. I know you're doing a calendar with firefighters in it. With puppies and kittens. Do you think my dad's picture can be with Simon's snake? It'll be cool to have it wrapped around him, especially without a shirt. Did you know he gots a tattoo on his chest? Right here." He put his hand over his heart like he was ready to say the Pledge of Allegiance. "That's not where girls would have a tattoo because that's where they have nipples. They feed babies. Do you have nipples?"

"Holy shit," Mac muttered as his eyes fell closed.

I blinked at Andy because that was a lot of words on different topics. I was so focused on the idea of Mac having a tattoo on his broad chest that I didn't process Andy's question about me having nipples.

Drew huffed out a laugh and set a long half-loaf of garlic bread on a cutting board. "Andy, how did you hear about that?"

"Allison's mom has a new baby and she feeds the baby with her nipples."

"Well, that's accurate, but private," Drew added.

"You want Simon's snake to be in the calendar?" I asked, redirecting. I knew he had no real interest in nipples like he probably would in about ten years, so I didn't give it any more attention.

Andy's eyes widened. "Yes! Can you imagine it all wrapped around Dad in the photo?"

I looked from Andy to his dad. Yes. Absolutely. I could see Mac shirtless with a snake wrapped around him. I imagined it, then what the snake in his pants might look like.

"The calendar is to show off animals who don't have an amazing owner like Simon taking care of him. Or her. Is the snake a boy or a girl?" I asked.

Andy frowned, then bit his lip. He shrugged his shoulders. "Don't know. But it's named Sparky."

"Well, don't you think other animals should be loved by Simon's of their own?"

He nodded vigorously.

"Then we'll let those who need adopting be in the pictures so someone will see them and want them."

"There are lots of pets that need 'dopting?" Andy asked, cocking his head.

I thought for a moment, hoping my answer didn't set him off on another tangent. "Probably."

Andy spun around. "Can we 'dopt a pet?"

Oh boy. I bit my lip.

"You have Richard," Mac said.

Richard?

"He hides and we never see him," Andy said with a pout. He even crossed his arms over his chest just like his father had at the meeting the day before when he heard something he didn't like. "It's no fun when your pet lives behind the dryer."

I looked to Mac for clarification. Did they have a troll? "Richard is an unsociable, snooty cat who only comes out from wherever he likes to hide when he's hungry. Lately, it's been behind the dryer."

"So do you have nipples that feed a baby?" Andy asked me. The boy could give anyone whiplash.

Mac stared at my chest and scowled as if I brought my nipples into the house to aggravate him. With a strange growl, he came around the counter, took my hand and tugged me through a door just off the kitchen.

"Mac, what–"

When he flipped on the light and shut the door behind us, I realized we were in the laundry room. And–

And then he kissed me.

And set his palms over my nipples.

Oh lordy. Now it was my biscuit getting buttered.

17

MAC

I COULD HEAR Dad talking to Andy through the door. That Georgia and I were probably looking for clean dishtowels in the laundry basket. I didn't hear a peep after that because it was Andy's job to empty the dryer and try to fold the clothes–at least try–but since he hated the assignment, probably hadn't done it and didn't want to point it out. I didn't give it much thought because my mouth was on Georgia's.

She came in the back door in a pair of black jeans with a pale blue sweater. Something soft and fuzzy. Her hair was in a ponytail but had curls in it. Little dark wisps framed her face. Her lips... yeah, I couldn't have helped but stare at them, were pale pink and glossy.

Everything about her was soft and sweet and her scent was all I could breathe. And her tits? Fuck me.

She was just the right size for me. Not just her tits, but all the rest of her, too. I didn't have to bend in half to kiss her. Or get a crick in my neck. Beneath my palms her tits were heavy and more than a handful. She was so blatantly feminine, so different than me. Where she was lush and soft, I was hard and angled. I was calloused and rough and she was silky soft and sweet.

I pulled back. Looked at her with her lips no longer glossy but swollen, eyes closed.

"You're driving me fucking insane," I said, my voice pretty much a growl.

Her eyes flew open.

"Wh... what?" she whispered.

I ran a hand over my mouth, wanting nothing more than to spin her around, bend her over the washer and fuck her. To make sure she forgot Smutters or any other guy who looked her way. I had enough blood left in my head to know now wasn't the time to take anything further. Andy was occupied for now, but not for long. And no way was I taking Georgia for the first time as a quickie in my laundry room. Richard would probably jump out from behind the dryer and claw my bare ass while I was balls deep.

"You stroll into my life with that pink luggage, all

pretty and kissable. Then you charm my six-year-old into believing you're his new mom. Then you end up in my garage apartment where I know you've got a purple vibrator you use to cram into that perfect pussy. Somehow, you also cast a spell on the fundraising committee and I'm somehow a topless model. The calendar's all anyone can talk about at the station. All I'm hearing is what they'll wear an innuendo about holding a hose, fully charged. Now you're about to eat my garlic bread."

"Shirtless, not topless, and I told you, it's going to be family friendly."

"After all that, that's all you have to say?" I asked, reaching up and tugging on my hair. I was usually in charge. That was what was required of a fire chief. Of a father.

But this woman who felt like sweet sin and smelled like a field of fucking flowers made everything go sideways.

"Is that all *you* have to say?" she countered.

"No!" I said, tossing up my hands. "Now Andy's talking about another pet because they need adopting. One aloof asshole cat is enough for this family." I turned away, then abruptly back. "Oh, and nipples! Why would Andy even mention nipples if yours weren't poking against your top?"

Instead of narrowing her eyes in anger, because I'd

be pissed as hell if someone spewed such irrational drivel like I was, she bit her lip clearly trying to stifle a smile.

"You shouldn't be worrying too much about Andy and nipples right now. You think you're going crazy now, wait ten years."

"I'm not sure if I'll make it that long with you around." I was thinking with my dick, had been since she landed in Montana.

My eyes narrowed. I knew I was being irrational. Ridiculous, even. Didn't matter. "You're laughing at me."

She shook her head, her hand going to cover her mouth. "No. Not laughing."

She was laughing. Even after that kiss!

Was she not as... as consumed as I was? I had to get myself together, or at least put her in her place. Which wasn't laughing at me with kissable lips and hard nipples, which actually were, poking against her top.

No question they were doing that on purpose.

"You're under the amusing assumption that you're in charge here," I said, although I wasn't sure if "here" was Hunter Valley, my fire station, my house, my son, my job, my cat... I crossed my arms over my chest. Maybe it would keep me from touching her again. "That even with all the chaos you've caused, I'll be led around by my dick."

She arched a brow and looked down at the front of my pants where the outline of my dick, which I didn't think had ever been harder, couldn't be missed through my jeans.

"You're the one who dragged me in here."

The sass on her!

"I won't be eating out of the palm of your hand," I added.

"It's not the palm of my hand I want you eating out," she countered, then bit her lip. Her cheeks flushed prettily. Hell, everything she did was fucking pretty because I doubted she even cried in an ugly way.

I groaned, then gave up the fight and tugged her close and kissed her again. This time, my hands cupped her ass and held her against my dick. My knee nudged hers apart and I could feel her heat against my thigh.

"Dinner's ready!" Andy's shout came through the door loud and clear.

I let her go once more. "Fuck," I breathed. Control? What control? I needed a six-year-old to keep me away from her.

Georgia swiped her finger over her mouth to fix her lipstick, then made her way to the door and into the kitchen. I couldn't follow her, not now. With clarity, I realized I still didn't have the upper hand. Because Georgia was in the other room with my family enjoying spaghetti and meatballs, I had to think about water pressure ratios in my head to cool off and to get my dick to go down.

Who was in charge? Not me.

FUCK!

18

GEORGIA

"MORE GARLIC BREAD?" Drew asked, holding up the cutting board by the handle.

I took a piece because... garlic bread and set it on my plate.

"Thank you."

Drew was across from me. I had a feeling he knew what we'd been up to in the laundry room, especially since we didn't return with any dish towels, but he didn't say anything. Andy was on my left eating a meatball off of the end of his fork. He didn't say anything either, but the mind of a six-year-old was thankfully easily swayed by his favorite meal. His mouth was ringed with marinara sauce and there was a drip of it on his shirt. On my right was Mac. He'd plowed through his plate of spaghetti and was poking at a cucumber slice in his salad. His knee bumped mine beneath the table. He hadn't said a word since he finally returned from the laundry room, a full five minutes after me.

I needed some time to get myself pulled together after those kisses, but I wasn't given any. I'd had to go back into the kitchen and face Andy and Drew with a lust haze and wet panties. Fortunately, that pageant facade of perfection paid off. I pasted on a smile and let Andy do all the talking. Still...

That kiss! Those hands! That ass grab!

Since when did I tell a guy *it's not the palm of my hand I want you eating out*? Where was the Georgia who'd been dumped by her ex for a younger, slimmer, fertile option? Was it being away from my regularly scheduled life that made me bold? Was it Mac?

Maybe it was the fact that he'd brought up my toy submarine/vibrator earlier. He needed a little payback.

Except now I was sitting beside a guy who didn't know if he wanted to strangle me or fuck me sideways.

"Tell us about yourself, Georgia," Drew said, offering a glance at Mac, who'd remained silent all through the meal. "Family back in Georgia?"

"It's funny you're named after a state," Andy said on a giggle.

I gave him an indulgent smile, then answered Drew's

question. "I have a mother and a sister, who is married and has two kids."

"You're an uncle?" Andy asked, wiping his mouth with his napkin.

"Aunt," I corrected. "Tommy and Sally Ann are five and three."

"Do they like to sled?" Andy asked.

I shrugged. "It doesn't really snow very much in Calhan. That's the little town where I'm from. I'm not even sure if they've ever seen it."

"Never seen snow?" Andy's eyes were wide, as if the concept was ridiculous. Since it was April and it was still on the ground here, I had to wonder if Andy ever *didn't* see snow.

"Nope."

"Does your mom let you stay up late?" he asked, then gave his father a little kid glare. "I can't stay up past eight."

"Georgia's a grown up," Mac reminded.

All I could do was stare at Mac's mouth that had been on mine. Firm yet soft. That mustache. I'd never been kissed by anyone with one before. I thought it'd be scratchy, but it was soft. It added another dimension to kissing and had to wonder what it would feel like sliding across my inner thighs.

"She doesn't live with her mother," he added.

"Actually," I began. My throat was suddenly dry so I

took a sip of my sparkling apple juice. The bubbles tickled my tongue and it was really sweet. "The past few months I've lived with my mother."

"Is she unwell?" Drew asked, his question more concerned than probing. It made more sense that she might be sick and need help instead of a thirty-five-year-old woman moving into her childhood bedroom because her life fell apart.

I shook my head. "She's fine. While my divorce was finalized six months ago, our house is still for sale, so I don't have my share of the profits from that yet. So I moved back home."

I didn't tell them that I was pretty much broke. Art had been the breadwinner for the two of us. I had my car. Some retirement socked away. But quitting didn't help, and pageant coaching wasn't raking in the cash. My half of the house sale would help, but I wanted to put it toward buying another place, although solo it would only be an apartment. And if I didn't have a job, then getting a mortgage would be impossible and–

"This 'vorce and home stuff sounds boring," Andy said, breaking me from my depressing thoughts. He finished his meal and had been sitting quietly listening. "May I be excused?"

Mac nodded. "Math homework," he ordered.

Andy's little shoulders slumped and he rolled his eyes as if it was the worst thing in the world. "But–"

"Let me know what Miss Mornay says tomorrow when you tell her it's not done," Mac said, calm as could be.

Andy's lips pinched closed. He climbed from his chair and carried his plate over to the counter, then ran out of the room.

"I heard about the calendar idea," Drew said. "I think it's great."

Mac made a funny sound, like a growl, or it could have been a burp.

His father ignored him. "Did you do a calendar like this back in Georgia?"

I shook my head and glanced at Mac, waiting for him to tell me the idea was stupid.

"You don't have experience with it?" Mac asked, eyes raised. His voice wasn't hostile, but maybe a little confused, as if I'd suggested something willy nilly to the committee.

"Not with a calendar, but with photo shoots and–"

"Modeling?" Drew asked.

I shook my head. "Pageants."

"Pageants," Mac repeated.

I nodded. "Yes, beauty pageants."

His mouth dropped open.

"I can see how that would cross over," Drew replied, filling the silence.

"I also worked for a PR company as an administrative

assistant. I'm knowledgeable in fundraising and orga-
nizing and–"

"Pageants."

It was possible I broke Mac.

"What's a pageant?" Andy asked, coming back into
the kitchen to grab a pencil.

I looked to him. "It's a contest for being pretty. And
poised. And smart. And confident."

He crinkled up his nose. "Pretty? So no boys are in it."

"Actually, there are some boys in them. A few. Your
age, too."

"I don't want to be pretty."

"You can be handsome and smile nice and big no
matter how nervous you are. You dress up, comb your
hair and–"

"That doesn't sound like any fun at all," he added.
"But you liked it? You're pretty and smart and... what's
posed?"

"Poised," I corrected.

He shook his head. "I don't want to be that."

"I think you're fine just the way you are," I told him. If
Momma had said that to me at any time in my life, I'd
probably not be such a hot mess.

He grinned, then ran off.

"Since you're here, that means you no longer work
there," Drew said, steering the conversation away from

Andy picking up pageants as his passion project. "Smart of James Corp to snap you up."

Drew gave me a smile and I imagined him to be my father. Kind. Easygoing. Quick to offer praise. I didn't know mine since he and my mom divorced when I was four and he didn't stick around, but since my mother only mentioned him by the term *sperm donor* and *waste of time,* I didn't imagine him being anything like Drew.

"My um, well, my ex-husband also worked at the company so I quit when we separated." I fidgeted because... yay! I loved talking about my failures. Especially in front of Mac.

I glanced his way. Yup, he was still staring. He'd kissed me. And fondled me. And... yeah, was slightly deranged, but I'd definitely liked how he'd been a little rough, as if he couldn't control himself. I didn't remember ever being kissed like that before. And we'd been dressed, with only a door separating us from a child. But I had no doubt it was an appetizer for what it would be like if Mac and I got together.

Maddening. Wild. Definitely intense and potent.

But the way Mac was behaving, like he was quietly having a stroke, I wasn't so sure it was going to happen again. Art made me insane and he was the last person I wanted kissing me. Hell, I left the *time zone* to get away from him.

"You quit?" Mac asked, finally rejoining the conversation.

My cheeks flushed with an equal mix of anger and shame. "He... well, he's the CFO and wouldn't quit just because we were divorcing. Besides, he had an affair with his secretary so she'd have to leave too in order to make that environment anywhere near comfortable."

Drew frowned. "His sec– I don't blame you."

"He cheated on *you*?" Mac asked, eyes wide.

I nodded. Yeah, that was a shame that made my cheeks hot. If they saw a picture of Pam, they wouldn't be so surprised. She was blonde and skinny and had perky boobs and thighs that didn't rub together, and I bet she was multi-orgasmic.

"I left because I didn't want to stare at them every day since they ended up getting married." I took a swig of the sparkling apple juice and wished it was something a hell of a lot stronger.

"They got *married*? Holy fuck," Mac muttered.

Both men had similar grim expressions. They looked at each other, as if they were talking without saying a word.

"This job got me out of town and away from them and my mother, who isn't as fun to live with the second time around." I bit my lip. "Actually, she wasn't all that fun the first time either."

It looked like thunderclouds had settled over their heads. All because of me.

Oh no. I put on my pageant smile. "Don't worry, everything's fine now. I'm here and things are moving forward with the fundraiser–" I flicked a gaze at Mac. "– quite nicely."

"What you need is a night out with some new friends," Drew said. He stood, picked up his plate and carried it to the sink. Coming back for more dishes, he asked Mac, "Aren't you meeting up with Theo at Kincaids?"

Mac looked at his watch. "Yes. I have to get going."

"Take Georgia with you."

"Um–"

"What?"

We spoke at once. I stood, grabbed my plate to help with the dishes. Drew took it from my hands. "I've got this," he said with a smile and tip of his head. "You get ready to go. Mac will wait."

I looked to Mac who didn't look like he'd wait at all. If his father wasn't looming over him, he'd probably bolt.

I didn't have too much choice. Saying no let them know I let Mac get to me. His surliness was because of me, definitely, but the calendar fundraiser was a good idea. Solid. Actionable and profitable. There was buy-in from everyone in town but Mac. As fire chief, he had a say, but he'd missed the chance to voice his opinion because of the emergency call. He arrived too late. By then, it was a done deal. Now he had to go with it. Be excited about it because he *was* the fire chief. He couldn't be Mr. Gloom and Doom in front of the town when it was *his* fundraiser.

But he could give me grumpy looks across the kitchen table. And man handle me in his laundry room.

I was going with him to this Kincaids place. I didn't have a choice. But the last thing I wanted was another man stuck with me when he didn't want me.

19

MAC

ALL I COULD THINK about as we drove to Kincaids was that I was going to kill Dad. Except I needed him to take care of Andy, so he was no help if I killed him. *Take Georgia with you,* he'd said.

That was the last thing I needed to do.

Did I want to spend time with her? Fuck, yes.

Did I want it to involve more than kissing and groping in the laundry room? Abso-fucking-lutely.

But I needed some epic control to keep my hands off of her. Having her in my truck, only a foot away and her scent swirling all around? Dangerous.

I couldn't touch her again. No way.

I'd tasted her. I wanted more.

But Andy looked at her as if she was a sparkly unicorn, in love with the idea of her being his mom. Hell, he might actually *be* half in love with her.

With him, she was all smiles and gentle looks. Wise words without being patronizing to a little kid. She knew just how to handle him to make him feel special, but not spoiled. She liked him and accepted every inch of his rambunctious, no-filter personality.

I couldn't blame Andy for his moon eyes and eagerness. I thought she was a sparkly unicorn of a woman, too. Her ex cheating on her with another woman was insane. Stupid. And that made him a total fucking asshole.

The guy cheated on *her*. What red blooded male would stray from someone so insanely sexy as Georgia?

She was everything I wanted in a woman but never knew. I was hot for her all the fucking time. It made it almost impossible to control my raging dick. I had to linger in the laundry room folding towels for the thing to go down! Not only that, she was leading me around by the balls on this fundraiser idea. Because of that kitchen fire, I'd missed the chance to say *fuck no* to the idea. Instead, the rest of the committee decided without me. Now, I didn't have a choice but to be Mr. January and I was sure she knew it.

She was subtle about it, her approach. A look and my dick was hard. Ridiculous talk about nipples had me staring at hers across the kitchen. With Andy and Dad present. A smile and the crew signed up to be in the calendar. From what I heard, puppies and kittens were immediately offered. Did anyone say no to her? Did anyone not fall under her spell?

I saw through it. Knew that sparkly unicorns like her weren't real. They were fantasy. While she was sitting in the truck beside me right now heading down Main toward Kincaids, she wasn't staying in Hunter Valley. She was temporary, flying her sparkly unicorn ass off into the sunset when the fundraiser work was complete.

Leaving me and my dick unsatisfied. Or well satisfied but alone.

Women left. They took your heart with them and Georgia was the perfect reminder of this. Out of all the women in my life who'd cut and run, at least she'd given advanced notice. I needed to be the smart one. Hell, the *only* one who didn't fall under her spell.

A car came in the opposite direction, giving a little honk of the horn on the way by. I couldn't tell who it was, but it was someone who knew me, and my truck, since it had a little light bar on top. Which was most people in town.

Georgia shifted in her seat. She'd grabbed a soft black coat and gloves from her apartment. Her hands were in her lap, holding a little purse that was the same blue as her sweater.

"You didn't have to bring me," she said.

While she didn't mention being cold, I reached out and angled the vents her way. That coat was more decorative than insolating.

"It's fine," I replied, glancing in my rearview mirror.

Out of the corner of my eye, I saw her looking my way. "When a woman says *it's fine,* it means anything but fine," she countered. "I figured, after being in your laundry room, since I *drive you fucking crazy* that maybe it really isn't fine."

I slow and come to a stop at an intersection and look her way. I keep my hands on the steering wheel instead of grabbing the lapels of her coat and pulling her across the center console and onto my lap.

"To a guy, fine means fine."

"And *you drive me fucking crazy* means *yes, I'm thrilled to hang out with you?*"

That sass was back. When she spoke about her dickhead ex over dinner, I saw her smile slip, her shoulders curl inward. The asshole had hurt her. Diminished her and that was fucking wrong. But the defeated look lasted only for a moment because suddenly she smiled and, well... it was possible I'd been dazzled. I was impressed by how she could change her mood so quickly.

It seemed this woman, the one in my truck who was giving as good as I gave, was the real Georgia. And I fucking liked it.

Problem. Big fucking problem. She should come with an emergency siren. A warning label that said DO NOT KISS OR GROPE!

"I shouldn't have kissed you. I shouldn't have–" I lifted my hands off the steering wheel indicating cupping her tits. "I don't want Andy to get any ideas."

"Because he's six and he shouldn't be learning about feeling a woman up quite yet?"

I glowered. "Because he's obsessed with finding a mom and has his sights set on you. I can't do anything or get involved with a woman who's not sticking around."

Reaching up, she brushed a tendril of hair off her cheek and nodded. "I would never do anything to hurt him." After a moment, she continued. "You're right. I'm only here for the fundraiser. No kissing. No big hands on my breasts and playing with my nipples."

Instantly, I remembered the feel of them. Their weight. The way her nipples had gotten hard as I ran my thumbs over them.

She hadn't forced me to kiss her. Or touch her. I'd done it all on my own.

A car horn stirred me. I looked both ways, then crossed through the intersection.

"No kissing. Nothing about nipples," I agreed through gritted teeth, although I wasn't sure if I was talking to her or myself.

"Doing that, or *not* doing that, and I'll make you less crazy?"

"Yes." I ran a hand over my hair. Was I going to be able to *not* kiss her or get her pussy to ride on my thigh? "No. Fuck, I don't know. You've stirred up my house, my work, my–" I bit off the word *dick* at the end although I was positive she knew it. No chance she missed how hard I was in the laundry room earlier when she was riding my thigh. "You're coming out with me because my father is acting like an old busybody."

I turned into the parking lot.

"You're in the truck," I continued. "We're here. It's happening. Theo James is Mav's brother. He's the local doctor and he helps out with fire trainings."

"Still..." She pushed.

"I'm sure Mallory knows now you're joining me and–"

"Mallory?"

"His girlfriend," I explained. "She's Miss Mornay to Andy."

"She's his teacher, right?"

I nodded. "Yeah. If Mallory knows you're coming out, then Bridget knows. If Bridget knows, then–"

"Meaning?"

"I'm sure you won't be the only woman there."

20

GEORGIA

Mac hadn't been wrong. I met Theo, the doctor. Dex, the hockey player, who was also Theo's brother. He was supposedly famous, but I didn't follow the sport, or any sport for that matter. That was it for guys. Then there was Mallory, Bridget and Lindy. Each was with a different James brother. Mallory and Theo, Bridget and Mav, although he wasn't here and Lindy, who was married to Dex. And Lindy was Bridget's sister. It was a little complicated, but pretty cool. On top of that, there was Melly, the town librarian. From the information Mallory shared–while Melly blushed–she just started a relationship with a guy who was fifteen years older, a lumberjack and oh yeah, her ex's dad. Daniel wasn't here because he was with his four brothers caber tossing.

I'd had to look that up on my phone to know what it was, but now I knew why Melly's cheeks were so red. If her man was as fit and gorgeous as the ones in the Highland Games photos, she was one lucky lady.

"I can't believe you all came out to meet me," I said.

The ladies were at one end of a long high-top table, the guys at the other. Mallory, Bridget and Lindy sat around me in a semicircle since I was on the end. Each of us had a glass of wine, except Lindy, who looked like she was going to have a baby any second, even though she waved her hand and said it'd be three more weeks.

"We have a group text," Bridget said, pushing her glasses up her nose. "Theo told Mallory you were coming and she sent out a group text. She heard a lot about you from Andy and none of us could miss getting to know you."

"No wonder Andy's been telling everyone he has a new mom," Mallory said.

When Andy looked panicked earlier when he would have to tell Miss Mornay he didn't do his math homework, I envisioned her to be a stern, old woman who used a beady eyed glare as a scare tactic.

But Mallory was far from old, probably mid-twenties, and she looked like she'd be an amazing teacher.

"At school?" I asked, covering my face with my hand. "Oh no."

She laughed. "You're so dang pretty it's no wonder he's been dazzled."

"I think someone else is dazzled, too," Lindy said, leaning in. She looked down the table and we all glanced in that direction.

There, at the end opposite mine, was Mac. Arms crossed over his chest. While Dex and Theo were talking, he was eyeing me.

"He's been staring since you sat down," Mallory added.

"Glaring," Bridget corrected with an amused smile.

"Glowering," Melly said.

"Eye fucking," Lindy whispered.

I gasped and the others giggled.

"That is not the look of a man who is dazzled," I whispered. But it *was* a look that made me hot. Made me remember how he kissed. How he'd dragged me into the laundry room because he couldn't hold off a second longer getting his lips on mine. And his hands on my body.

"Not him, his dick," Mallory said simply.

I sputtered on a sip of my wine. "I *dick dazzle* him?"

In unison, they nodded.

I dick dazzled a guy? And not just any guy, but Mac?

Impossible. I definitely hadn't dick dazzled Art. A

guy who was dick dazzled didn't cheat because his dick was so happy and satisfied.

"Are you taken?" Bridget asked. "Is that why you're not interested in him?"

My eyes widened. "Oh, I'm interested because... look at him. And I'm recently divorced, so ridiculously single."

"Well, they say the best way to get over a guy is to get under another," Lindy offered, waggling her blonde eyebrows. "The way Mac's eyeing you, he wants you under him."

"Over him, too," Mallory added with a giggle. "Why wouldn't he? You've got a rockin' body and that hair..."

She and Bridget eyed me up and down, or at least what they could see of me above the table. "Yeah, how do you do that?" Bridget asked.

"What?" I asked, glancing down at myself. Had I dribbled some wine on my sweater? Shit, it was dry clean only and red was a bitch to get out.

"Your hair. It's in a ponytail like mine, but I look like I finished a run, all snarled and wispy."

Lindy reached up and playfully tugged on the end of Bridget's. They'd said they were sisters, but Lindy was probably my age and Bridget in her early twenties. They didn't look much alike either.

"Yeah, and your makeup, sheesh, do you have a YouTube channel or something?" Mallory added.

I blinked at her, confused. YouTube channel? Me?

"She even makes me look like a slob," Lindy piped in, but she had to be joking because she looked so put together.

I was a little embarrassed at their scrutiny. "My momma always said you don't leave the house without your face on and well, I need all the help I can get."

"Help? You're insanely pretty. It's kinda hard not to look at you. You could be Miss America with the way you're all put together," Mallory suggested. "Right?" She looked to the others. "All she needs is an evening dress and a sash."

I frowned. "Actually, I did pageants for ten years."

Mallory set her hand on my forearm and looked at me with anticipation. "Say you were Miss America."

I shook my head. "I didn't make it further than runner up for Little Miss Calhan because I wanted to baton twirl instead of sing the *Battle Hymn of the Republic* my momma expected, which is ironic because in my hometown, the Civil War isn't over."

"You can baton twirl?" Melly asked, eyes wide. "I tried once, and it hit me in the head."

I laughed. "Absolutely not. Thus, being runner up. Sing? Yes. But I never got close to another tiara again."

"I knew it!" Mallory said. "You have the poise for pageants. And the hair. God, I need the name of your shampoo. Do you use a keratin treatment?"

"Little Miss Calhan?" Lindy asked, her eyes practically twinkling. "I bet you were adorable. If this watermelon turns out to be a girl, then maybe she can do pageants." Her hands rested atop her huge stomach.

"Pageants aren't for everyone," I advised. "Trust me. I was seven at the time of the baton twirling incident. If only I'd sung, then I'd have the little tiara to put beside all my sister's trophies and tiaras from her wins. But as I got older, I got these..." I pointed to my chest. "And hips. And an ass that got to be more than the pageant norm. You might think I rock an evening gown, but I don't rock a swimsuit."

"Whatever," Bridget said. "Who rocks a swimsuit anyway? They're expensive and besides, you can wear one for like two weeks here in Montana. Anyway, who says you have to be stick thin to be stunning?"

"My mother and sister," I answered immediately. "Who is stick thin and was Miss Georgia. Also, my ex, who traded me in for a lighter model."

"My mother's a gambling addict alcoholic," Mallory shared, as we were having a crazy mother contest. "Mothers don't know everything."

"My mother had an affair with the mayor," Melly said.

"Mayor Mary?" I asked, wide eyed.

Melly shook her head. "A few mayors ago."

"Who cares about being skinny anyway?" Lindy asked. "I haven't seen my feet in two months."

"Exactly," Bridget said. "Your ex is obviously a jerk. Can you imagine if men were judged by wearing a swimsuit?"

"While wearing heels and twirling in a circle? And a baton?" Lindy added, grinning. "Although Dex wears skates like they're an extension of his body so I bet he could do heels."

"What's that, sugar?" Dex asked her, hearing his name.

"Nothing." They kissed and he turned back to the guys. God, they were insanely cute to watch. Happily married and any day having a baby.

A baby. I was instantly jealous of her and all she had. A guy who wouldn't stop touching her. Called her *sugar* and was clearly all-in for a family.

"Is that where you got the idea for the fundraiser calendar?" Mallory asked, stirring me from my thoughts. "Because of the pageants?"

"Calendar?" Lindy wondered. Obviously, their group text didn't cover everything.

I filled them in.

"I love it!" Lindy said, absently rubbing her belly. "She should ask Eve to be a sponsor."

"Our friend Eve, who's married to Silas, runs Steaming Hotties," Bridget explained.

"The coffee shop? I saw the place yesterday. It's across from the fire station. I'll stop in tomorrow and introduce myself."

"I'll buy a few and put them up at the library," Melly offered.

"So Mac's going to be in the calendar?" Bridget asked.

I nodded and gave Mac a quick glance down the table. "It's optional, but as fire chief he feels obligated. He's not too thrilled about the entire concept," I admitted, thankful the music in the bar was loud enough that the guys couldn't hear what we were talking about.

"Mac in bunker gear and *only* bunker gear?" Lindy asked, fanning herself and grinning. "He doesn't need to smile. Hell, that grumpy as hell face he's giving Georgia right now works *juuuuuuust* fine."

We glanced down the table again to Mac. That wasn't his grumpy face. That was the look he gave me as he kicked the laundry room door shut behind him and kissed me.

Oh my.

"Totally dick dazzled."

21

MAC

I STARED at Georgia sitting between the other women. She was laughing at something Mallory said, her mouth covered with her hand. The mouth I'd kissed a few hours ago. The one I wanted to kiss again. The one I wanted to see wrapped around my dick.

The women turned to look at me as one, as if I was a curiosity in the zoo.

"You're staring," Theo murmured.

"They're staring," I countered.

He noticed, then ignored them. "You're eyeing her like you want to swipe the drinks off the table and fuck her over it."

He wasn't wrong.

"So is every other man in here," I growled. I didn't miss the way she had every guy's attention and she didn't even know it. They weren't sipping their beers and thinking about taking her to church because all I could think of was defiling the hell out of her. Even after I'd been the one to tell her no more kissing.

I'd started it. I'd ended it. Yet, I wanted more.

After the way she responded in the laundry room? Fuck, she'd wanted it, too.

"She keeps sneaking glances at you," Dex commented. Sitting beside his wife, he had a hand on her thigh. "I feel like I'm in the lunchroom in middle school."

"Yeah, well, I kissed her." As if that explained this stare off.

"She's not a cookie to lick and say it's yours," Dex added, continuing on the juvenile theme. Although I did want to lick her and do it in front of the entire bar so everyone knew she was mine.

But she wasn't mine. No. Fuck! I wanted her but couldn't have her. Yet, no one else was going to touch her.

Theo laughed and I finally looked his way. He'd been a grumpy asshole when he moved here last fall. He'd gone from big city surgeon to small town doctor, gained an amazing girlfriend. And he got happy.

"What?" I asked, studying him. "You're scaring me with your laughter."

"It's payback time," he said, grinning.

I frowned. "What the fuck are you talking about?"

"I was the cranky fucker sitting in this bar and you were laughing your head off at me because I had my head up my ass about Mallory."

"And I'm the cranky fucker now?" I pointed to myself.

"Oh yeah."

"Let me ask you two a question about women."

Dex grinned. "We are the experts."

I ignored that. "What does a woman do in the bathroom in the morning for forty-five minutes?"

"Hell, if I know. Mallory's in and out in thirty."

"Thirty?" I asked. I showered in five, shaved in two and I was done.

"Lindy spends forty-five minutes in the morning. Shower, moisturizing, drying and styling hair, makeup."

So Georgia hadn't used her vibrator. That would probably add another few minutes, right?

Theo slapped me on the shoulder. "You want her, even if she's that high maintenance, I say go for it."

I swiveled on my stool to face him, to get him to understand. "She's not from here."

"Right."

"She's leaving as soon as the fundraiser is done."

"Exactly."

"She's the one who came up with the calendar idea."

"Don't hold that against her. It's a really great idea," Dex added.

"Fine, but I was all for a chili dinner. Then another biggie is that she's staying over my garage."

"I know. Easy access. So what's really the problem? Sleep with her and get her out of your system." The way Theo looked at me, he couldn't see an issue. He had an advanced medical degree with years of additional training. I figured he was smart enough to grasp the situation, but no.

"Andy's in love with her."

His brow winged up. "That's the competition you're worried about? A six-year-old?" said the man who didn't have, and didn't want, kids.

"He can't fall for someone who's not going to be around."

His look changed because he was sympathetic toward a kid, not me. At least he and Dex recognized the challenge when it came to Andy.

"He or you?" Theo countered.

I glowered.

"Parents are allowed to have sex. Or I hope so because I'm going to be one in a few weeks," Dex said. Clearly he knew what he was doing in the bedroom since his wife's current state was a blatant example of his virility.

"Yeah," Theo added. "Like you said, she's leaving.

Andy's going to be sad whether you sleep with her or not. Have fun. Have sex. You remember what that is, right?"

I glowered some more.

"I told her on the way here that the kiss was a mistake. That it shouldn't have happened, and it can't happen again."

"One thing women know about men," Dex said. He was like a happy golden retriever, always smiling and easy going, as if he shit rainbows. Although, I'd seen him play hockey and he was a different person on the ice.

"Yeah?" I asked, waiting for him to share his wisdom.

"We're always wrong."

Theo chuckled. "I bought Mallory a house when I wasn't supposed to. I can vouch for that statement."

Georgia got up from the table and went toward the bar carrying her empty wine glass. I watched her progression, watched various men eyeing her on the way. Arlo, Mallory's brother and the owner of the place, was behind the bar. He came over to her, offered her a smile. They spoke for a moment, then he winked and went off to fill her order.

The man seated at the bar turned toward her. Eyed her like a steer at auction, then began to talk to her.

"He's hitting on her," I growled, after watching them for a few seconds.

Dex and Theo followed my glare.

Dex laughed. "That's one of the dads from the PeeWee league."

Since everyone in town knew Dex played pro hockey, he'd been wrangled on occasion to help coach with the kids' programs at the skate center. It wasn't consistent, yet, but as soon as he retired, he'd probably take up the role full time. He said a few more years with the Silvermines, but I had a feeling he'd be quitting sooner than he thought once he became a dad.

"Looks like they're hitting it off," Theo commented.

Like hell!

"She came here with me," I snapped.

"So? She's not yours. She's fair game," Dex advised.

I stood up. "She's *not* fair game," I added.

"Professional advice?" Theo tossed out before I could storm over there and beat up the PeeWee dad.

More advice from the James brothers. Were they the experts? Maybe they were since all four of them had somehow gotten women to fall in love with them. "Sure."

"Listen to your dick."

My dick was saying *get over to the bar, keep that fucker from shooting his shot, toss Georgia over my shoulder, and take her somewhere so I can sink into her sweet pussy.*

Fine. I was wrong earlier. We could kiss. I could play with her nipples. I didn't have to marry her. I didn't have to keep her, but she sure as hell wasn't going home with that guy.

Theo was suggesting that Georgia was the perfect solution to a sex drought. No strings. No hard feelings. No running into her at the grocery store after things were over. We could fuck and forget each other. Hell, she'd be in a different time zone.

Maybe Theo wasn't too dumb after all. Or I was just slow. Or protective. Maybe both.

Eyeing Georgia, I got between her and PeeWee Dad.

I arched a brow, hoping that simple gesture conveyed everything my dick wanted.

"Um, excuse me?" the guy said.

I ignored him and focused solely and completely on Georgia.

The corner of her mouth tipped up and she arched one perfectly curved brow in return.

I took her hand.

"Sorry," I said to the guy. "She was never going to be yours."

Then I led her out of the bar.

This was happening.

My dick was so fucking smart.

22

GEORGIA

MAC DIDN'T SAY a word until we were standing beside the passenger side of his truck. Instead of opening the door for me, he set his hand on it. I turned to face him, and he stepped close. It was dark out, but the parking lot was well lit. Still, he was cast in harsh shadows. It was freezing and our breaths came out in little white puffs.

"I was wrong," he said, reaching up to stroke my hair.

The gesture raised goosebumps along my neck.

"Oh? About what?"

There was a long list of things he was wrong about so it was important I knew which one. The calendar idea. Being Mr. January. The kiss.

"Kissing." His gaze dropped to my lips. "And touching."

Suddenly, I wasn't cold any longer. And I agreed with him.

"So wrong," I agreed, nodding. I'd dick dazzled him and I wanted his dick.

"We need to kiss. And I need to touch your perfect tits again. Cup your ass." With every word, his head dipped closer and closer to mine until I could feel his breath on my cheek. "Not PeeWee Dad."

"Who?" I wondered.

"Exactly. This is happening, Gorgeous."

"Okay. Kissing. Groping. What else?" I asked breathlessly. Why wasn't he kissing me now? COME ON, KISS ME!

"I have a fucking list." His lips brushed my jaw, feather light. I angled my head.

I wasn't sure if he meant he had a Fucking List or just a list that was really fucking good. Didn't matter either way. "Good. I do, too."

23

MAC

I CLOSED the door to the garage apartment behind us, and as I'd held her hand since I helped her from my truck, I tugged her into my arms. And finally fucking kissed her.

We hadn't said a word on the drive home. I'd had to focus on the road, not her, otherwise I'd have driven onto the curb. She was too much of a temptation, even with her curves hidden behind her coat.

Shifting, I turned us so she was pressed against the door.

What was it about this woman? Her taste. Her scent. Her body. She was fucking intoxicating. Yet, it seemed she'd come to town to mess with my life. The fundraiser. My son. She was even at my dinner table.

Yet, I couldn't control myself around her. And I was always in fucking control. I had to get *in* control, and this was the way to do it. To bend her to my every want. To control *her* in the only way it seemed I could.

So I slid my hand into her silky hair and gave a slight tug.

She moaned.

Fuck yes.

"Like that?"

She blinked her eyes open. "Oh yes."

"You want it a little rough?"

"Do you do this... or anything else any other way?"

I shook my head, stared at her swollen lips. "No, gorgeous."

"Good."

Good. I claimed her mouth as mine because right now, she was. She liked it a little rough, I was the man. I could get used to this, to kissing her. Being with her. This was like my reward for putting up with her insanity. For making my life crazy.

But while all the blood had flowed south to my dick, I had to remember she was just passing through. She wasn't from Hunter Valley. Wasn't staying, either. She–and this between us–was temporary.

So I'd kiss and fuck the hell out of her while it lasted.

"Mac," she whispered against my lips when I finally let her up for air.

"No strings," I said, working the buttons on her coat open. I was going to see what was beneath that soft blue sweater.

"What?" she asked as her hands dropped and started to open my belt buckle. The same belt I'd used to keep her suitcase closed.

"This. What we're doing. No strings," I repeated. "You're leaving and I can't–"

"Just sex," she agreed immediately, her gaze focused on my pants.

I nodded once. Fuck, it was so hot watching how eager she was to get to my dick.

"Just sex."

Good. She understood. Then I went about ridding her of her clothes.

24

GEORGIA

I WAS DOWN to my bra and panties. Mac stepped back to stare. He ran his thumb across his lower lip as he looked me over from head to toe.

I'd been hot until now. Too hot. Too needy to even think things through.

Mac was seeing me. Almost all of me and while my gray panty set had pretty lace and mesh, it didn't hide all of my imperfections.

I raised my hands, then lowered them, then raised them, alternating back and forth like windshield wipers across my body.

"What's the matter?" he asked.

His shirt was gone. His belt hung open. Same with his jeans. The little V there showed plaid boxers. Of course he had no idea what the matter was because he had an insane body. While he wasn't more than six feet tall, he had thick muscles. There was no question he worked out. He had to be fit as a firefighter and he no doubt was a leader not only on the job but as an example for overall fitness.

He was the perfect calendar model. He was... perfect.

While I didn't want to think of Art while I was standing in my underwear ogling Mac, I had to take one moment to compare. Art was officially scrawny. With a paunch. His chest hair was a little mangy. No muscle tone. He was... pathetic all around. Why had I been upset in losing him? I couldn't remember now.

I was blinded by the Mac's washboard abs and V thingy that led to a huge dick. I hadn't seen it and couldn't say for fact, but this guy? Big dick energy meant big dick.

Then there was me. How was he even here with me? Was it because I was easy? Well, I was for him. Also, easy access. I was staying over his garage. But–

"I've never seen so much thinking going on. And what are you doing with your arms?" he asked. "Don't go all shy on me now."

I looked up from his abs and met his gaze. "I... um,

well, it's been a while, and the last guy I was with–my ex-husband–dumped me for his secretary." I wasn't telling him he married and impregnated her, probably on the same day. Standing here vulnerable and naked was enough.

25

MAC

RIGHT. Her dipshit ex-husband.

Georgia, standing in only frilly and feminine bra and panties, was sexy as fuck. Her tits, which were more than a handful, filled out that lace and fabric to perfection. Clearly, she didn't think that.

"Let me guess," I said on a huff. "The secretary slash new wife is probably a twig."

She nodded and her lower lip stuck out in a little pout.

I took a step closer to her so I could look down that tempting line of cleavage. I could get lost in there. Smothered. I might die in the deep valley.

What a way to go.

"Bony," I continued, guessing what the other woman was like. "Little tits that can probably go without a bra."

Another nod.

Reaching out, I brushed her long hair over her shoulder, then played with the bra strap.

"Eats salads for every meal and has an ass your ex bounces a quarter off of."

With a head tilt, she tried to shift away. Bingo.

"Oh no, you don't," I said, hooking my finger in the strap to keep her in place. "First off, your ex is an idiot. Anyone that would even *think* about cheating on you has to be mental. Doing it with someone you work with? Dick move."

Her eyes widened and I continued. She needed to hear this.

"Second, I don't want a bony woman. Look at me, I'd break her." I let her go, puffed up my chest and patted it in a *Me, Caveman* gesture. "I don't want little bug bites for tits. I want a handful. Hell, more than a handful. Ones that bounce during sex. Plump nipples that like to be sucked on and tugged. An ass I can grab onto while I fuck. I love thick thighs and curves, Georgia."

Finally, she looked up at me with those gorgeous brown eyes. Her lashes were so fucking long. I knew my words were getting to her because she was panting, those perfect tits jiggling with each breath.

"Really?" she asked.

I took her hand, set it on my chest and then moved it down my body, turning it so our overlapping fingers faced down. Into my boxers they went. I wrapped our hands around my dick.

My rock hard, eager-for-her-touch, dick.

"Fuck..." I breathed. It had been a long fucking time and her little hand felt insane. "Really," I repeated.

I pulled our hands free, then stepped back. Separating from her touch wasn't what I wanted, but I didn't want to embarrass myself by coming from a quick handy. I was patient. Maybe. We could fuck right this second against the door and it would be amazing. I'd make sure it was good for her but if she had even a trace of doubt about how hot she was, I was fixing that right fucking now.

As I moved to the bed, I said, "Now, be that feisty woman from the laundry room earlier and rule my world."

"How... do you want me to do that?" she asked.

I licked my lips. "Easy. Come sit on my face."

I watched as her eyes widened. Her entire body flushed at my dirty words. I had to wonder if her ex ever went down on her before, which I didn't want to think about, but also wanted to rectify if it was true. A woman needed to be eaten out good and thoroughly. And often.

"Sweetheart, earlier you were under the assumption

that you were in charge," I said. "I'm in control. The only thing you can do tonight is call it off. Anytime you want. So unless you want to stop, get over here and climb on."

26

GEORGIA

"You don't want to... have sex?" I asked. What he was asking pushed every one of my triggers. He'd see me naked. He'd see me *down there* REALLY up close and personal. I'd be sitting on him. I didn't have small thighs and I wasn't light. I could literally smother him to death.

I didn't pull out a mirror or anything... well, okay, I had that one time when Keely took some weird women's empowerment class in college and had to explore our femininity for homework. She'd gotten me in on the concept, although we'd done the exploring in separate bathrooms.

The view was... weird. I definitely wasn't a lesbian and why any guy wanted to go down there was–

"Fuck yes, I want to have sex. But I don't have a condom. Do you?"

I laughed at the irony of it all. We'd been driving each other crazy ever since I arrived, the need for his dick had been so powerful ever since I'd been on my knees in the baggage claim and he'd taken his belt off. But now I couldn't have it. Or at least not the way I wanted it.

"Yeah, no." The last thing I'd expected to do in Montana was... this.

He crooked a finger and I walked closer. He was being patient, but I felt like it was only going to last so long, like once he got his hands on me, he wouldn't be able to hold back.

That worked for me.

Reaching out, he hooked a hand around my waist and pulled me in close so I stood between his spread knees. The air was warm, but goose bumps still rose on my skin. I gave him credit for holding my gaze when my boobs were right at eye level. They ached to be touched by him again. My nipples throbbed for his attention.

"Is your apprehension about me going down on you in general or sitting on my face?"

I licked my lips. "You said you wanted thick thighs and curves. I just don't want to kill you with them. Your department would show up and I really don't want to explain what happened."

"What a way to go." He grinned, then nodded. "I know what the problem is and it's my fault."

"Yours?" What could he have possibly done wrong?

"You're thinking too much." His eyes raked down my body and settled on my boobs. "I'm going to solve that right now."

Pulling me into him, he set his mouth over my nipple. Yes. *Yes.* Even through my bra I felt it. The tug. The pull. The–

"Oh dear Lord."

He wasn't gentle, but I didn't want that. I needed to know he craved me as much as I did him. And this was only his mouth on me.

I felt his grin as he kissed along my cleavage and then gave my other nipple the same attention. Back and forth he went until I was writhing, my fingers caught in his hair.

"These tits. Fuck. I've fantasized about them so much."

The clasp was undone and he moved away only long enough for my bra to fall to the floor.

He growled, eyes darkening and heating in turn. A *fuck yes* escaped his lips before he went back to work. The feel of his mustache against my skin only enhanced the sensations. Raspy. Tickling. Soft. His calloused hands cupped. Kneaded. Fingers brushed over my nipples. Tugged.

"Ohhhhhh," I moaned.

He turned and tipped me so I was on my back on the bed and he loomed over. The feel of him pressing into me was potent. He was solid. Sturdy. I felt small and feminine and overpowered–in the good *he's going to claim me* sort of way.

His attention didn't waver from his task.

I had no idea how long he played with my breasts, but it was a while. Minutes. Hours. I didn't care. My fingers yanked, then pushed him closer. Then tugged. I was close to coming from just this alone. How was that possible? Oh Lord, it felt so good. My pussy ached, lonely and wet. Why wasn't he giving the rest of me any attention?

Eventually, he kissed across my bare stomach. YES!

Fingers hooked into my panties and they slipped down my legs as he worked his way lower. I lifted my hips, helped him slip them off.

Somehow, watching him toss a scrap of lace over his shoulder was really hot.

When I was bare, he finally lifted his head, looked up my body at me. "Fuck, you're gorgeous."

Lifting up onto my elbows, I met his gaze. I could only imagine what I looked like, my nipples all wet and hard from his mouth and fingers. He knelt on the floor between my legs. He could see my pussy. All of me.

Then he leaned in and gave me a lick, as if I was the

tastiest of ice cream cones. I sure as hell was dripping like one, melting in the heat of his gaze.

"Mac," I whispered, arching my back.

He stood.

"No!" I gasped. One lick was *not* enough.

"Don't worry, I'll give you more."

He dropped onto the bed beside me, which made me bounce. He manhandled me as if I weighed nothing, moving me so I straddled his chest. I hovered over him, my legs straddling his narrow hips. His hands went to my breasts and he cupped and played with them some more. My back arched and I stared at the ceiling.

He was definitely a boob man.

"Come higher, gorgeous."

I shimmied up his torso but either not fast enough or not the way he wanted because his hold moved to my hips and pulled me up so I knelt over his face. I had to admit, just the way he was moving me around was a turn on.

I looked down at him. "What about you?" I asked. He was still tucked away in his jeans. I'd felt it earlier and he had to be uncomfortable.

"You want to suck my dick?" He turned his head and kissed the sensitive skin on inside of my thigh.

I bit my lip. I wasn't going to think about how it had been in the past with Art. Mac asked about *his dick.* Yes, I wanted to suck it. I was hovering over his head, my pussy so close to his face that his warm breath fanned my heated–and very wet–center.

I couldn't be nervous or embarrassed any longer. Not with how he touched me. Looked at me. Made me feel.

"Yes." Was that my voice? The one word sounded sultry and deep.

"Turn around."

I frowned, then caught on. Oh yes, please.

Carefully, so I didn't knee him in the head, I shifted to face his feet.

"Good girl." He groaned. "Your ass is perfection. Take me out."

He lifted his hips so I could push his jeans and boxers down enough so his dick sprang free.

"Oh my stars."

He was big. Porn star big, although I'd never seen porn, so maybe he was just normal sized, and Art had only sported a baby pickle in his pants. I licked my lips because suddenly my mouth watered. Dicks weren't that attractive, but Mac's? Plum colored. Long. Thick. Bulbous head. The skin was smooth and taut and he was hard. It curved up to his navel and there was a drop of fluid at the slit.

My mouth watered. I had to taste it.

So I did.

He hissed and tensed. I licked the slit again, then swirled my tongue around the crown. "This looks just like a fireman's hat," I said, taking the tip into my mouth.

He laughed, but then growled at the same time his dick pulsed against my tongue. A salty burst of pre-cum coated my tongue.

"Who's in charge here?" he asked when I gave it a little suck.

I giggled, hovering right over him. I felt pretty and desired and a little bit of a tease. "Me."

I gasped when he grabbed my hips, pulled me down and put his mouth on me. The hot feel of his tongue was so incredible.

"MAC!" I shouted and rolled my hips as he licked me right up the center and swirled around my clit. He found my clit. No road map. No instruction manual. "Please, don't stop."

"Get my dick in that sweet mouth and I won't."

27

MAC

GEORGIA.

Holy fuck.

I'd been crazy for her since the airport. Since I saw her bra and that vibrator. Since she smiled at me. Since I saw her curves. Then she moved into the little apartment and was the organizer of the fundraiser. Everything she did seemed to push my buttons, to drive me a little more insane with every fucking smile. What was it about her and those smiles? It was like a superpower. A weapon to get anyone to do whatever she wanted.

I thought getting her here, my hands and mouth on her, I'd tame her. Soothe this need I had to get her to bend and submit.

It did the opposite. She was insatiable. Gorgeous. Wild. And once she got over her hang-ups and shyness, she rode my face like she was trying for the Triple Crown. She became untamed.

It was really fucking hard focusing all my attention on her needs when she had my dick in her mouth. I wanted to figure out if she liked her clit licked on the left or the right the best. If circling made her pant. If a flick made her drip.

I couldn't think of any of that. Hell, I couldn't think at all because the suction of her mouth was like the sweetest, wettest vacuum. She was fucking good.

I knew she had to come first. That wasn't something I had to remember. Georgia always came first. But she sure as hell tested that because my balls had been tight, my spine tingling with the need to come. I held back, held back, held the fuck back until she was writhing and moaning around my dick as she came.

Only when she dripped on my face did I let go, shooting my load. Her greedy mouth swallowed every drop I pumped down her throat.

I couldn't see. My ears rang. My fingers were numb. Did I have toes? And being smothered by pussy with my dick in her mouth would be an amazing way to go. Hands down.

Holy shit. It was the best sex I ever had, and we didn't even have sex.

I thought I was in control of every situation. But this? I might have told her what to do and she submitted beautifully, but I was in big fucking trouble here. One taste of those tits, that pussy and I was hooked. The way she moaned and screamed my name? I was screwed.

Theo said to sleep with her once and get her out of my system. Get my dick wet. Empty my balls. Whatever.

But this? It wasn't a one-time thing. No way. I was addicted.

So it was my new mission to get her naked and make her mine as often as I could before she left. Send her on her way back to Georgia with a sore pussy, a satisfied smile on her face, and hopefully a big *fuck you* to her ex.

28

GEORGIA

WHEN I WOKE UP, I was alone in bed. Mac was gone.

I wasn't sure what to feel about that. Hurt?

We made no commitments. The opposite in fact. We'd agreed to no strings.

Glad? A little, because I wasn't sure what to say to him. *Thanks for the orgasm and I'm glad I didn't suffocate you?*

Well, I was thankful for the orgasm and I was glad I didn't kill him with my pussy. I giggled to myself as I stumbled into the little bathroom. The pedestal sink wasn't big enough to fit all of my moisturizers and makeup, so I had my case on the top of the toilet tank. It was clear Mac hadn't considered a woman's morning and night routines when planning the remodel.

I saw myself in the mirror. Gasped.

"Oh!"

Now I was thrilled he'd left, hopefully while it was still dark. The night before, I hadn't done my nighttime routine because, well, Mac. My makeup was still on, smeared and scary. Raccoons had nothing on me. And my hair! One side was flat, the other sticking straight up like I was in an eighties big hair band. Thank the good Lord he didn't see me like this. He'd run away screaming as if it was Fright Night before Halloween.

Spontaneous sexy times and makeup removal and moisturizing didn't go together.

I turned on the shower. I had work to do.

29

MAC

WE'D ALREADY BEEN on two calls this morning plus discovered the brush truck's pump gauge was broken. The station's industrial dryer had a lint clog and had to be disconnected and the vent line cleaned out. An order of latex gloves was somewhere in Utah instead of being delivered yesterday.

None of that could get me down. Not when I had Georgia sucking the cum from my balls like a porn star. She'd been all shy and tentative because of the number her ex did on her, but when I got my mouth on her pussy, she'd gone all in. Forgotten about any hang-ups the asshole gave her and her passion and uninhibited nature came out.

She blew my mind... along with my dick.

So yeah, I had a spring in my step and a smile on my face.

"What's wrong with you?" Flowers asked, sticking his head in my office. He assessed me as he would a patient on scene.

I looked up from the budget spreadsheet. Even those numbers didn't bother me today.

"What?"

"You're smiling. It's scaring me." He turned his head. "Van Routen. Get in here and bring a med kit."

"Jesus, does everyone think I'm a cranky asshole?" I asked, pushing my chair back from my desk and crossed my arms over my chest.

When I realized what I did, I dropped them.

Van Routen came in as I asked and he and Flowers said, "YES!" at the same time.

"Not an asshole, chief," Van Routen confirmed. "Just cranky. Not today though. We're not used to seeing you smile so much. It's like you got l–"

Barks and shouting cut him off. It was a good thing, too. While we were all really close, this was a place of work and there were clear sexual harassment rules in place. We were cautious about coed living since both men and women were on shift together and my sex life was not up for discussion.

I wasn't going to kiss and tell about my night with Georgia. Not with any of them.

A black streak ran by my door.

"What was that?" Flowers asked, sticking his head out my door.

A woman ran past. "Benji!" she hollered.

"That was a dog. And that"–Van Routen pointed–"is another."

This one was gray and black, tongue lolling in his open mouth, as he casually sauntered into my office and sat on my foot.

"It's the first day of the calendar shoot. Smutters is here for his pics and Maria, if we don't get any calls, will do hers, then Cleary."

Georgia walked past, then backed up and stopped in the doorway. "There he is," she said, pointing at the dog. She gave him a look similar to the one I employed with Andy when he'd done something wrong, but it was more amusing than disastrous. "That's Corky."

I left Georgia's bed this morning before dawn. It was dark in her little apartment and I didn't get a chance to study her while she slept. One, it was a little creepy, and two, I'd been behind. I had to sneak into my house, shower, and put my uniform on before Dad got up. Yeah, I told Georgia the night before I wasn't going to be grounded if I was caught in her bed, but I didn't want

Dad to think differently of her. Our no-strings activities were our secret.

I didn't want to have a conversation about my sex life with *anyone* before coffee.

So the last time I had a look at her, she was sprawled beside me, sated and completely uninhibited. Naked, hair a mess, lipstick smeared. I'd done that to her and I was fucking proud. I wanted a medal and a trophy.

Now, I couldn't look away. What was it about her? Why was I drawn to her like this dog Corky and my foot? It was electric.

"Hi," she murmured to me, then looked to Flowers and Van Routen. "Hey there. Busy morning?" she asked them.

As they shared the morning's events, I took in her black pants, white blouse, which was untucked, and the tails peeked below the hem of a red argyle sweater. Her lipstick was a bright red that matched and reminded me of the ring I found around my dick in the shower this morning.

DON'T THINK ABOUT THAT! Building code violations. Root canals. Flooded basements. Anything but the way I'd stared at my dick in the shower and didn't want to clean that Georgia-made mark off.

"–so Maria is opening the back bay door to let light in for the shoot," Georgia said to the guys. "Corky here will be in her pics and Benji, if Kennedy from the animal shelter caught him, will be with Peter. There's a litter of kittens in a cat carrier that can be used, too."

Smutters. Georgia was going to be with him. Probably without a shirt on. Smutters, not Georgia. No fucking way. I was the only one seeing her bare.

Nothing was said for a few seconds.

Van Routen cleared his throat. "So, since you two are having a staring contest, we'll just... yeah, you two can–"

"Later, Chief," Flowers added. "Come on, Corky. Let's go find you a treat."

The dog woofed and I felt him move away, but I only saw Georgia.

They left. She stepped into the room.

Finally. Fucking finally. I moved around my desk and went to my door. Shut it. Locked it.

Turned and pulled her to me. Kissed her.

And fuck yes, she kissed me right back.

30

GEORGIA

THE KISS WENT from hot to inferno in a matter of seconds. He turned me, pressed my back into something hard.

"I have to make you come."

"Mac," I breathed, because I wasn't averse to the concept, but we were in his office. At the fire station.

"Be a good girl and widen your legs for me." His voice was a murmur in my ear. Rough and deep, but only for me to hear.

His deft fingers opened my pants and slid the zipper down with a skill and speed I shouldn't take time to consider. I didn't, because the next second his fingers were sliding down the front of my panties and parting me.

"Oh my God," I breathed.

"Shhh," he whispered. "Can you be quiet, or do you want me to take my fingers away?"

I shook my head, looked up at him. "I'll... I'll be good," I whispered.

"That's right, you will."

This wasn't playtime. This was like the final minute of a football game and the team needed to make it all the way down the field and then score before the time ran out.

A finger slid into me while another circled my clit. In, out. Round and round.

I rolled my hips into what he was doing and bit my lip.

"Fuck, you're so wet. Is that all for me?"

I nodded, whimpered.

"Your pussy's clenching on my finger so good. I'm the only one to make you feel this way, aren't I?"

"Mac," I hissed, when he curled his finger inside me in just the right spot. Where had that spot been my whole life?

"Not Smutters. Me."

I blinked. "Smutters? What?" Why was he talking about him now?

"Only me." He was pushing me to orgasm quickly so there was no doubt who was giving it to me.

"You," I said.

"That's right. Fuck, I can't wait for that to be my dick inside you. Come for me, gorgeous. I want to watch."

Of course, I did what he wanted. I came, pulsing on his finger, biting my lip to stifle the sounds I wanted to make. It felt good. Soooooo good. And doing it in his office where I had to stay quiet, where he could get a call at any time and I had a photo shoot to run, was hot. The whole thing pushed me over. I went from *hi* to *fuck yes* in an embarrassingly short time.

Once I caught my breath, he pulled his hand from my panties, and I watched as he licked his fingers clean.

"Fuck, that was just mean," he said with a heated glint and a grin.

I frowned. "What?"

"I can't do anything else. Just watch you as you come. And taste you. Fuck, you're gorgeous when I get you off." He licked his lips. "I can't bend you over my desk. I can't get you on your knees. I can't press you into the door and get on *my* knees."

"Mac," I whispered.

He growled. "Flowers is worried about me since I'm smiling too much. It's your fault. That mouth of yours seems to be my undoing. That pussy. Fuck, your sweet taste."

I laughed and tried to come out of my pleasure stupor.

"What?" he asked. "It's true."

"And Smutters?" I asked. I'd been too aroused to think about why he was talking about him, but now it made sense. Was he jealous? Sure, Peter was handsome, but he had *nothing* on Mac. Somehow, I got hot for a growly, jealous guy.

He frowned. "Fuck Smutters. Wait, no. Don't fuck him. Just–"

"I can handle the guy." I ran my thumb over his lower lip.

"What are you doing?" he asked.

"Red lipstick doesn't go well with your mustache," I told him.

He grinned. I wasn't used to his smiles. To see him anything but moody and a grump. But this? My ovaries did backflips at the sight. But I liked it.

31

MAC

IT SNOWED OVERNIGHT. Dad got Andy to school no problem since he parked his SUV in my spot in the garage and was able to drive through the snow to the cleared street. Nothing had been shoveled. I never let him because I went on enough calls for falls or heart attacks from shoveling. Now that Georgia was in the garage apartment, I couldn't wait until later to get the job done. I had to make sure the path was clear for her to even get out the door and down the steps.

No way was she getting hurt.

I got out the shovel and went to work on her outdoor stairs, flinging snow over the railing. When I got to the top, she opened the door. Warm air and her luscious scent washed over me. I was working up a sweat from the workout even though it was below freezing. Unlike me, she was all fresh and pretty in–

"What the fuck are you wearing?" I snapped.

She glanced down at herself. "What?"

She wore jeans and a thick black turtleneck sweater. Her hair was down, tumbled over her shoulders and today her lips were a vivid red. She looked fucking perfect. How did she do that? Look so damned pretty all the time?

I hadn't seen her since my office the day before, but I heard all about her from those who'd had their photo shoots. Plus, the mayor who updated me on the number of calendars already ordered. She was thrilled. The town was excited about the concept. All because of Georgia.

But I was the one who licked her pussy flavor off my fingers. The one who looked her over and got cranky all over again.

"Those." I pointed at her feet.

"My boots?"

"Those aren't boots," I countered, suddenly crankier with her than I would be at my dad if he had a shovel in hand. "They have a heel and–" I ran a gloved hand over my face. "Are they *suede*?"

She picked up her foot and bent her knee to scope

out her footwear, as if she was looking to see if she had shit on the bottom.

"What's wrong with them?"

I waved my hand in the air to indicate the winter wonderland, even though it was April.

"We have a foot of snow. You can't wear those today."

"Why not?"

"You'll fall. A heel?" I shook my head. They were sexy as fuck, but completely useless today, except to get my dick hard. "Get your snow boots on."

She crossed her arms over her chest and the move plumped up her tits. Tits I knew were big and soft and lickable and insanely responsive.

"I didn't bring any. In fact, I don't actually own any."

I propped the shovel in the corner of the railing, set my hands on my hips and sighed. "Get your things. We're going shopping."

She reached just inside the door for her coat and pulled it on.

"For what?"

"Winter boots. Is that the coat you're wearing?"

She rolled her eyes. "Obviously, since I'm putting it on and the one I've worn it since I got here. It's warm."

"Now there's snow. It's wool. If it gets wet, you'll freeze."

"I don't plan on getting it wet."

We could stand here and bicker or I could shut up

and get her to the store. I sighed, knowing sleep was delayed. No way could she go to work dressed like that. I wouldn't be able to sleep for worrying about her. I had an obligation to keep her safe even if she didn't.

"Let's go, gorgeous."

32

GEORGIA

THE GUY always seemed to be growling at me. As if I drove him crazy, just like he'd said in his laundry room while he was kissing me for the first time. We were in his truck, the interior warm. He'd gotten off shift a little while ago and instead of going to sleep like I learned he did in the morning after he worked, he was driving me across town.

"Busy night?" I asked, trying to think of something neutral to talk about. Clearly, my shoe choice angered him. I had to admit, snow boots sounded really cozy right about now. It was cold. Like really cold. With flurries lingering in the air, the town was picture perfect, like a postcard. The plows had been busy, but the roads were still covered. Everything was white.

"This isn't too much snow, so people know how to drive, but we did have to pull one car out of a ditch. Not because of bad driving but because of a deer."

This wasn't too much snow? If it snowed like this in Georgia, the state would be shut down. The grocery store shelves would be bare. Havoc would ensue. Here, it was just another day.

"It's, um, great your dad takes care of Andy like he does."

The corner of his mouth tipped up. "Yeah, I couldn't do it without him."

"What happened to Andy's mom?" I asked. Shit, bad thing to ask. Maybe it was a bad breakup. No, maybe she *died*. Lord, that would be horrible, and I just stirred up heartbreak. "Never mind. It's none of my business."

He shook his head as he glanced in the rearview mirror. "It's okay. I'm actually not his dad. I'm his uncle. He's my sister's son."

"You have a sister?" I wondered.

"Tracy. Four years younger." I didn't miss the way his fingers gripped the steering wheel. "I... we... haven't seen her since a week after Andy was born. She's a drug addict. Got pregnant by mistake and she somehow stayed clean for the pregnancy, pretty much because I had her on lockdown at my house, but ultimately couldn't beat it. We had an intervention, and she chose drugs over her own kid and–yeah."

Well, shit. That was awful. For all of them.

"I'm so sorry."

With a shrug, he said, "I have full custody of Andy. He's mine. So the three of us make do."

He was quiet for a minute. I thought they were getting by just fine. Andy was smart, funny and very well adjusted. But I understood now why he was so crazy about me being his mom. It wasn't me specifically, I knew, but he was in a phase where any woman might fill that role. He probably met and heard about other class-mates' mothers and felt like he was missing out.

"What about you? You have siblings?" he asked.

I smiled. Even though his dad asked me about this the other night over spaghetti and meatballs, I answered again. "Yes, sister. Sassy."

"Sassy?" He glanced at me and grinned.

"Welcome to the South," I said. "Her name's actually Sue Ann but has always gone by Sassy. She's two years older. Pretty. Perfect."

"I doubt that," he said with a huff.

I laughed. "Oh, she is. Or thinks she is. She was Miss Georgia about ten years ago."

"Wow, impressive." He braked at a stoplight and looked me over, as if he was seeing me differently. "That explains a lot, doesn't it?"

I frowned. "What?"

"The other night, you said you were in pageants, too."

"That's right, but not to the same success." I rolled my eyes. "Some parents make their kids learn piano or play a sport. I thought I'd be pretty good at soccer, but my mom put us both in pageants. To give us poise and countenance. Her words, not mine. I tried to be as talented as my sister, but I don't have the... good southern daughter personality that does whatever her momma told her."

He grinned. "Oh, I believe that."

I pursed my lips. "My momma and Sassy are two peas in a pod. I could never keep up with Sassy, no matter how hard I tried." I looked down at my gloved hands. "I'm thirty-five years old and still failing."

"Failing?" He slowly pulled through the snowy intersection.

"No Miss America sash for me," I said, sounding a little dejected. While it had never been my dream, but Momma's, it had been ingrained in me not to lose. "Not even Little Miss Calhan. No job. No husband." *No baby.*

Out of all of those things, the baby was for me. He or she would be mine. Something everyone saw as an accomplishment, but I saw it as unconditional love. I didn't seem to get it from the others in my life.

"No job? You said you quit because you worked with your ex and his new wife. Right?"

I nodded.

"Why the hell would you stay there and torture yourself?" He blinkered and turned into a parking lot.

"Why would I let myself go enough to lose him in the first place?" I countered.

He whipped his head toward me and his eyes widened in surprise. "Let yourself–"

Before he could say more, I took in where we were through the windshield. Gave him a pageant smile because... here? "Oh look, we're... we're getting boots at the Seed and Feed?"

33

MAC

THE SEED and Feed was the store that carried almost everything. Including women's winter boots. I didn't doubt there were similar stores in her hometown, but I doubted Georgia ever went into one. Not unless she was interested in purchasing salt licks or baby chicks and she didn't seem the type to get her hands dirty.

I'd been in the store a thousand times, but never with a woman. And never with one who revealed more about herself than what she said aloud.

It sounded like her mother and sister expected things from Georgia that she didn't want to give and put her down because of it. She didn't fit their mold and shamed her for it. Her ex? If he went for a different woman, then

Georgia didn't fit his mold of a wife either. Her confidence took a hit and that was clear, especially the other night when she tried to hide her luscious body from me.

Whatever her hang-ups and doubts, I didn't see them. To me, she was perfect. And I'd tell her until she started to believe me.

"Like I told you, your ex is an idiot to let you go," I said. "I don't know your sister, gorgeous. Or your mother. If they don't see you as strong and brave and perfect just the way you are, then that's their loss."

"You haven't seen my sister," she countered, sighing deeply. If Georgia thought she was a hideous creature that needed to walk around with a bag over her head so she didn't scare the town folk, then her sister must be a supermodel, or Georgia needed glasses.

Who could look prettier than Georgia? It was fucking impossible.

I shook my head. "No, I haven't. I'm not interested in her. I'm interested in you."

She huffed and I reached out and lifted her chin with my fingers so her eyes met mine. I saw the hurt there. This time, it wasn't me who put that look there, thank fuck. But I still didn't like it. I never, ever wanted her to be less than confident.

"I didn't make that clear the other night?"

She glanced away. I thought I had, but not enough. This was going to have to be repeated until it sunk in.

"Hmm," I said, dropping my hand. "I think you might need a little reminder."

She glanced around. "What, here?"

We stood between a display of women's long under-wear and wool socks. Canned country music came from hidden overhead speakers.

I grinned. "You have a dirty mind. I was going to tell you how fucking gorgeous you are. That those boots, while ridiculously impractical, are hot and I want to fuck you in them and only them. But don't worry. I'm not going to pull my dick out by the long underwear display so you can see how hard you make me. All the fucking time."

Her gaze drifted downward and I closed my eyes for a moment. That wasn't helping.

"Oh," she said.

I closed the space between us, tucked her hair behind her ear. "You're driving me crazy, gorgeous. All I hear about at work is *Georgia this* and *Georgia that*. At home, Andy won't shut up about you. My dick is pissed I had to work and leave your bed yesterday morning. And nothing drives me crazy. Usually. Until you showed up. Got me?"

She studied me, her cheeks flushed. "Yes."

"Good girl," I said, stroking her cheek with my knuckle. So soft.

I watched as the hurt in her eyes lifted and she

smiled. Fuck, she was like a flower that needed water, wilting until it was given the attention and praise it needed to thrive. It seemed every time I called her a good girl, called her gorgeous, I saw the doubt lift.

I'd build up that confidence, even if it meant getting over my issues with the calendar. Or I could fuck her until she knew how pretty and perfect she was to me. That was a much better idea. She'd go home feeling beautiful and know she was a sex champ.

"Hey, Chief!" someone called from the next section over.

I raised my hand in a wave but didn't look away from Georgia. People saying hello to me happened to me all the time. I learned I could only wave otherwise I'd be pulled into random conversations all day long. And right now, all I saw was Georgia.

"Let's get you those boots," I told her. "You've got a calendar to work on."

The good news was, I'd see her later for a fundraiser committee meeting.

The bad news was, I'd see the first of the calendar photos. Then I'd know what I was in for. Body oil. A waxing like Theo mentioned. An inappropriate pose with a fire hose.

Juuuuust great.

34

GEORGIA

By the time we were done buying my new snow boots...
and puffy coat... and hat, the roads had been plowed
enough where Mac thought it was safe for me to drive
myself around town for my meetings. It was hard for me
to be put out that he decided what was best for me, but
to be honest, it felt good.

He was thinking of my safety. Mac no doubt saw my
being southern as a weakness, not having snow boots or
a proper Montana coat or the skill to drive in snow. But
his alphaness came from concern and safety, and I hadn't
had someone take care of me in a long time. And the last
thing I wanted to do was get in an accident and he get
called out to rescue me.

Sure, Mom and Sassy worried about me, but not for the same reasons. They worried about me because they thought I couldn't do anything right. That I failed at pageants, my weight, my marriage. I didn't have a husband and two point five kids and a picket fence and a minivan and a husband to satisfy with chicken and dumplings on the table at six and a blow job before bed.

Without all that, I wasn't doing life right.

I was tired of being shamed by people in my life. Momma and Sassy, even Art. Yes, I'd let them, but I hadn't taken the time to step away and see it. Like *really* far away. Like Montana.

So I spent the day reveling in Mac's *good girls* and concern. I'd had my first man-made orgasms in a long, long time. He helped me pick out sturdy, thick–and cute–boots with fake fur trim. A pink coat. He'd rolled his eyes at the color but approved the down fill count.

I was wearing both, plus a cozy hat with a fake fur pompom on top, when I went into the same meeting room at the fire station as last time and opened my laptop for everyone to see the first images. The photographer had shared with me the folder of all the images and I narrowed it down and selected a few for each month for the committee. These were the ones I thought were the best, that showed each of the firefighters' personalities and where the pet they were holding was behaving.

I was nervous because while everyone but Mac was

excited about this fundraiser alternative, I wanted them to like the progress. If they hated it, I could organize a chili dinner. But I'd feel like a failure. Or feel like *more* of a failure.

I needed this to work. I left Calhan with my tail between my legs. I didn't need to leave Montana the same way.

Today it was Mac, Maverick James and Mayor Mary in attendance. Patrick was on shift, and they were out doing fire inspections.

Like Monday, I stood in front of the conference table. Like Monday, I was nervous as hell. Yet, I had my pageant smile on and exuded all the fake confidence I had when twirling that baton trying for the Little Miss Calhan trophy.

I spun my laptop around to face them. "Mayor, if you'll just click the right arrow, you can scroll through the images."

She shifted in her chair to reach the keyboard. Maverick and Mac flanked her and they leaned in.

"The goal of these photos is to portray that the Hunter Valley Fire Department is friendly, confident, competent, but also down to earth," I began, ensuring they understood the perspective and reasoning behind the shots.

As I spoke, I studied their expressions. Mary's smile grew as she clicked through the photos. Maverick and

Mac looked like they were in a poker game, not wanting to give any tells as to the cards they held.

"The animals aren't an add on to make the images cuter," I continued. "While they do, it's more to show them as loveable as possible and clearly people friendly and adoptable. The–"

Maverick held up his hand.

"These are really great," he said, looking me square in the eye. He was a really attractive, really large man in a Steaming Hotties pink t-shirt. "Very impressive. You're right. The dog, especially in this one... could you go back an image, Mary?" he asked. She did and he pointed. "It's almost like he's on shift as part of the crew."

"Such fun," Mary said. Her eyes were still on the laptop display. "This one, with Peter, that's done well."

Mac humphed, leaned back and crossed his arms over his chest.

Oh no.

The mayor and Maverick looked away from the laptop and to him. "You can't possibly have a problem with these," Mary said to Mac.

"Still think they're objectifying your crews?" Maverick asked, circling back to what Mac complained about on Monday.

"No," Mac replied. "These photos..."

I held my breath. When I realized my smile was slipping, I pasted that fucker right on. Just because we'd, yeah, done some serious oral the other night and he'd fingered me to orgasm right down the hall in his office didn't mean he was going to like the photos.

"...are really great," he finished.

I exhaled and my fingers actually tingled. He liked them. Thank the good Lord. The smile now was genuine. "Good. I heard your concerns on Monday with regards to this project steering clear of sleazy or inappropriate. The importance of this, besides raising money for a worthy community cause, is to showcase that the fire department *is* the community. It's made up of brave, kind and approachable locals."

"She and the photographer have done a damned fine job," Mary added. She looked to Mac, her gaze running over him in his uniform. The shiny badge on his chest had CHIEF across the top. "Why do you look like you're constipated? That's the look everyone in town would have the day after the chili dinner."

She laughed and Maverick's mouth twitched.

He dropped his arms and gave her a weak glare. "Because now I have to be Mr. January."

35

MAC

THE MEETING DIDN'T LAST MUCH LONGER after our review of the photos. Georgia had the approval she needed to continue and she'd get back on whatever schedule she'd put in place to get the calendar done on time. The community event was still on for the same date and time as the initially proposed chili dinner.

I didn't get to talk to her before she left the building. While I wasn't on shift, I'd been called out to join the crew doing building fire inspections because an older warehouse was flagged. This meant we had to mark that it was potentially unsafe until repairs and codes were met, but we had to notify Hunter, the police chief. While the chances of there being an issue with that unmanned building in the next few days until it could be repaired was small, we didn't operate on chances.

So I didn't get a chance to tell Georgia that I'd been wrong about the calendar. The photos were good. Tasteful. Everyone had their shirts on. No glistening bodies or sexy leers. Nothing of the sort. In my favorite one, Liz from B shift was in the driver's seat of the engine. While the photo was taken from the side, Liz looked forward as if driving. A dog was in her lap and staring ahead as well, as if both of them were focused on getting to a call. They looked determined, but somehow the photographer made them look friendly and warm.

There was no tension or anticipation coming from them as we felt riding to a call. Just... what the hell did I know? I liked it. That was the reaction they were going to get from the community as well.

Then there were Smutters' photos. He looked buff and fierce with a hose slung over his shoulder. His images were of him in motion, as if tugging the line for a fire. But sitting on top of the hose on his shoulder was a kitten. I had to admit, Smutters with a kitten was perfect. Instead of the chip on his shoulder, he had a cat.

I was impressed and proud of Georgia. Sure, the photographer deserved credit, too, but I didn't want to get in her pants. Only Georgia's. I'd tell her how pleased I was, then I'd fuck her.

36

GEORGIA

I PARKED my car on the street in front of Mac's house and walked up the driveway. It was dark and I could see inside. The lower level was lit and I stopped at the base of the stairs to my little apartment and looked through the kitchen window.

There was Mac at the counter, flipping open the lid on a pizza box. Andy was jumping up and down, waving napkins in the air. Drew was there, too, saying something I couldn't hear. I couldn't miss their smiles and the way they interacted. It made me smile myself to watch.

While the dynamic wasn't part of a Norman Rockwell painting, they were a family. Three generations of men. They were a unit. They loved each other just the way they were.

That had my smile slipping and even in all the thick, cozy layers of down and fleece, I was chilled. I looked up at the pitch-black sky, wondered all of sudden what the hell I was doing here. Standing and watching a family in their happiness while I was all alone.

I'd never felt so lonely than in that moment, seeing what I always wanted but could never have. I was shut out, literally, in the cold. What I saw was something I could only see and long for, but nothing more.

I was the no strings woman who'd leave Montana and Mac's life would be less crazy.

He was right when he said he didn't want to start something with me. I was leaving. When the fundraiser was finished, and at the rate it was progressing, the end of next week. I'd be back in Calhan as a pageant coach. Back to listening to Sassy talk about her perfect children. I'd hear about Art and his new wife and his soon-to-arrive child. To Momma pointing out what I had and gave up.

What I'd never have now.

Maybe I'd be hired on in Denver at James Corp head-quarters. Hopefully, this contract job was a test. But even if I succeeded, I wouldn't be staying here.

While the MacKenzies had welcomed me into their home, I wasn't family and never would be. Fooling around with Mac was fine, but this? Seeing them tucked warm and safe in their kitchen with pizza and laughter and love? It was too much. It was best to remember that now. To protect my heart from a little boy's toothless grin. From a kindhearted older man. From a sexy, protective firefighter.

I climbed the steps, saw the note tucked into the door that invited me to join them for pizza. I stared up at the night again, swallowed hard. They didn't know it, but their invitation was cruel. A tease.

Because I failed at no strings. Sure, when I told Mac "just sex," I'd believed it then. I'd never done a casual thing before, always being in some kind of relationship. Or I caught feelings when there really wasn't any.

Like now. I was catching feelings not just for Mac but his family. His life.

Why couldn't Mac have been just a guy I fucked? Nothing more.

But no. He had to have the perfect house. Perfect son. Perfect dad. Live in a perfect town with perfect... Yeah, everything was perfect.

Except for me.

With one last glance down to the family who was now eating at their kitchen table, I turned and went into the apartment, leaving the lights out.

I didn't want Andy to notice I was home and come up. Sure, they'd see my car out front, but hopefully assume maybe I got picked up and was out somewhere. Or asleep.

I stripped off my outerwear and slid to the floor, my back against the door.

I dialed Keely.

"I'm in trouble, K," I said when she answered.

"Tell me."

So I did. I pretty much vomited everything that happened since I arrived.

"Why didn't you tell me about Fireman Mac Hotstuff before now? You're pretty much staying at his house and didn't share?"

I rolled my eyes. "He's always grumpy with me. Growling, like I pissed him off. Especially over the calendar."

"Is he actually angry at you?" she asked. "I mean, he's not going around badmouthing you and your work just because he doesn't want to be Mr. January, is he?"

"No. He's... grudgingly going along with it and at the meeting this morning, said he liked what I'd done. But he doesn't have any choice. The others want the calendar so unless he wanted to be an asshole, which he's not, he has to be for it."

"Oh, I bet he has a choice but secretly knows your idea's a good one. So jerk or not?"

"Not a jerk," I told her immediately. He was a nice guy. "He's... sweet, but don't tell him that. I mean, he calls me *gorgeous*. He bought me boots. Was going to drive me around today if the roads weren't clear."

"Ate you out like it's an Olympic sport," she added.

That made me smile because yeah, he had talent. "That, too. And got me off in his office at the fire station."

"That's really freaking hot. So he's a good guy. And dirty."

"He has a mustache," I added, as if that explained everything.

"Holy shit, woman. I'm fanning myself. But I haven't figured out why you say you're in trouble."

I sighed and rubbed a hand over my forehead. "Because I've been here four days and while we agreed to no strings, I'm falling for him. And his family."

And this cute little apartment. And what Mac and I did in that bed.

"Oh." She knew I wanted a child of my own. That a hot guy with a magical tongue was easier to find than a guy who liked and wanted a kid, or already had one. Mac was amazing with Andy. Dedicated. Hell, the boy was his nephew and not that he shouldn't treat him like his own, but he was committed to raising him up right.

"Yeah, oh."

We said our goodbyes because what else was there to say?

Next, I texted Bradley who needed to help me out. Somehow, he got me into this mess.

Get me a room at the James Inn. Now.

If I was just a no strings woman, then I needed to be out of their backyard and not invited in for pizza. I needed to protect myself. Coming to Hunter Valley was supposed to get me away from my troubles, not make more. A minute later, he texted back.

Room 204

GEORGIA

"HI GEORGIA, THIS IS DREW."

"Hey," I said, the usual southern response to a greeting where the word was somehow dragged out to be two syllables. "Is everything all right?"

I was at the fire station for another photo shoot. We had already gotten through half of the months and the plan was to finish within the week. Leanne, the part-time admin support for the station, pulled me from the photo shoot to take a call. Learning it was Drew made me worry. Why would he ask for me?

"Actually, no. I was trying to reach Mac, but he doesn't answer his cell and Leanne says they're on a call.

She knows you're staying with us and told me you were available."

I set my hand on my chest. As soon as he said *no* my worry started.

"Yes, he's been out all afternoon," I told him. "They've been gone since before I arrived. And yes, I'm available. Are you okay?"

"Well, I seem to have broken my foot."

I gasped. "What? Oh no. Are you at home? Are you alone? Do you need me to get you? Did you fall? Hit your head? Chest pain?"

He laughed. "Nothing like that. I was at the grocery store and stepped off the curb wrong or caught a little ice. My foot twisted. There were people around so don't you worry about me being alone. John Tranquil drove me to the ER."

I didn't know who John Tranquil was, but I was thankful he offered assistance. And I was so glad the injury wasn't anything worse.

The night before, after Bradley sent me the room number at the James Inn, I packed a small bag for what I might need today–there was no way I could carry my huge suitcase down the stairs–and drove to the James Inn. It was posh and understated and as amazing as it was supposed to be. But it wasn't the cozy, little apartment in the MacKenzie backyard.

And that was the point. I needed distance and staying across town was what I needed.

"I'll be right there." Immediately, I thought about where my purse was. My keys. The hospital. Where was the hospital? I was in the fire station. Leann would know.

"You are sweet, but I'm fine," he reassured. "It's Andy I need help with."

"Andy?" My blood pressure spiked at something being wrong with him.

"I pick him up from school and I can't... obviously. Mac's busy and–"

"I'll get him, no problem," I said immediately. "We'll come to the hospital and stay with you. Bring you food. You must be hungry. A ride home."

"I'm all right. I'm waiting for the x-ray results, but everyone thinks I broke a little bone on the top of my foot. Not a big deal but from what they say, I'll most likely have to wear a boot for a few weeks." He didn't sound too excited about that. "Theo's here and said he'd give me a ride home."

Right. Theo was a doctor. Drew was in good hands.

"All right, but don't worry about Andy. I'll get him no problem. We'll go for hot chocolate. What time does school end?"

An hour later, I made it to Andy's school. Instead of getting in the long pickup line, I went inside to meet him in person. I offered my ID to enter, but the front office knew who I was, knew I was doing the calendar, knew I lived in Andy's garage apartment. They said they were expecting me because Drew had called.

"Miss Georgia!" Andy said, when I stuck my head in the open first grade room door. The kids were in line, coats and backpacks on, ready for the bell to end the day. Andy rushed from his place and came over to hug my legs. "This is my new mom!" he shouted, gleefully telling all of his classmates.

With an arm around his shoulders, I squeezed him back, but looked to Mallory over his head. Yikes, he hadn't gotten past the new mom thing. Not one bit.

The bell rang and we moved out of the way for the kids to head outside for pickup. While they'd been calm and quiet before, pandemonium broke loose in the hallways as the kids were done for the day.

"Show me your classroom," I said when he looked up at me with his toothless grin.

He spun about, took my hand and showed me everything. His spot with his name on it. The reading nook. The finished work basket. The calendar. The class chore chart.

When he ran out of steam, I pulled out a little kid chair and sat down. I needed to get him to see that my being here was *not* because I was his new mom. When I relocated to the James Inn the night before, this was one of the reasons. Yet, it didn't seem to have made a difference. I was pulled right back in. I was in Andy's classroom and he'd just announced I was his new mom.

Yeah, I was in all right.

"Come here, sweetie," I said. He stood directly in front of me, eyeing me with pure joy. I hated to dampen his spirit, even the littlest of bits. I wasn't going to tell him about Drew. Not now. I didn't want him to worry and I wasn't sure if Drew downplayed his injuries or not.

But we did have to talk about me being his new mom. I just wasn't sure how to begin.

"Did you know that I grew up with just a mom? No dad."

His little brow puckered. "You didn't play catch or build a tire swing?"

I shook my head, imagining my mother putting a tire swing in our yard. "Nope."

"That's okay. You can share mine."

"Thank you. I told you I have a sister. Her name is Sassy."

"Sassy?" He giggled.

"Do you have a sister?"

He giggled again. "You know I don't."

"Is it okay you don't have one?"

He shrugged his shoulders, but the move was barely noticeable under his heavy coat. "She'd probably put pink stuff all over."

I laughed. "Probably."

"Everyone's families are different," I explained. I was no psychologist and I had no experience with kids, so I hoped I wasn't making things worse. "You've got Grumpy and your dad and you. I've got my mother and Sassy."

Mallory was at her desk, trying to look busy but definitely listening in. That was fine with me because she was in this–watching out for Andy–for the long haul as his teacher. I wasn't.

"What I'm trying to say is that you don't need a new mom because your family is perfect just the way it is."

"That doesn't mean we don't want one," he countered.

Inwardly, I rolled my eyes.

"When the right woman comes along, I'm sure she'll make the perfect mom. But honey, that's not me."

His smile slipped. *Yeah, buddy, I felt that too.*

"I'm only in Hunter Valley for a very short time." I pushed on, telling him and also myself. "For a job. Then I go back to where I live."

"To your house?"

I bit my lip. Nope. To my mother's.

"To your job?" he added.

Nope. To filling in as a pageant coach with Sassy's overflow clients. Lord, was I depressing.

I didn't know how to answer either of those questions, so I didn't.

"To be your mom, then I have to be with your dad," I

pointed out. "We have to love each other and trust each other and–"

"You do!"

I shook my head. "Have you heard the way your father is cranky all the time? I think you're calling the wrong person Grumpy."

"That means he likes you! I think he likes you a lot."

I was surprised by this. Did he know about what we did in my apartment? Certainly not the... interlude in Mac's office at the fire station.

"Oh?"

"He made garlic bread for you. Garlic bread's special. And you went out with him the other night. Like a date. And he thinks you're pretty."

I bit my lip. He was so earnest. "He told you that?"

"Dunno. But he looks at you funny. And when a boy looks at a girl funny, that's how babies are made."

I blinked at him. "I... I didn't know that," I murmured. I was not the one to talk about the birds and bees with him.

"That's what happened to Allison's mom," he explained.

Ah, the one with the new baby sister or brother from the nipple conversation on spaghetti night.

"So since my dad looks at you funny, then he wants to make a baby with you."

I felt my cheeks flush. Oh dear Lord in heaven. The

idea of making a baby with Mac made my ovaries explode. And my heart.

I was *not* going to tell him he was mostly right. He only wanted to *practice* making a baby. With a condom on and my IUD as backup birth control.

"Andy–

"Don't you want children?"

He was six and so very sweet and innocent but knew exactly how to ruthlessly wound me. His question was the ultimate trigger. I took a deep breath.

"Yes, I do. Very much," I said, swallowing hard. "But your dad gives me cranky looks because at work, I'm making him do something he doesn't want. I bet you give him cranky looks when he makes you pick up your room."

He frowned. "Yeah."

"And if your dad looks at me funny, we're not going to make a baby, okay? That's when two people love each other so much that it can't be contained and that extra love spills over makes one."

I cleared my throat and willed back tears. My words were true. So true. But I hadn't considered them when it came to me and Art. Looking back, we never had enough love for a child. He never had enough love for me at all.

And I had to wonder if I ever loved him like I was supposed to.

"But we can be the bestest of friends even if I can't be

your mom," I said, wanting to reassure him. He didn't know I was staying at the James Inn now, but one thing at a time. Perhaps when he found out this would be reinforced.

He looked skeptical. I had to turn this around. Waaaaay around.

"I want to be your best friend. Because best friends like me pick you up from school and get hot chocolate together."

"Hot chocolate?" His eyes lit up like I offered him a million dollars.

"Mhm," I confirmed. "I like marshmallows in mine."

"Me too!"

Thank goodness for the ability to redirect a six-year-old. I gave Mallory a look and she offered me a sympathetic one in return.

I reached out and booped his nose. "See? Best friends."

38

MAC

WORD about my dad got to me when we climbed in the engine to head back to the station. I checked my cell and read through his texts telling me what happened and then updating me that he was at the hospital, that he was waiting on an x-ray, and so on. The latest was that he had a boot on his foot, a script for pain meds and a ride home from Theo, who must've coincidentally been at the hospital.

I had Van Routen, who was driving the engine, drop me at the school on the way back to the station. If Dad wasn't getting Andy, then I needed to. He wasn't out front, so I bolted inside, making my way to his classroom. I got some looks since I was in my bunker pants and boots, having ditched my coat, but everyone knew me and Andy so they didn't panic that the building was on fire.

I stopped outside the first-grade door when I heard Georgia's voice, then Andy's giggle. Peeking in, she was in one of the little chairs, her knees crunched up–wearing the boots and pink coat I bought her–as Andy stood in front of her. He was dressed to go outside, his Spiderman backpack over his shoulders.

Obviously, the one text Dad forgot to share was that he'd gotten her to pick up Andy.

I hadn't seen her since the meeting the day before and hadn't had a chance to tell her how much I liked her work on the calendar. But the night before when I peeked out the back window to the apartment over the garage, the lights had been out. While I'd wanted nothing more than to climb in bed with her, if she was asleep, I didn't want to wake her.

I left for the station early, but her car was already gone, meaning she was off to work before me.

I was about to walk into the classroom, but then I heard what she told him, how gentle and kind she was with his tenderhearted emotions. How I was making my dislike of the calendar that obvious. That I looked at her funny. Thank fuck that wasn't how babies were made because she'd be popping out kids left and right. I couldn't do anything *but* look at her with the need to show up at the garage apartment with an entire box of condoms so we could finish what we started.

So I leaned a shoulder against the wall and eavesdropped.

Finally, she mentioned hot chocolate and everything about making babies and being his mom was forgotten. They were friends. Marshmallow lovers united.

While I didn't think the issue with Andy wanting Georgia to be his mom was over, she'd appeased him for now. For that, I was thankful.

I ducked into a neighboring classroom so they didn't see me as they made their way down the hall. The radio tucked onto my bunker pants began to squawk and I instantly turned it down.

Andy was fine. Safe. I trusted Georgia with him and I didn't want to interrupt their hot chocolate date. I was a little jealous. But the only thing I had a taste for was Georgia herself.

I couldn't stay away. I didn't even want to try any longer.

Like Theo said at the bar, Andy'd be sad when she left regardless of whether I slept with her or not. One orgasm hadn't eased my need for her. It only made it worse. In fact, my dick was hard just thinking about it.

I needed more time with Georgia. Alone time. Adult time. But when?

39

MAC

"This is a nuisance," Dad said, shifting on his couch, crossing his arms over his chest... just like I did. I couldn't blame him. His broken foot was in a huge walking boot propped up on the coffee table. He had to wear it for the next three weeks, maybe longer. "It's the end of the pickleball season at the community center."

He frowned and shifted a pillow behind his back.

From the elementary school, Mallory gave me a ride to the station. There, I grabbed the fire station's incident command SUV and drove to Dad's house. I was still on shift and if a call came in, I could leave right from here.

"Thankfully, it wasn't worse," I said.

He didn't need crutches, but he'd have to take stairs carefully. He could've hit his head or broken a hip.

"True," he agreed. "I didn't even do anything except step off a damned curb."

"We went on a call yesterday for a guy who threw his back out sneezing," I said with the hopes of making him feel a little better.

"I can't drive with this thing," he complained, shifting his boot back and forth on the coffee table. "That means I can't take Andy to and from school."

I waved away his concern. "We'll carpool."

"You can't reciprocate," he reminded. He was in a mood, and I didn't blame him. "Carpool means taking turns."

"I'll ask Flowers to help out. You know he will."

"Yes, but Flowers is usually on shift with you. That means more work for his wife."

I had a feeling nothing I could say to make things better were going to work. And, he had a point. Even on days I wasn't on shift, I was on call. While a big call was rare, they happened, and when they weren't expected. I couldn't leave Andy home alone if I had to rush to a fire and he had to be at school, nor could I take him to the scene. We needed guaranteed coverage for him.

"I won't be able to do your stairs either."

Shit.

Keeping an eye on Andy was one thing, but if something happened to Andy upstairs in our house, it would be a problem. Or if there was a fire at night and they had to get out quickly. Dad wouldn't be able to get to him to offer help, and I was a stickler about safety.

Fortunately, Dad's house was a rancher. There were only two steps down into the garage and he could handle those, especially since there was a railing.

I sighed. I didn't realize how reliant I was on Dad helping with Andy until now.

"Then we'll–"

The front door flew open and Andy barreled in, snow boots clomping on the wood floor. "Grumpy! Miss GG said you hurt your foot. Wow, that's a cool thing you get to wear."

I reached out. "Careful!" I called before he was too rough. "Don't jostle him."

Andy stopped just short of the elevated leg. Frowned. "I can't sign it."

"No, it's not a cast," Dad told him. "I broke a little bone on the top of my foot and this is what I get to wear. I feel a little like Frankenstein."

Andy giggled.

Georgia closed the front door and came into the room at a more normal pace. She took in his foot and my father's overall appearance. "How are you?" she asked. "I bet your pride took a hit as much as your foot."

"That about sums it up," he replied, offering her a

smile. He was cranky with me and gave her all the sugar. "But like Mac said, it could be worse. Thank you for collecting Andy."

"We had fun!" he said. "Miss GG–"

"Hang on, how come you get to call her a special name?" Dad asked him. "Does it have something to do with the chocolate mustache you have?"

Andy licked his upper lip. "We're bestest friends 'cause we both like marshmallows in our hot chocolate. Best friends call each other nicknames."

"What's your nickname?" I asked him.

Andy rolled his eyes. "Andy, of course."

I glanced at Georgia who was biting her lip and trying not to smile.

"We went to Steaming Hotties and the lady in the pink shirt gave me extra marshmallows because I was so polite."

He glanced at Georgia as if seeking confirmation, who nodded. "That's right. A perfect gentleman."

Andy smiled with pride as he shrugged out of his jacket. "Can I have a snack, Grumpy?"

"A snack? Do you have a hollow leg?" he asked.

"I think we're getting pizza again. I'm on shift and–" Shit. Fuck.

Andy.

Dad couldn't tackle my stairs and Andy couldn't stay here tonight, even though he had sleepovers often enough. I picked up Dad's prescription and knew he was on some good painkillers for a few days. He'd be asleep early–and asleep hard–once he had the next dose.

I looked to Dad.

Dad looked to me.

Then to Georgia.

Georgia.

GEORGIA

"I REALLY APPRECIATE THIS," he said for the tenth time. Instead of pizza, Mac picked up deli sandwiches after leaving his dad's. Since I didn't know my way around town like he did, I followed him in his fire department command truck back to his house. Since Andy wasn't allowed to ride in that vehicle, he'd been with me in my rental car again. Happy as could be.

Then, like a little family, we ate at the kitchen table and listened to Andy talk about school. Even though Mac was on shift and his walkie talkie sat by his water glass, he'd stayed to eat.

Then it was bedtime for Andy. Mac asked if I could stay with him in the house instead of in the garage apartment since he had to go back to work. It was clear Drew wasn't an option, even though the older man didn't want to admit it. The boot he had on his foot was large and cumbersome and I expected would take some time to get used to. Andy was caring and thoughtful, but there was no way Drew could keep up with him tonight. And he'd taken his pain meds before we left him and was probably sleeping hard by now.

So it was me. In Mac's house. First dinner, then a sleepover.

Fuck. Shit. Crap. A pageant queen didn't swear, but I wasn't a pageant queen and if there was a time for swearing, this was it.

Mac didn't know that I moved to the James Inn. That I'd made a decision to distance myself from them as a family. It was one thing to have Mac come to my hotel room and have some no strings sex, but being in his house? Upstairs? Taking care of Andy and *staying* in the guest bedroom.

Completely and totally opposite of my intentions. This was the opposite of needing space.

I sighed. I didn't know what else to do. I'd have to tell Mac about relocating to the inn and my reasons for it. He'd know I was catching feelings then he'd get all cranky again. Maybe even toss in an *I told you so* about the importance of no strings. Laugh at me. Maybe not sleep with his secretary on the side like Art, but I didn't

even want to have him look at me in the same way. A
look that told me I wasn't worthy of everything and
laughably couldn't even do no strings right.

It wasn't only Mac that I was falling for.

Picking up Andy at school and taking him to
Steaming Hotties for hot chocolate was hard enough.
School pickup? A stab to the heart. Having him chatter
from the backseat of my car? Another stab. Sharing hot
drinks and marshmallows? Stab, stab, stab!

Now it was going to be making breakfast, homework,
bath and story time.

Ugh!

Yet, all I said for the tenth time with a big smile was,
"No problem."

Mac opened the guest bedroom door for me.

"No! That's Grumpy's room." Andy rushed down the
hall, sliding across the hardwood in his socks. He put his
arms out to block my way, as if there was some kind of
HAZMAT scene in there.

"It's the guest room," Mac corrected.

Andy vigorously shook his head and took my hand,
tugging me back down the hall to–

Lord, help me over the fence.

Mac's room.

Andy pulled me all the way in. Mac followed.

There was a very large bed taking up most of the
space. The bed was made, but just by tossing the

comforter up and over the pillows. A shirt was flung over a chair in the corner and the door to the closet was open. Mac's scent filled the room.

This was bad. Very bad.

I'd gone from the apartment over the garage, which I thought was too much, to Mac's bedroom.

"Moms and dads share a room. She stays in here with you!" Andy said.

I blinked.

Really, really bad.

Nothing I said to him in his classroom earlier stuck. No Miss GG and marshmallow sharing best friends.

Andy *wanted* us to stay together. I glanced at Mac and tried not to smile because the one person we were trying to be discreet with was the one who wanted us to share a bed.

"Andy, bud, she's not–"

"I know what Miss GG said. What you said. But try it. Maybe you'll like it."

He ran out the door, pulling it shut behind him as he went.

I stared at the door for a long moment.

"You heard what he said," Mac commented, coming closer with a sly grin. "Let's try it. Maybe we'll like it."

41

MAC

I was *all* for trying it. I knew I'd like it. Pulling her in my arms and kissing the hell out of her. Stripping her of her clothes.

I'd spent the past few days thinking about how we'd gotten each other off in her little garage apartment. Then, fuck, in my office. Every time I walked in there, I got hard and I would until I fucking retired.

"Now?" Georgia asked, wide eyed. She was surprised, but I couldn't miss the heat and need in her gaze. Behind my closed office door was one thing. Behind a bedroom door with Andy telling us to try it was another.

I shrugged. "Andy'll make himself scarce..." It could

work. "Maybe you could get that toy of yours. We could have a little fun with that."

She coughed. "My... toy?"

I grinned.

"Right. Let's start with my dick first."

I had to reach down and shift myself in my navy work pants. Just the idea of giving her every inch of my dick was torture.

But I didn't want to have a conversation about the birds and the bees with Andy yet and if he was telling his entire class that Georgia was his mom, I didn't need him telling the same kids how his dad got naked and did illegal things to Miss GG. And with her toy submarine.

So...

I ran a hand over the back of my neck. "Fuck, no. Not now. Let's at least get him to sleep and then—"

A call came in with the familiar shrill chime on my walkie talkie.

I closed my eyes. "Shit."

Now? Really? My balls were going to be so fucking blue.

The dispatcher gave a few codes and an address.

"I have to go," I growled. I moved to the door, opened it and pointed to the linen closet down the hall across from the guest room. "Sorry, but the clean sheets are in there."

"Go," she said, being calm and completely understanding about the inconsistent and urgent nature of my work and that I was leaving her with changing my bed alone as well as babysitting for Andy.

"I'll be back in the morning after my shift."

I closed the distance between us, kissed her hard and swift before I left.

42

GEORGIA

I woke up hot. Stifled. A furnace was at my back and a heavy arm was–

Oh sweet Lord above.

Mac.

I was in bed with Mac.

Or, I was in Mac's bed. With Mac.

The night before, after Mac left for the emergency, I gave Andy some space. I'd already had one discussion with him about me not being his new mom that hadn't stuck, so I'd had no intention of trying again. Especially when I found him asleep in Grumpy's bed. Obviously, his plan was to keep me from sleeping in there. The little guy forced me into Mac's bed. There was no way I was sleeping in Andy's little race car bed or the couch downstairs.

For being six, Andy was *really* focused on his New Mom Agenda. If I wasn't his main target, I'd be impressed.

There was only one option. I changed the sheets on Mac's bed and eventually fell asleep. I definitely tossed and turned, imagining Mac in here. And how he'd wanted to have some fun with me and my vibrator. How he just wanted to fuck.

Gah!

If that wasn't enough, my mind wandered to other questions. Did he sleep naked? Was he a snuggler when he slept with someone or did he sleep sideways and take up all the space? Did he bring other women to his bed? Was I the only one pitiful enough to make it to his king-sized lair and be all alone?

That one had me punching the pillow and trying to settle longer than any other thought.

I must've conked out because I completely missed Mac coming home sometime during the night and climbing in bed. And pulling me into his arms.

One thought answered: He was a snuggler when he slept because we were like two spoons in a drawer with his muscled arm flung over my waist. And yup, that was his big palm cupping my breast through my pajama top.

I swallowed hard, tried not to breathe or move or do

anything to wake him. Because I was cataloging every hard inch of him–and I meant *every* hard inch–along my back. It felt so good to be in someone's arms again, to feel protected. To be wanted even when asleep.

Because Mac wasn't moving at all. His arm was a heavy band over me. I felt his warm breath fanning my neck.

There was soft gray light coming from the window, indicating it wasn't yet dawn.

"Mac," I murmured.

"Hmmmm," he replied, not stirring.

"You're smothering me."

His arm over my hip slid back and I could roll over.

"Not used to a man in your bed?" he asked, his voice rough from sleep.

I frowned, but he couldn't see me. He asked as if this was the only way two people slept together.

"My ex slept like a starfish so we each had our own side." More like he had most of the bed and I had the edge.

This was... nice. He *wanted* to be in bed with me. Knew I was here and held me even when he wasn't awake. I wasn't relegated to the side, but we were together right in the middle.

Mac asleep was so different than him awake. He was still big and rough-edged, but he was relaxed. Peaceful. Snuggly.

Mac, a snuggler. Who knew? The winter wouldn't be too bad if I had a man like him to keep me warm all night.

I smiled, eyeing his mustache. From the other night, I knew *exactly* what it felt like between my thighs.

"I can hear you thinking," he said. "I have a feeling you should share those thoughts aloud."

How did he know I was having sexy ideas that involved him? And me. Us.

"Andy will find us," I said.

His lids opened and that dark gaze held mine. "He told us to try it. Well, I did the other day and I like it. He's a smart kid."

"I thought you were supposed to be at work," I prodded. It was too dark to be the end of his shift.

"We had to get a second crew for the call. Everyone heard about my dad and even though he's doing okay, Smutters offered to finish my shift for me."

"That was nice of him," I said. I knew how much the guy made Mac cranky.

He raised his arm, looked at his watch. "We have at least an hour before Andy wakes up. Come 'ere."

He pulled me in so our bodies pressed together again, my arms caught between us. My head was tucked beneath his chin.

He was bare chested, definitely, but I couldn't tell if

he was wearing underwear or not through my satin pajamas. I *could* tell he was *very* hard.

"Fuck, I really like waking up to you."

Warmth seeped through me from his words, not just from his body.

"Georgia," he said.

"Hmm?"

"I think there's something else we should try that I *know* we'll both like."

I couldn't help but giggle. "Oh yeah?"

He shifted, rolling me onto my back and then coming up over me.

"Yeah."

43

MAC

Georgia, in my bed. Under me.

Fuck. I groaned and kissed her neck, her silky hair brushing my skin. The scent of her filled my nose. I felt the thrum of her racing heart against my lips.

Her fingers tangled in my hair as I moved lower, kissing across her collarbone. Her pajamas were a pale color. It was too hard to see exactly what in the dark room, but they were satiny and while completely covering her, were sexy as hell.

Her being in my bed: sexy. Waking up to her in my arms: sexy. Her breathing: sexy.

I opened one button at a time, exposing more and

more of her creamy skin. It glowed in the moonlight. The fabric parted and slid to her sides.

"Gorgeous Georgia," I murmured, shifting to suck one plump nipple into my mouth. I felt it harden beneath my tongue. Felt her breath catch. Heard her gasp.

When she whispered my name, I lifted my head. "I'm calling you GG from now on, too."

She looked down at me. "Don't stop."

Bossy little thing. Did she really think I could walk away from her in my bed? I couldn't help but grin. "Yes, ma'am."

I gave her other nipple the same attention, then laved and licked both, going from one to the other. I played with them until she was writhing beneath me and a loud moan slipped out.

"Shh," I said, kissing down her soft belly. Andy was usually out cold once he fell asleep, but little kids were wild cards when it came to, well anything. He might have encouraged us to sleep together, but I didn't want him to get an eyeful.

"One of these days, you can be as loud as you want. For now, you gotta keep things quiet."

She bit her lip as if that would silence her.

"Good girl."

Pulling the waistband of her sleep shorts down, I worked my way lower on the bed, taking the blankets with me. I was far from cold and Georgia's soft skin was so warm. Tossing her sleepwear over my shoulder, I looked my fill. Sure, I saw all of her the other night, but she was in my bed. My fucking bed.

She laid there quiet, waiting, her breath catching.

"My GG."

She studied me, then pushed up to sitting. "I want to see you."

I couldn't help but grin at her boldness and pushed my boxer briefs off. When I got home, I took a shower in the hall bathroom so I didn't wake her, then put on underwear. While I had her in my bed, we hadn't yet talked about sleeping together full-on naked. Sure, she'd had my dick in her mouth already, but that had been when she'd been conscious and had been right there with me.

Now I had her consent and those briefs were gone. My dick bobbed free and there was no question–if she had any doubt whatsoever–that I wanted her. I was hard as a fucking fence post.

"Please say you have a condom," she said, her gaze affixed right on my dick as if she liked what she saw and wanted to take it for a test ride.

Leaning to the side, I set one hand on the bed and reached into my bedside drawer with the other and pulled out a brand-new box. I sat it on the bed beside her.

She eyed it with surprise. "Wow, um, that's more than one."

I gripped the base of my dick and gave it a hard squeeze. If I was going to last, she had to stop being so fucking perfect.

"I told you I had plans and we're going to need a hell of a lot of condoms to get through them all. I got this box the other day."

"These plans," she began, biting her lip, her gaze raking over my body. "Which one do you want to do now?"

The list was long. Varied. Filthy. "Any that involve getting my dick in you. You want mouth or pussy first?"

44

GEORGIA

MOUTH OR PUSSY FIRST?

Oh Lord.

My mouth watered and my pussy clenched at the question.

Watching him slowly pump his dick was so hot. It was virile and potent.

I didn't want to think of Art, especially right this second, but watching Mac?

Who the hell was Art?

He was utterly and completely forgettable. Secretary Pam could have him and his shitty job in bed.

Seeing a bead of pre-cum, I couldn't help myself. I leaned forward and licked it up.

"Mmm," I said. The salty tang coated my tongue, just like it had the other night. I'd loved having him in my mouth. The thick feel, the taste, the way he responded.

"Fuck," Mac said, tangling his fingers in my hair.

I took as much of him as I could take, then sucked. His hips bucked, just like last time.

"Oh, you good girl," he hissed, then tugged on my hair to pull me off.

It was rough and it hurt oh so good. My nipples were pebbled hard, my pussy was wet and swollen and ready for him. My lips had to be swollen. We eyed each other for a second, then he pounced.

I gasped, my back hitting the soft mattress and the hard, hot feel of him over me. His chest hair was soft against my skin.

With urgent hands, he spread my legs and settled between them. His hard length nestled in my slick folds.

"That's all you get with that sweet mouth, my GG." Reaching out, he grabbed the box, ripped it open and got to work on getting us both protected.

The entire time, I watched, totally aroused at being manhandled. This was happening. I ached for him to slide into me, to feel all of him as he stretched me open. It was going to be tight, taking him. The man was generously endowed–or better known as fucking huge. My pussy clenched with anticipation.

"You wet and ready for me?" he asked when he was done. His gaze met mine, then slid down my body.

I nodded. I was so wet. So ready.

He arched a brow. "Oh, I'm not so sure."

What? Not sure? I was so wet. Needy. Achy. I had the taste of his dick and pre-cum on my tongue. I WAS READY!

He settled between my legs, tossed one over his shoulder and licked me from bottom to top. Then circled my clit. His mustache tickled while his tongue was magical.

"Mac!" I gasped, my eyes falling closed. "I'm wet. I am. Please."

"You beg so nicely. You'll come first, then you'll get my dick."

As if it was his mission in life to get me off, he went back to his task. Or I was so desperate to be pussy licked that I was easily pushed to orgasm. Maybe both.

He was single minded, deliberate and ridiculously talented. Flicks and swirls with his tongue, then he got his fingers involved. They slid in and out, mimicking what I hoped his dick would do very, very soon. But then they curled and–

Was that my g-spot? Holy–

I gripped the sheets, arched my back and came–as quietly as possible–all over his face. This time, I didn't think about what my pussy looked like. What it tasted like. What I looked like when I came. What I looked like when I didn't come.

None of that.

I just bit my lip, stifled my moan... and came. And came.

Only when I slumped on the bed in a way that indicated every bone in my body had dissolved did he stop and kiss the inside of my thighs and tickle me with his mustache. Then worked his way up and kissed me on the lips.

I tasted myself on him. His mustache was actually wet. From me.

He wasn't a shy or mild lover. No, he got into it. As in right there, not afraid to get covered in my cum.

He met my gaze.

"*Now* you get my dick."

I nodded. Oh yes. Finally. I spread my legs wider in invitation. He hooked a knee and with one talented shift of his hips, he slid home.

45

MAC

HOLY. SHIT.

I was balls deep in Georgia. Hot. Wet. Tight.

Her pussy felt like home. Like it was where I belonged but never knew. It was the place I'd been missing my whole fucking life. Holy shit.

"GG," I hissed. Her inner walls clenched and rippled around me as she adjusted to my size. Some caveman gene in me made me want to pound my chest in satisfaction that I got her on her back, got my dick in her. Filling her and taking her. Satisfying her body with mine.

Up on one elbow, I loomed over her. Watched her face as I pulled out then slammed back in. How her eyes widened in surprise, then fell closed. Her hands went to my ass, cupped it. Pulled me deeper.

"More," she breathed.

Yes. I'd give her more. Always.

And then I stopped thinking and just fucked. She lifted up into my thrusts. I pushed a knee up and back to go deeper. Then I hooked the leg over my shoulder. Then leaned back on my heels so I took her at a different angle, shallow and rhythmic.

Then I pressed her into the bed, chest to chest. Every position was good. Better than the next. And this was only missionary.

Georgia met me thrust for thrust until we were sweaty and whimpering. Whispering dirty words.

Harder. More. Yes, just like that. You feel so good. I'm close. Again. Right there.

As the bed bumped into the wall, I was hanging on by a thread, trying to hold off coming so fucking hard I knew I was going to go blind, but GG wasn't there yet. It didn't seem like she could make it with only my dick, so I reached between us, found her clit and circled it with my thumb.

"That better?" I asked as I rolled my hips, watching her closely to see what worked best.

Her eyes were closed and she nodded.

But it wasn't going to be enough.

I pulled out.

Her eyes flew open and she looked at me with confusion and panic, as if I was going to stop. "Mac!"

"Shh," I said, sliding down her body. I found her clit. It was swollen and hard, so I sucked on it with my mouth in little pulls. Obviously, her clit needed a little extra attention for her to come.

"Oh Lord," she whimpered, thrashing on the bed. Her hands tangled in my hair. That was better. Thrashing and her pussy walls starting to ripple and clench was a good sign she was getting closer.

I only stayed there for a second or two, then moved back over her and slid deep.

Reaching between us, Georgia worked her clit as I filled her with more shallow thrusts. I'd found her g-spot earlier and I wanted to hit it with my dick.

"Like that," she whispered, nodding her head, her fingers moving in quick circles. "Yes. Oh God. Right there."

Yeah, she liked having her g-spot stimulated. I could totally fucking do that.

"I'll pull out if you don't come," I taunted as sweat dripped down my brow.

Her eyes flew open and her hand moved faster.

"No!" she said, eyes pleading. "I'll do it. I'll be your good girl."

Oh, those words. There was no way in hell I was pulling out of her clenching heat. But the possibility of it got her hotter. Even through the condom I felt her get wetter.

"That's right. Then come, GG."

And she did.

All over my dick as she clenched and writhed. Her nails dug into my lower back.

I was done. It was too much. She was too much. Too tempting.

My balls drew up and emptied. "Fuck," I growled, burying my face in her neck as I came and came and came.

While I was trying to catch my breath, I couldn't imagine doing this with anyone else. I'd only crossed one thing off my list.

My dick was still hard, ready to take her again in the next fun way. Once wasn't enough.

46

MAC

WHILE WE HAD fire trainings every Saturday morning, this was the one weekend a month Theo participated. The first time he helped back in the fall, he'd been a pretend patient in a vehicle extraction. He'd been a good sport, even bought everyone lunch.

Six or so months later, he was still a good sport and he still bought everyone lunch. That was why we were sitting across from each other at Kincaids waiting for our burgers to be served. We were at the end of the long table and the B shift crew filled up the rest. We'd finished up a medical station rotation where everyone recertified in CPR, practiced IV sticks and diabetic patient assessment. I saved these kinds of trainings for when Theo came because he was the expert and gave more insight as a doctor than the paramedics on staff.

For a guy who lived in Montana, he still dressed like a big city doctor. Usually, he wore khakis and a button down with his doctor's white lab coat and stethoscope, but today he was dressed casually in jeans with his button down. I had yet to see him in flannel.

Everyone was talking about the calendar since Liz, who sat at the far end, had already had her photos done. Cleary, too. Everyone ribbed me about seeing the photos at the meeting the other day and not sharing, but I'd stayed quiet about how they came out, other than saying they looked good. We'd agreed as a committee that the photos wouldn't be shared until the fundraiser event and the big reveal.

"So you aren't against the calendar any longer?" Theo asked, kicking my foot under the table, stirring me from my thoughts. I'd been easily distracted this morning.

It was no wonder. After that mind blowing sex we'd had in my bed, I dragged Georgia to the shower and washed her from head to toe. Saw her without makeup. With her hair wet and far from styled.

She looked different, but still my GG. I had a feeling I was the only one who ever saw her that way. While I had no factual data on this–and I wasn't asking–I doubted she let her ex shower with her. If he'd been fucking around on her, why would she share this intimate side of her with him?

I felt lucky. Special. And a horndog. Because after I soaped her all up, paying very thorough attention to her perfect tits and her greedy pussy, I pressed her against the tile, dropped to my knees and ate her out. Then I fucked her up against the tile.

Oh yeah, my kind of shower.

Unfortunately, I had to get dressed and leave for the training. Those two rounds were all we were going to get in because Andy woke up when I was making coffee.

Theo kicked my foot again. What had he asked? Oh yeah.

"From what I saw, Georgia's got a good eye. She and the photographers are doing a great job."

"I didn't think I'd hear you say that," he replied.

I picked up my water and gulped some down. "Yeah, well, I can't knock the calendar or what she's doing with it."

"But?"

"But I'm still not thrilled being in it."

"You don't have to be in it."

I gave him a look. "Yes, I do. I'm the chief. Of course, I do."

"So no sexy spread for Mr. January?"

I had to smile. "Hardly."

"Well, I can't wait to see the final product. What

about your dad? How's he doing?" Theo asked, changing the subject. The other end of the table was talking about the new chainsaws that were being delivered. Pearsons Tree and Landscaping were going to take us into the woods for next weekend's training to learn how to use them.

"Stopped by his place this morning," I said. "He's fine. Cranky."

"That's to be expected."

"I think he's more annoyed than anything else. He can't drive or take care of Andy like he usually does."

"Where is Andy this morning?" he asked.

"Birthday party. GG dropped him off."

"GG?" he asked, eyebrow up.

Yeah, GG.

"I'll get him in a little while," I said, not telling Theo why I called her my Gorgeous Georgia, and maybe I needed to keep it to myself. "The mom knows if I'm late that I'm on a call and he can hang out."

"Need long term help? Verna told me to tell you she can send out a fill-in schedule."

I was used to the community spirit in Hunter Valley, but I was usually one of the ones doing the helping. It felt different–and nice–when others were willing to pitch in and assist in return.

"Tell her thanks, but Georgia's volunteered to do the things Dad can't."

His brow went up and squeezed a slice of lemon over his iced tea. "Is that right?"

He studied me as if my usual fire uniform was telling him something. While I wasn't on shift today but worked the training, I wore the same clothes as if I was, in case we got a call. We didn't always put on our bunker gear, so we needed to be identifiable to everyone as part of the department.

I grinned, thinking about how Andy put us together the night before. He had no clue what he'd done, but I sure as fuck was thankful. So was my dick. So, so thankful.

He set his forearms on the table and leaned in. "You're smiling. That can only mean one thing."

My grin was answer enough. I shrugged, down-playing it. From when she walked out of the secure area of the airport and I got my first glimpse of her, I wanted Georgia. My dick was like a homing beacon, a tuning fork that aimed straight for her. Fucking her was a fore-gone conclusion, but I never expected to do it in my bed. And this morning? When I finally got inside her?

Holy. Fuck.

It'd been a while, sure. But it hadn't been mind-blowing because I'd been pussy deprived. No, it had been Georgia herself. The mix of tentative and wild. Responsive and fucking perfect. Every inch of her was made for me. That ass. Those tits. Her smiles. Her moans. The way she'd said she'd be a good girl for me. Her–Georgia Lee Gantry–was tailor made for me with everything I ever wanted in a woman.

The jolt I got from our handshake at the airport hadn't been all floofy and froufrou like some sappy, streaming romcom movie. It had been a thing. Because the connection with Georgia during sex? Like we were one. Best sex ever.

I cleared my throat and had no plans to tell Theo that. He was a doctor and would tell me I needed medical intervention. Psych evaluation. Or just laugh.

Whatever I help needed, I didn't want. I liked how I felt when I was with her. And I wanted to do it again. Except–Andy. Except–she was going back to Georgia as soon as her work was done. Casual meant whenever sex. Fun sex. Hot. Heavy. Hard. Dirty. I never expected her to be in my bed. My shower. It made things complicated. Especially when I didn't want to go back to sleeping alone when she felt so damned good in my arms.

While Andy was going to be thrilled his dad and *new* mom were sharing a bed, it was a horrible idea when it came to his well-being. It'd only be validating his whole new mom obsession when all it was was me being a greedy fucker who wanted easy access to Georgia.

"Wait until I tell you what happened."

He held up a hand. "I don't need the play by play."

The server dropped off our burgers, the scent of grilled meat hit my nose and made my stomach rumble.

As I put my napkin in my lap, I said, "Listen, you fucker."

I told him about Andy and how he put us in the bedroom together, slammed the door and told us to try it.

By the time I was done, he was grinning.

He reached for the ketchup and poured some on his plate beside his fries. "Sounds like you need some kid-free time with her."

I shrugged and tucked into my burger. Andy hadn't ever crimped my style with a woman before. Not that me having a kid bothered Georgia. I had to wonder if she liked Andy better than me. No, it was that Andy was a little chaperone. While he was all too eager to put us together, she and I couldn't do any of the things I wanted. Like get her naked and get her on her knees. Or riding me. Or bent over my couch. Or anything else on my ever-growing list entitled Ways to Fuck Georgia into Forgetting Her Name.

"Kinda hard with my dad out of commission," I said, snagging a salty fry.

"We'll take him tonight," he offered. "A sleepover."

I almost choked on my burger. I swallowed hard. "You two? You guys have sworn off having kids."

He and Mallory didn't want children of their own. Among their friends, they'd made it known. From what he told me, Theo had a dick dad and didn't feel like he had a good role model. And, up until last summer, he'd been a more-than-full-time surgeon where kids never came up. As for Mallory, she was a teacher and had kids around her all day. That was enough for her.

"Having them." He popped a fry in his mouth. "We like them just fine, but we also like giving them back to their parents. We're planning on rocking the aunt and uncle role."

Right, because Dex and Lindy were having a baby in the next few weeks.

"I thought this was casual," he said, using his napkin to wipe his mouth. "When we saw you at Kincaids, we told you to fuck her, not marry her. She's only here for the fundraiser project."

"That's right."

"No feelings being caught?"

I shook my head. "Nope."

Sure, I was ready to put on my lights and siren and get to her so I could take her again as fast as possible, but I knew better than to catch feelings. This was casual. No strings. She hadn't been here a week yet and we were hot and heavy. She wouldn't be here long. My dick didn't have distance vision. It was only interested in the here and now. And in Georgia.

Theo had told me to listen to my dick. Well, I was.

I was used to people leaving. My mother. Yeah, she

died and I still grieved her loss all these years later. Then Tracy. She'd made a choice and it hadn't been her family. Then there'd been Teri. It was easier to be in control, have the expectations set up front. I'd done that with Georgia. She knew the deal here. I was her post-divorce rebound.

I'd let her go when it was time. No big deal.

"And Mal and I will talk to him about his obsession with her being his new mom," he said, reminding me I had a child that was having a big problem with no strings.

"Thanks. I need all the help I can get with that."

In the meantime, a night alone with Georgia? No meddling Andy? No keeping her moans and screams quiet? The chance to cross bend her over the couch off the list?

Fuck, yeah.

47

GEORGIA

"I CAN'T BELIEVE you want more pizza," I told him. I meant the night I'd watched him with Drew and Andy through his kitchen window and then moved to the James Inn to get distance. For only one night. Then, I ended up in Mac's bed.

We were at a little place a few blocks down Main Street from the fire station, tucked in a corner table with a sausage and mushroom pizza between us. I had my plate raised for him to slide a slice onto it. It smelled so good. Garlic. Tomato sauce. The windows had condensation on them from the heat of the brick oven.

"There's always room for pizza," he replied, tossing in a wink.

I agreed. I took a bite. Especially something this good.

He'd somehow tracked me down to one of the study rooms at the library, coming in just after five and telling me I was done for the day. Not asking if I was finished but *telling* me. He'd grabbed my laptop and my bag. While that was gentlemanly, I'd refused to let him carry my purse. No man, especially with all the testosterone and pheromones he had, was carrying my pink purse. I loved how it matched my new puffy coat. It definitely didn't match his.

We'd ditched my rental in the library lot and he'd driven us to the pizza place. He'd updated me that Andy was spending the night with Theo and Mallory and Drew was fine with a friend over for dinner. It seemed he had a counter full of dropped off desserts and more casseroles than he could eat by himself.

That meant we were alone.

And we were on a date. Dinner meant a date, right?

While he didn't exactly ask me, it was more along the lines of chest beating, grunting *you* and *me* and *pizza* and *now*.

So here we were with a guy named Otis making us the best pizza I'd had in a long time.

"Besides, you need your strength for what I have planned for later," he murmured, leaning across the small table. "And if we ate at the house, well, we wouldn't eat." His gaze darkened and heated.

I knew exactly what he wasn't saying.

We'd be having sex. Probably on his kitchen table. Maybe this wasn't a date after all. Perhaps it was preventative planning. We needed fuel for what he had in mind. I squirmed; my pussy eager for more. I'd gone from a sex dry spell to a deluge. My panties weren't going to be able to handle it.

"How's the calendar coming?" he asked, then took a bite of his slice.

"You want to talk about the calendar? You do realize it's almost your turn to be photographed. I don't want to turn you off your food."

He chewed, then wiped his mouth. Those lips I knew could kiss so well turned down. "Right. No work talk."

"Right," I confirmed with a nod. He wasn't grumpy right now. In fact, he seemed downright... normal.

He had on jeans and a blue flannel. His hair was combed, face shaved. No walkie talkie attached to his hip. I had all his attention.

He took a sip of his soda. "You mentioned you used to be in pageants."

I took extra time to chew the bite in my mouth. Then swallowed hard.

"That's what you want to talk about?" I asked, licking my lips.

He shrugged, his gaze following the motion of my tongue. "Sure. It's not like I know anything about them."

I took a sip of my drink, the ice clinking in my glass.

"Well, it's like any other kid activity." I gave him a casual shrug. "Soccer or violin lessons. You practice and then there's a big game or recital or whatever and you try to be the best."

He studied me. "I don't see you playing soccer, but maybe you did the violin?"

I laughed. "No violin. Tap lessons were first, but me practicing on the kitchen floor when I was six threw my mother over the edge. Too loud and I was horrible. Then she put me in dance, but I have zero coordination. Then singing lessons."

His eyes widened. "You sing?"

I nodded. "I do."

"How old were you when you started in pageants?"

"Five."

His eyes widened. "Five? Wow."

"My sister started first and so I tagged along and then my momma got me in on it, too."

"How'd you do?"

I sighed. "Not good."

"No sash and tiara for you?"

I shook my head. "Runner up. Little Miss Calhan."

He laughed. For a split second, I thought he was

poking fun, but he wasn't. He was only amused. "I can see a young version of you up there giving them hell."

"Me?" I paused, my pizza slice halfway to my mouth. "I'm too ladylike for that."

He sobered and looked me over. "You are. I'm guessing you stopped at some point."

And this was where the conversation always turned sour for me. So I made my response short and sweet. Like a pageant question and answer session, I had what I wanted to say down pat after years of practice.

"The better Sassy got, I quickly learned it was harder and harder for me to keep up. Perfection is pretty hard to follow. I stopped when I was fourteen." I took a big bite so I didn't have to say more.

He held his slice of pizza in his hand and cocked his head. "Who wants to be perfect?"

I laughed. "Sassy. My momma. The pageant judges are looking for perfection, too."

"Fourteen. That was a long time ago. You still trying to keep up with her?"

I shrugged. "She's married. Has two kids. A Miss Georgia crown."

"And you've got–"

"What do I have?" I asked, cutting him off. "An ex who cheated on me. Who–" No, I wasn't going to say that he was having a baby. "A job I had to leave. I'm in Montana."

This was not a fun date.

He grinned.

Why was he grinning?

"That's right," he confirmed. "You're in Montana. In Hunter Valley. Eating with me." He leaned in so only I could hear. "You've got on a kickass pair of snow boots and you're the only person around who can rock a pink coat. If you finish your dinner like a good girl, I'll give you a really big treat when we get home."

Home.

I didn't have a home right now. The house with Art was being sold. Momma's place definitely wasn't mine. I was only temporary here. Even in Mac's bed.

He hadn't meant it the way my little aching heart took it. So I focused on what he meant to make me hot instead. "Really big treat?" I asked.

He waggled his eyebrows like an idiot. "You know it."

I had to shut down the pageant chat. Talk of Sassy. Momma. Art. All of it. Mac was right. I was here with him, the guy who gave me multiple orgasms and didn't seem to care I wasn't perfect or hold my past against me even after twenty years.

He'd seen every single bit of my body. Saw me bare faced. Bare assed.

And he wanted to see it again. As soon as I finished my dinner.

What was a smart girl to do? I ate that pizza in a hurry.

48

MAC

"THAT'S IT. TAKE EVERY INCH," I said, curving my body over hers as I fucked her over the back of my couch. Just the way I'd imagined all day. All week.

We'd barely made it in the front door when we were all over each other. There was no way we'd make it my bed, so I turned us, bent her over it pulled her pants and panties down to her knees and took her hard.

"Mac!" she cried.

"Be as loud as you want, gorgeous."

We were loud. She was wet. I was so fucking deep. *Slap. Thrust. Smack.*

"Please, I need it," she cried, her hands trying to find a place to grip on the couch cushion.

I need it.

Those words. The filth behind them. She needed my dick. Needed to be fucked. To be taken hard. To be needed so much that we hadn't made it ten feet inside the house.

Like a teenager getting inside a hot, wet pussy for the first time, I came. Just like that. Pulsing and filling the condom as I buried myself so far inside her I didn't know where I stopped and she began.

"FUCK!" I shouted, the sheer bliss of coming was overwhelming.

When I could see and hear again, I realized I sucked as a lover. She hadn't come.

I'd been greedy and selfish.

"Fuck, GG," I said, trying to catch my breath. "I'm sorry. The way you begged for my dick pushed me over."

I pulled out and helped her up. "Don't fucking move," I said, heading to the kitchen and chucking the condom in the trash.

I tugged up my jeans but didn't zip up. I was still hard.

She had her pants still lowered, her pretty pink panties tucked into them. Her shirt and sweater were long enough to cover her pussy, but still, those creamy thighs exposed and knowing she was swollen and bare and–

I walked back to her, not stopping. I leaned down

and tossed her over my shoulder, just like the good fireman I was.

"Mac!" she cried as I carried her up the steps. Her hands gripped the back of my loose jeans. "What are you doing?"

"Taking you to bed and making you come," I told her. "Multiple times. While my performance just now doesn't prove it, I'm a gentleman and I take care of my woman."

49

GEORGIA

FOUR ORGASMS AND A NAP LATER, we were in Mac's bed. We lay on our sides facing each other. Naked. The house was quiet. His bed was warm. Cozy. Like we were in our own little world.

Mac had proven himself the gentleman, or *not* a gentleman with all the inventive ways he'd fucked me and pleasured me. I hadn't minded that he'd come first downstairs. It was oddly flattering that I'd made him come quickly. He'd been so into me–well, literally and figuratively–that he couldn't control himself.

I loved it. It made me feel sexy and pretty.

He reached out, tucked my hair back behind my ear. "What are you thinking about?"

His voice was deep, but soft. It wasn't laced with frustration or moodiness. It wasn't gravelly with need. This was Mac, pure and simple.

I didn't want to go over why I hadn't felt either sexy or pretty lately. Sure, makeup and being nicely dressed gave the outward appearance of success and poise and all the things I learned doing pageants. But it didn't make you feel attractive.

Eons ago, the dresses my mother put me in for pageants were never my style. Lots of yellows and sherbet colors with flounces and sequins had been in play. I looked horrible in yellow, but it stood out up on stage when in a line with other contestants.

Then, because of Art, I felt rejected. Being kicked to the curb for a younger, slimmer woman made me feel unattractive. Unwanted. Sad. Lost. Worthless.

No, I didn't want to tell him any of that. So I redirected far, far away from all of that. To Mac himself.

"That I know everything about Andy–"

Mac grinned. "He doesn't know a stranger."

"–but I don't know all that much about you."

"What do you want to know?" His hand moved to lazily slide over my hip, as if he couldn't stop touching me. In fact, he didn't even look me in the eye, but watched the path of his fingers.

"How come you never got married? I mean, you're a catch."

That had his gaze meeting mine. "A catch?"

"You're the fire chief. Obviously, you're smart, fit, interested in helping others."

"I can't say that I haven't dated," he said. "A few times serious, but then Tracy had Andy and I became a dad overnight."

"And?"

"And," he continued. "Not every woman wants someone else's kid."

"True." Usually this scenario was reversed, where the woman had a child and a man wasn't interested in the extra baggage. "It's just... you're you and–"

"What are you getting at, GG?"

"GG? You sound like Andy."

He shook his head. "GG is short for Gorgeous Georgia."

And I melted. Right then and there.

Especially when he followed it up by a gentle kiss.

"I haven't found the right woman yet, that's all."

Lordy, that hurt. I was naked and in his bed, my pussy sore from being fucked six ways to Sunday. And *he hadn't found the right woman yet.*

Sure, I was temporary. A week or two fling. Fun.

I pasted on a smile because I'd been caught with my guard down. Orgasms did that to a girl. I belonged at the James Inn, not here in Mac's cozy, big bed without a six-year-old chaperone. Savoring something that wasn't really mine.

I cleared my throat.

"Your work makes it kinda hard to do that. Everyone I talk to raves about you," I told him. He was well known in Hunter Valley. Needless to say, he met many people through the emergency calls he went on. He knew the hospital employees, I was sure. At least the emergency department. The police department. Everyone at Andy's school. The older crowd who were friends with Drew.

Everyone.

"Well, it sure as hell keeps me busy," he said.

"Did you always live here?"

"Born and raised."

"Did you ever want to work for a bigger department? I mean, a big city where there's all kinds of action."

He reached for a curl, pulled on it and let it go.

"Nah. I don't need have any interest in going anywhere else. Maybe the beach for a break from winter, but Hunter Valley has everything I could ever want."

That smile stayed right on my face. Because what he wanted was in Hunter Valley and that didn't mean me. I was leaving in a week, or whenever the project was done. Bradley could get me a flight out of here whenever I needed.

"This place is growing on me," I said, trying to be light and neutral. And it was true. Hunter Valley was an amazing town. I'd met such nice people. "Even the snow."

I could see staying. But I had no job after next week. I was only contracted for this role and then I'd be gone. Easy. Tidy.

Except until it wasn't.

"Even the snow? I'm glad to hear that," Mac said, cupping my neck and pulling me in for a kiss. That didn't stop. At least while he was kissing me, I didn't have to fake smile.

50

MAC

THE NEXT FEW days went by in a whirlwind. When I wasn't working, I did stuff with Andy. I took him and a friend to play basketball at the community center. Grocery shopped. Worked on the drywall in the kitchen.

Georgia worked. She had more photo sessions and meetings with the graphic designers and event coordinators. She ate dinner with us at Dad's.

When I worked, Georgia covered for Dad with Andy, taking him to school, picking him up.

In between all that, I snuck her into my bedroom after Andy went to sleep. Sure, we stayed quiet, but those first nights having her in my arms, I wasn't having it any other way. And what we did before I pulled her into my arms to sleep wasn't half bad either. In fact, we'd made it through one box of condoms and onto the next.

We were making a pretty good dent in my fantasy list. Georgia was... insatiable. A generous, uninhibited lover. Whatever hang-ups she had that first night were long gone. Her ex was far, far away and I did my damndest to fuck him from her mind.

Other than Dad being laid up, it was amazing. Everything was great. The only bad thing on the horizon was my turn posing for the calendar.

Oh, and Georgia leaving. But that was expected. Planned. I'd fuck her out of my system before then.

51

GEORGIA

I CAME in through Mac's kitchen door from my little apartment. While I never gave up my room at the James Inn, I hadn't stayed there more than that one night. I'd been in Mac's bed, sneaking in late and leaving early before Andy woke.

Was I stupid? Probably. But what woman would turn down Mac-made orgasms and being held in his arms all night because her job was almost done? None.

They'd gird their emotions and savor every passionate, pleasure filled second. Then, they'd go home and work their way through pints and pints of ice cream but with the sinful memories.

That's what I was doing. Enjoying myself knowing

binge eating and extra battery purchases were in my future.

"Ready," I told him breathlessly. It wasn't as cold tonight, indicating that spring might actually happen. The snow was still on the ground, but it had melted. Slightly.

With my fake fur trimmed boots and my pink coat, I barely noticed it any longer. The snow *and* the cold.

Mac turned from the sink where he'd been scrubbing a plate.

"You went up there an hour ago," he said, closing the dishwasher.

I shrugged, shutting the back door behind me. "I told you I had to get ready."

The look on his face was one of complete confusion. "To change your clothes." His dark eyes raked over me. "You look great, by the way, but what the hell have you been doing for an hour?"

"Getting ready," I repeated. He had no idea what it involved. None.

"Well, you look very nice," Drew said. He was at the kitchen table with his friend, Ralph, who I was introduced to earlier, and Andy. They were playing cards and peanuts were in the middle of the table as if they were playing for snacks.

Yesterday, I ran into Lindy and Dex in the produce section of the grocery store. They seemed oddly amused by the squash and invited me and Mac over for dinner tonight. Now.

"Are those flowers for me?" Mac asked.

I looked down at the seasonal bouquet I got at the store. I blushed because that meant he might be thinking this was a date, although it was the guy that usually gave the girl flowers. But, nope. This wasn't a date. This was friends asking me to dinner and inviting Mac as well because I was staying at his house. Well, they thought in his garage apartment, not knowing I was now in his bed.

"For Lindy. A hostess gift, although being pregnant, she probably would have liked the sparkling apple juice as much as Andy."

Mac nodded, went around the counter to Andy and ruffled his hair. "We'll be back in a few hours."

Drew looked up from his cards. "We'll be fine."

Ralph nodded and took a card from the deck. "If this guy doesn't clean us out of peanuts."

Andy giggled and put a two down on the table.

With exaggeration, both men groaned at whatever the card meant. With a grin splitting his face, Andy leaned across the table and pulled the peanuts toward him. It seemed it meant they lost.

Between Drew and Ralph, Andy'd be well covered.

Once done collecting his winnings, Andy climbed from his seat and ran over to me and wrapped my legs in a hug. "Bye! Tell Mr. Hockey I said hi."

I laughed and gave him a squeeze back. This, this right here, was perfect. And painful. It was like a typical night when part of a family. Mom and Dad going out and the son spending the evening with his grandfather. Andy knew me leaving now was only for a night out and that I was coming back. That part of his feeling of safety and belonging included me. He hadn't hugged his dad. He hugged *me*.

I swallowed hard. "Will do."

52

MAC

"I CAN'T BELIEVE you had a tree fall on your house," Georgia said, looking around Lindy's kitchen. While there was fresh paint and new appliances, the room still seemed to be a throw back to when her parents were still alive and this was their house.

Lindy and Dex spent most of their time in Denver since he played for that city's professional hockey team, but during breaks and off-season, they stayed here.

Lindy was in one of the kitchen chairs, rubbing her big belly. Dex refused to let her get up. "I know," she said, looking around as if she could still see the tree. "It's crazy, isn't it? Mac, you were here."

Georgia turned to me, wide eyed. "You saw it? The

tree really came through the roof and all the way down and into the kitchen?"

I nodded. "We got here before Lindy, actually. A branch came in through that window, too. It went right through the stove."

Georgia looked around as if trying to picture it.

"Yeah, I was at the grocery store–"

"With me," Dex added, handing me a beer.

Lindy winced and Dex didn't miss it.

"Another one?" he asked her, setting his hand beside hers on top of her belly.

"You're in labor?" Georgia asked, setting her glass of wine down on the table and looked as if she needed to do something. She'd barely had a sip.

We'd only arrived a few minutes earlier. A lasagna was in the oven and there was a charcuterie board to nibble on. Lindy had put Georgia's flowers in a vase in the center before Dex forced her into the chair.

Lindy waved her hand. "For about three days now, I've had contractions. The OB says it's normal and–"

"Three days?" GG asked.

Dex ran a hand over his neck, clearly nervous. He might be a pro on the ice, but this baby thing was something new–and scary–for him. "Crazy, right? We were at the hospital that morning and they smiled at us and sent us back. I guess they're used to crazy first-time parents."

"Are you missing games?" I asked him. Spring was

toward the end of the pro hockey season. Playoffs were about to begin.

He shrugged, leaned down and kissed the top of Lindy's head. "Fortunately, we were playing at home in Denver the night before and I flew up for a quick visit. Now? I'm not leaving until this baby's born."

"I wanted to have it here," Lindy explained. "Bridget's here. My friends. This is where we'll ultimately raise him or her. Being in this place is important."

"You still don't know what it is?" I asked.

Lindy stood, Dex taking her elbow to help her. She walked to the stove and grabbed an oven mitt, turning to glance back. "Nope. I'm so excited to–"

Her eyes widened and she bent over and groaned.

"What? What is it?" Dex said.

I went on alert.

"Okay, now *that* was a contraction." She winced and her face looked like someone just stabbed her in the back. And front. Maybe kicked her crotch, too. "And it's still going. And going. Holy shit."

Georgia looked to me. I looked to her.

I took the oven mitt from Lindy and turned off the oven. "Let's get you to the hospital."

"C'mon, sugar," Dex said. He was grinning and nudging her along. "I got you, let's go have that baby!"

He started to steer her toward the front door and Lindy dropped into a squat and made a sound like a pissed off bear mixed with a blood curdling scream. Her face went red from the strain and she blew out a hard breath.

"Holy shit," Dex said. The smile was gone and he looked like an entire front line of a pro hockey team was barreling down on him.

"That's another one," Lindy said.

"What? No. They're little, tiny things that made the nurses laugh," Dex said.

She groaned again. "THIS IS NOT THAT! Oh, shit. I either peed myself or my water just broke."

53

GEORGIA

ONE OF THE experiences I didn't expect to have in Montana was to watch a childbirth.

One second Dex was handing me a glass of wine and we were eating little gherkins from a charcuterie board, the next Lindy was in serious labor. Those laughable baby contractions she had for a few days changed in a second. Like a finger snap and she was in excruciating pain.

Before she made it to the front door, her water broke, soaking her leggings and the floor.

Her contractions were so powerful they seemed to be one on top of the other.

"Okay, momma," Mac said, holding the front door

open. He had his keys in hand. "Let's get you to the hospital super-fast. They're gonna take real good care of–"

"Hospital?" Lindy said, whipping her head up to glare at Mac. "This baby is coming NOW." Her jaw was clenched and she looked fierce. A hand was on the underside of her belly as if keeping it in. "Oh God, I swear the head is coming out of my crotch."

"Now?" Dex asked her, his eyes bugging out of his head. He knelt beside her and held her hand. "You've been in labor for sixty seconds. That's not how the class went! The doctor said–"

"The doctor was WRONG!" Lindy snapped right in his face as if she'd been possessed by a demon. If her eyes could glow, they probably would. "THE CLASS WAS A WAY TO RIP US OFF."

Dex winced. "Ow, sugar, my hand."

"Don't *sugar* me," she snapped. "That's how we got into this mess."

Dex didn't even understand that a baby didn't follow any kind of rules. He also didn't know about the grip strength of a woman in labor. But Dex himself was far from calm. He was looking around as if a doctor would magically appear. He was also a touch irrational. I didn't blame him. If he went to birthing classes, he expected breathing techniques and an epidural and a focus point and other shit that definitely wasn't going to happen now.

"We'll get in the car and drive fast and the baby will come with all the doctors and nurses and–"

Lindy patted him on the face, but it was a little harder than a reassuring pat. Maybe she was between contractions now and her face wasn't etched in pain. Her voice was calmer when she told him, "I think the baby's head is coming out of my crotch. I am not having this baby in an SUV while you drive down Main Street."

Dex nodded like a bobble doll. "Okay, okay. Then–"

She tried to push to standing and he helped her up. She made it a few steps, then bent over again, groaning and panting and shouting at Dex and the world.

I looked to Mac because he was the fireman and knew what to do in emergencies. But this wasn't a house burning down or a heart attack. He seemed to be assessing the situation because he hadn't approached the couple.

"Have you delivered a baby before?" I whispered when I moved closer, not wanting to add any more concerns to the mix. Dex might lose his mind if he discovered we were a group of people with no clue on how to deal with a speedy baby.

He shook his head, but then took charge. "Okay, Dex, looks like you're having a home birth. Carry Lindy up to the master bathroom." He pointed toward the stairs. "I assume after the tree remodel you've got a nice big bathtub."

Dex looked relieved to have someone tell him what to do. "Yes."

"That's the best spot for you two to meet your new baby. Go."

Dex scooped his wife up and did as Mac said.

Mac turned to me. "Call nine-one-one and tell them the address."

I ran for my purse which was by the front door but spun around.

"I don't know the address!"

"Shit," Mac murmured, then yelled up the stairs. "Dex, what's the address?"

His booming voice carried and Dex shouted it down to us.

"Tell the dispatcher it's a precipitous birth. That the baby could be here before anyone shows up." He pulled his phone from his pocket and handed it to me. "Then call Theo on here and tell him the same thing. He may get here before anyone else since he doesn't live far away. Hopefully, he's at home."

Theo! Yes, a doctor! Good. A doctor would be really, *really* good.

I nodded, trying to get my fingers to hit the right numbers on my phone.

Mac ran upstairs, but he was calm. How could he be like that? It seemed Lindy was going to have a baby faster than the lasagna took to cook and he wasn't panicking.

This was his job. Okay, maybe not babies, but emergencies.

And I was standing here freaking out. *Get your shit together!*

I talked to emergency services and they said a crew was on their way. Theo answered–thank the Lord in heaven above–and was coming as well. Both were calm and sounded completely competent, which was reassuring.

But they weren't here now and I was *not* reassured.

Especially, just like in the movies, the deep groan of a woman in labor came from above.

Shit.

I ran up the stairs, ready to help in any way I could. The bathroom–thankfully–was spacious and well-lit and the tub was a huge whirlpool one big enough for two. If a baby wasn't coming, I'd compliment them on the remodel.

"I'm not letting you see my wife's pussy," Dex snapped. Lindy was in the tub and Dex knelt beside her on the tile, glaring at Mac. "Get your own."

I bit my lip and tried not to smile at Dex's insanity.

Mac had his hands up as if warding off a robbery. Or an angry soon-to-be dad.

Lindy groaned, hooked her hand around Dex's neck and tugged him close. Their eyes met, only inches apart. "Mac is a paramedic and he's not looking at my pussy, he's going to be looking at the baby that is coming out of my body RIGHT NOW."

Dex stared at her and his mouth fell open. "Now? As in *now?*" he squeaked and shifted down the bath to look between her parted legs. "Holy shit. Mac, look. There's, there's–"

Dex pointed with a shaky finger.

I'd never seen Dex so freaked. I had to imagine a man who always looked at a woman's pussy with the desire to put something *in* it was now going mental because something was coming *out.*

Lindy had gotten her leggings off and she was propped back as if she was taking a relaxing soak.

Mac moved Dex down to the foot of the tub and out of the way and patted his shoulders as if saying, STAY! "Yup, looks like your baby's got blonde hair like her momma."

The baby really was coming out?

Mac looked to me. "Find me towels. Lots of them."

I yanked two off the towel bar beside the shower and passed them to him, then went into the hall and pulled all there was from the linen closet.

Lindy groaned again. Her hands that gripped the side of the tub turned white with her strain.

"*Ohmygod*, I have to push. Oh, I have to."

"Okay," Mac agreed. "As you know, you're crowning,

so whenever you want, just push. You're doing great. So great. Your baby's going to be here before you know it."

He was calm and in control. I went to kneel beside Dex, set a hand on his arm. His eyes were wide like saucers as he watched his wife give birth in their bathtub.

Lindy reached down between her legs. "Oh God, the head." She started to cry, to groan and then push all within one breath.

"Good job. That's it," Mac praised. He opened a towel and reached into the tub, letting nature work. "One more and–"

Lindy groaned. Dex gasped. I stared, wide eyed as the James baby slid into this world like a prize from a t-shirt cannon launch.

"It's a girl!" Mac said, grinning. He rubbed the baby down with the towel, then wrapped her up in it.

Then she cried.

And then I exhaled.

Mac set the towel-swaddled baby on Lindy's chest and grabbed another and set it between her legs.

Dex scurried around us and squatted by Lindy's head. "Sugar, oh look. Holy shit, you did it. I'm so proud of you. She's so beautiful." They were crying and kissing and eyeing their new baby. It was a precious moment.

I heard noise downstairs and with Mac still tending to Lindy, I went out to meet the help. The fire department came in first, carrying medical bags and leaving the door open behind them. I recognized the two who came in and saw a few others waiting by the engine. I directed them up the stairs and Theo ran in directly after them.

He looked to me expectantly.

"It's a girl," I said, then burst into tears.

54

MAC

HOLY SHIT. What a night.

Once Theo, with help from Liz and Contreras and the others from B shift, finished with Lindy, Dex carried her down to the gurney waiting at the base of the stairs. Theo followed, carrying his new niece, who was wrapped in a fresh green towel, then gave her back to her glowing mother.

Lindy was all smiles and Dex was over the moon. And a little in shock.

They didn't even see Georgia in the living room, wiping tears from her face, as they went out to the ambulance for a ride to the hospital.

"You two good?" Theo asked, standing in the entry, eyeing me, then Georgia.

I nodded, but I couldn't speak for Georgia. "Congrats," I told him, shaking his hand. He grinned. "Go. We'll close up here."

He nodded. "Mom and baby seem fine, but they'll stay overnight for observation." Theo slapped me on the shoulder. Grinned some more. "Thanks for being there, although I don't think they're gonna name the baby after you."

"Probably a good thing." I laughed. "Lindy did all the work. She's a rock star."

He left, closing the front door on his way. I had no doubt he'd be spreading the news to the others in the James family.

I crossed the room to Georgia and pulled her into my arms. She went easily and cried into my chest. I held her, stroked her hair.

"You did so good, gorgeous. I'm proud of you," I murmured, then kissed the top of her head.

Pulling back, she looked up at me. Her eye makeup was smeared and her cheeks were splotchy. Adrenaline was a potent thing. It allowed someone to perform amazingly well under tough situations, but the crash after was tough.

"How are you so calm?" she asked.

I shrugged. "It's my job."

I was used to it. Most of the time. Every once in a while, a call got to me, but this was a good one. It was probably time to add a pregnancy and labor training to the Saturday rotation.

"Why are you crying?" I wondered. "Lindy and the baby are going to be fine. Looking back, she'll be thrilled she didn't labor for two days."

She looked away. Sniffled.

"I... I..." she began but didn't finish.

"GG?" I prodded.

"My husband and I were married for seven years. I wanted a baby. At first, he said we were too young. Then he was settling into his job. We bought a house so there wasn't enough money. There was always some excuse he came up with that delayed the family I wanted to make with him."

Every single time her ex came up, I liked him less and less. I had a pretty good idea of where this was going and I wanted to go to Georgia and beat the shit out of the guy. I'd think Dex, after delivering his kid in his own bathtub, would be up for taking the entire Silvermines front line and helping me.

"It's my fault." She turned away and crossed the living room. I let her go because she wasn't looking at me and she'd know I was pissed.

Her fault?

"I should've caught on well before seven years that he didn't want a baby with me. Seven years!"

She flung her arms up.

"He was your husband," I reminded. "The guy you committed your life to, who should've been right there with you. It's not your fault he–"

I bit off the rest of my words. I was going to say *It's not your fault he cheated on you.* Except I didn't know the full story. Georgia wasn't a cheater. I knew that. But I didn't want to point out things that happened in their marriage I knew nothing about.

She turned to me, her eyes glittering with tears. "That he fell for his secretary? Dumped and divorced me, then married her and got her pregnant within a month?"

Oh shit. Okay, I was right after all. I hated him even more. But getting this new woman pregnant? Fuck, he was cruel, too.

"They're having a baby?"

Her throat worked as she swallowed hard. "Yes. It seems it was *me* that was the problem all along."

I crossed the room and pulled her back in my arms. "No. That's not fucking it at all." I wasn't keeping quiet now that I knew the rest. "He's a dick. A manipulator. A cheater. What's going to happen to the secretary when he cheats on her next?"

I had no clue if he would, but once a cheater, probably always a cheater.

"Yet, here I am," she continued. "Watching someone else have the one thing I can never have."

I pushed her back, set my hands on her shoulders and searched her face.

"You know that? A doctor said you can't have one?"

She shook her head. Even after helping with a baby being born, her hair was still perfect. "I'm thirty-five."

"So?"

"So my ovaries are getting tired. Besides, I need–" She paused, wiped under her eyes with her fingers to swipe up the dark smudges, then looked to me.

"Need what?" I wanted to take away her hurt, to carry her burdens for her. But I couldn't fix her past. I couldn't help her with her future either. She only had a few days more work on the fundraiser calendar before it went to the printer and then she'd be gone. No strings didn't mean a baby. It meant the opposite.

No commitment. Nothing but fun and orgasms.

A baby? That made lesser men run away screaming. I never thought I'd have another child because Andy was plenty. Hell, I never imagined having him. But life was complicated and while I never expected to have a newborn nephew become my own, he had.

The older I got, the chances of me finding a woman

who'd want more was slimmer and slimmer. There still wasn't a woman on the horizon here in Hunter Valley.

"Nothing. Lindy and Dex, the new baby, it made me a little emotional." With a chin lift, she smiled.

"You're going to find a man." I didn't like saying those words and I was fucking jealous of someone who didn't even exist. But I had to say it. To make her feel better because she hadn't said she would stay in Hunter Valley, to give something, a relationship even, a try that was more than no strings. She hadn't said one word about wanting more from our *thing*. Or staying here. Or... anything but getting the job done.

We looked at each other and I waited. I gave her the opportunity to speak up, to tell me she wanted more. But no.

So I swallowed down my jealousy and continued, "I know there's a guy out there for you, because you're one hell of a catch, Georgia from Georgia. And if he treats you bad and doesn't give you all the babies you want, you let me know. I'll kick his ass."

The smile grew and I was suddenly dazzled. There was my gorgeous unicorn. The one that was going to slip through my fingers and be gone for good soon enough. I had to remind myself she wasn't for me. She wasn't for Andy. Hell, she'd arrived without boots or a proper coat. She sure as hell wasn't right for Montana. Or me.

"I'm sure you would." She took a deep breath, let it

out. It seemed her tears were done and thank fuck for that. I liked her smiling so much better.

"I think this night wasn't what you expected when asked to someone's house for dinner," she continued, wiping her cheeks and heading for the kitchen. "I bet Lindy and Dex are going to be hungry when they get settled at the hospital. Why don't we dig up some plastic containers, pack up a lasagna dinner and deliver it to them at the hospital?"

55

GEORGIA

"Hello, Momma."

"There you are. I thought maybe you were eaten by a bear in that God-forsaken place."

Ah, my mother, the southern drama queen.

"I think they're all hibernating now," I said. I went to the switch on the wall and flipped on the gas fireplace. Every room at the James Inn had one. "And I'm not living in a tent in the woods. This is a town. With buildings. Heat. Hot water."

"There are perfectly good towns in Georgia," she countered.

"Yes, there are, but the job is here. I'm sorry I didn't

return your call earlier, but I was busy working and then... you won't believe it. I helped deliver a baby."

She gasped. "I told you it was the wilderness. You helped to deliver a baby? Don't they have hospitals?"

"Sometimes a baby wants out on their own time," I replied. "In this case, it was fast. Too fast."

I'd cried all over Mac. That had been an error on my part. Then I'd told him about Art and how I'd wanted a baby. For a moment, I feared he'd think I was preparing to trap him. That I was sobbing into his flannel about popping out weak eggs and that I needed his super sperm immediately. To snare him into eighteen years of childrearing all because I'd missed out before now. That hadn't been the case.

Seeing the love Lindy and Dex had for each other, the excitement, the fear and the pure joy of seeing the person they made...

It had been moving. And it hurt. And it made me cry.

What was I doing? Falling for a man who'd made it clear the amazing sex we had was casual. That it was a Montana fling for me. Fuck a firefighter for a few weeks, then go home. Forget him and his family.

No big deal. Like delivering a baby. It was a job to him. Something to tackle, control and resolve. Nothing more. Nothing less.

It wasn't his fault I felt more for him than I was supposed to. It wasn't his fault I witnessed the amazement of childbirth with him. It wasn't his fault it made my biological clock tick louder.

I'd done all of that on my own.

We took food to the hospital and as Mac expected, Lindy's room was packed. Dex sat on the bed beside his wife, holding the new baby in his arms. They'd named her Justine, after Lindy's mother who passed away years ago.

They radiated pure joy and happiness. Around them was Theo and Mallory, Bridget and Maverick and Silas and Eve. They were all first-time aunts and uncles.

Maverick had passed Mac a cigar and he was the man of the hour for his birthing skills.

We didn't linger, thankfully. Even though I'd had drinks with most of them when I first arrived, and Mav was my boss on the fundraiser project, and I'd offered up my towel support during the birth, I'd felt completely out of place, an outsider.

This was a family moment and I hadn't wanted to intrude.

Mac drove us back to his house and the fact that I didn't belong, even with the MacKenzies, became so glaring.

While Mac had wanted me to stay with him like I had been the past few nights, Drew was going to stay the guest room. It was one thing to fool a six-year-old, but I wasn't going to share Mac's room with Drew across the hall.

While Mac had said he was thirty-five and wasn't going to be grounded for being with a woman, it wasn't happening. Especially since it had been made more than clear I was just a fling.

And for that I was thankful.

I needed some room. Space and time to think. I was still shaky from the birth. From the abruptness of life. Of change. It was a stark reminder of how much I'd been kidding myself. I was an all-in kind of girl. Even when I agreed to just sex, I couldn't do it. I'd caught feelings.

Stupid Georgia.

So I snagged some clothes from the garage apartment and went to my barely-used room at the James Inn. Andy and his father and grandfather were tucked in bed on the other side of town. New parents Lindy and Dex along with baby Justine were being safely observed at the hospital.

I was tucked in cozy, a fire in the gas fireplace, me in a plush robe and slippers after a hot shower. I'd never look at a bathtub the same way again.

I'd even savored the chocolate that had been on my pillow.

Alone.

And my momma wasn't letting me forget it.

"You'd have a passel of them now if you kept Art

happy," she said, and I could clearly see her in my mind shaking her head with her usual disappointment.

I had Good Girl Syndrome, the need to please even if it was to my disadvantage. To sit quietly by and put others' feelings and needs first. I always let my mother walk all over me in order to keep the peace.

"Art was never happy with me," I admitted. It was the truth and was obvious if he strayed. "That's why he's Pam Buttermacher's problem now."

"Maybe if you lost some weight or served dinner when he got home from work instead of working yourself," she added, knowing just how to make me feel bad. To make it my fault.

"Then I'd be worse off than I am now," I countered. "I'd have no job skills, penniless and no children to show for it. Because it's quite hard to make a baby when your husband is sticking his dick in someone else."

"Well, I never," she huffed.

"What is it you called about, Momma?"

It had been such a long day. Overwhelming. Emotionally exhausting and she was only making it worse. So much worse. Because after spending time with Mac and him telling me I was gorgeous and proving it to me by fucking me every which way he could, my mother's jabs were even more glaring.

I heard her breathing, as if she had to collect herself.

"I wanted to know when you're returning from that

silly job. Sassy needs help with some pageant clients and I need to tell them when you'll be available. They won't be getting the best, but some of these girls won't ever wear a tiara, but their mommas continue to hope and are willing to pay for it."

Like she still did with me.

It was my turn to collect myself. She didn't ask how the fundraising project was going. If the James Corp thought I was doing a good job. If the community thought I was. No. Not once.

"I'll have to get back to you. Good night, Momma."

I hung up. Because no matter what I said, nothing was going to change.

I wanted this calendar to succeed because, obviously, I'd suggested it. The last thing I wanted was to have it fail and the department find better success with a chili dinner. But I also needed to prove to myself I was competent and capable, that I was better than what Momma and Art and any other doubter thought of me. Bradley believed in me and I needed to believe in myself.

Now? I wanted to succeed because I needed so badly for James Corp to hire me full time. I needed to be in the Denver office, not back in Calhan. I needed to find my place, my spot in life that wasn't in Sassy's shadow, wasn't my Momma's warped view of an overweight divorcee and wasn't Art's second choice. For so long I let others dictate my wants and happiness. I stayed in places where

I knew I didn't belong. Like continuing to linger in the MacKenzies' lives hoping for scraps. All of these issues were my mistakes I repeated over and over. No more.

The calendar had to be amazing. I had my life riding on it.

56

MAC

"Morning," I said, heading for the coffeemaker. I just got out of the shower and Andy was stomping around upstairs trying to find his favorite socks.

By the time I got home the night before, it was late. By the time I updated Ralph and Dad on what happened, it was even later. Ralph went home and Dad said he was content sleeping over so I didn't have to go back out.

Now, Dad was up before me and at the kitchen table with the newspaper. He'd tackled the stairs fine, but the clomping of his walking boot woke me.

"Morning."

"Georgia coming down to take Andy to school?"

I shook my head and filled my to-go mug to the brim. "She stayed in the apartment. I told her last night I could take him. I'll go on to the station from there. Today's my photo shoot. I'm the last one."

He smirked and I glared.

"The project's wrapping up then," he said. "I think Georgia said she was going back home on Friday?"

I shrugged. We never talked about the actual date she was to go.

"Guess so."

He put the paper down and stared. "You guess so? She's leaving town for good and *you guess so?*"

I took a sip of the steaming brew. "We're not in a relationship, Dad."

"She's been sleeping in your bed."

He knew and he wasn't an idiot. There was no doubt Andy told him *all* about Georgia staying in my room.

I was thirty-five. Still, I blushed.

"Because Andy put her there." That was my excuse and it sounded flimsy.

"She's been taking care of him," he reminded. "Driving him to school, staying with him when you work."

"Because you broke your foot."

"She helped you deliver a baby."

"That's my job."

He sighed. "Your job? You helped bring your friends' baby into the world. It's joyous! You have a woman who is in love with Andy. That's really special. She cares for you. Maybe even loves you."

I blinked, then shook my head. Love? "No. Nope. She's looking for a guy to give her a baby."

"She said that?"

I nodded. "Last night."

"And he can't be you?"

"Me?" Was he insane?

"Yes, you."

I shook my head. "She's going back to Georgia. This has been... between us, well, we both went into this with our eyes wide open."

"So you don't care about her."

I sighed. "She's leaving, Dad." How many times did I have to say that to everyone? "I'm trained to not get emotions involved."

"Because of your job," he said, repeating my words back to me.

I nodded.

Andy clomped down the stairs and dashed into the kitchen. "Found them!" He held the socks up. They were green and didn't seem all that special, but what did I know?

"Grumpy made you breakfast. It's on the table," I

said. "As soon as you're done, we're taking him home on the way to school."

Then I was going to my photo shoot. With an adoptable puppy or kitten. This wasn't what I had in mind when working for the fire department, but sacrifices had to be made. Right?

57

MAC

"YOU CAN KEEP THE SHIRT ON," Georgia said, holding a wiggly little mutt. She wore the pink puffy jacket and even the cute hat I bought her, the one with the little pompom on top. The way the little guy was licking her face made me jealous.

Miranda, the photographer, stood beside her and looked through the camera lens, then fiddled with some buttons.

Thank fuck they'd wanted the engine parked behind the station so there was at least some privacy. I felt like a dumbass getting my photo taken and I didn't need the crew on shift to be pestering me.

They would, too.

But I wasn't the first who'd been photographed. In fact, I was the last. Yeah, I'd put this shit off for as long as I could and I was the only one being a stubborn ass about this project. Seeing the photos of the others made me feel better that I wasn't going to be slicked up with cucumber wax and doing something sexual to a piece of fire equipment.

But I didn't like to get my photo taken. I didn't like to be the center of attention. And I definitely didn't want to be in calendars on walls all around Hunter Valley for the next year. Hopefully, if I was Mr. January, they'd forget about me by February.

"I saw some of the photos last week, but did the others have their shirts on?" I asked.

"They did," Georgia confirmed. She studied me. "You know, you don't have to be in the calendar. I have a backup list I can–"

"No," I said, holding up my hand. No way was I backing out of this. "I'm the fire chief. I have to be in it."

"Right," she said, sharing a look with Miranda. "Maybe we should have you hold a bowl of chili instead of the dog?"

Oh, the sass. I glared. She smiled.

"The other day, Smutters was talking about his bunker pants pushed down his hips like he was in Play-girl. The liar." I'd seen his photos in the meeting and knew for a fact he was talking out his ass. I let him because ultimately, the calendar would prove him wrong.

Georgia rolled her eyes and gave the gray dog a scratch behind the ears. He leaned into the touch and closed his eyes. Yeah, doggie, I knew what her hands on me felt like.

"Remember, this is a PG calendar," she promised. "Kids will see it. I promise you, there was nothing inappropriate in any of the other photos and won't be with yours. That's not what it's about. Okay?"

I frowned but nodded. I had on my bunker pants with red suspenders and my navy HVFD t-shirt beneath. My bunker coat and chief helmet were tucked under my left arm.

She came over, handed me the little dog. "Here."

I couldn't help but smile when it licked my chin. "What's her"—I held the dog up with my free arm and inspected its undercarriage—"*his* name?"

"Roscoe."

"Why don't you..." Georgia looked around and bit her lip. She was focused and thinking. "There. Go sit on the back."

I went that way and Miranda followed. I heard the camera click but didn't know why. I was walking away. How exciting was that?

I dropped onto the back running board, set my coat and helmet down beside me. I couldn't feel the textured metal through my thick pants or that it was really cold. Sitting the dog next to me, I looked down at him.

Click.

My head whipped to Miranda and I glared.

"Don't mind that look. He's always grumpy," Georgia told her. "You look like you're really uncomfortable. Why is your back so straight?"

I gritted my teeth. "Because I don't want to look slouchy."

She rolled her eyes and laughed. "Relax. This isn't the DMV."

Roscoe woofed and sat and posed for the camera like he was a natural. The little fucker.

I settled back onto the platform and tried to get comfortable.

Miranda took some photos, but it was weird.

This was weird.

Georgia came over. Stepped close. I wanted to wrap my hands around the backs of her thighs and pull her near so I could set my head against her soft tits, but I held off. Barely. I'd missed her last night. A few nights sleeping with her in my arms and I wasn't only grumpy about the photo shoot.

"Remember the other night when you were watching me use my toy?" she whispered.

My head snapped up to look at her.

"What?" I said, instantly hard.

A glance at Miranda told me she wasn't paying us any attention. She was fiddling with something on her camera.

"Remember?" she asked again.

I cleared my throat. "Yeah."

"You sat in your reading chair and watched me on your bed. The look you had was what gave me the nerve to do it. The way you watched got me hot."

"Yeah?" I was reduced to monosyllabic talk because watching her with her legs spread wide as she made herself come? Hottest fucking thing ever. Gone was the shy woman from that first night I got her bare.

She bit her lip and nodded. "Later, you can find out what color panties I'm wearing. For now, you're going to sit there, look at me and wonder."

With that, she stepped back. Then again. Her eyes held mine until I lowered them, taking in her jeans, sweater and thick coat. I couldn't see her shape at all. But I knew what those tits looked like. What they felt like in my palms. I pictured it.

Click.

How swollen and slick she got from her toy so she was ready for me. How she tasted.

FUCK.

Click.

The dog nudged my hand, so I picked him up, set him on my thigh, all the while staring at Georgia.

Click.

Fuck, I was sweating, even though we were outside. The boots, the bunker pants. Looking at Georgia and imagining her in pink lace. No, black mesh so the panties didn't do a thing to hide her pussy. Was she wearing a thong?

I grabbed the hem of my t-shirt and lifted it to wipe my face.

Click.

I glowered at Miranda. She was keeping me from tossing Georgia over my shoulder, carrying her to my office and locking us in again and showing her what I did with a bad girl for teasing me. At least my bunker pants hid my hard on. When I saw her next, she better be ready.

I had plans.

58

GEORGIA

I OPENED the door and found Mac on the other side.

"Hiding from me?" he asked, arching a brow as he leaned on the casing.

In fact, I was. After the night before and the new baby–which was the talk of the town–I thought it best if I gave Mac some room. He'd literally said to me, *"You're going to find a man"*. He never, for one second, thought it could be him. That I may have found the man I wanted to be with in a grumpy firefighter in Montana.

No. If he wanted me for something permanent, he'd have said anything but pretty much tell me I was going to find another guy.

Then, later, my mother chimed in about how I couldn't keep a husband. She seemed to think that if I'd been a better wife, I'd have the life I wanted with Art. The baby, too. I saw the way Dex and Lindy looked at each other and Art *never* did that with me. Not once.

I wanted that. The moment they shared where their love was so great that it spilled over and made a child, exactly as I'd told Andy.

This morning at the photo shoot, Mac was back to his old, cranky self. While he'd shown up and sat with a dog on the back of a fire truck, that wasn't all it took to make him Mr. January. The photo had to be good, not proof he tried.

So I'd had to pull out some teasing. Coaxing. Sure, I didn't coax my pageant girls I coached the same way, but sometimes everyone needed a little motivation. Mac's was through sexy times.

It had worked. The pictures we'd gotten with him were appropriate, but smoldering. The one where he wiped his brow with the hem of his t-shirt? Holy shit. Now that hadn't been PG and that had gone into my thumb drive. That image was only for me.

I hadn't meant to tempt him. Okay, I had. I felt powerful and feminine when I teased Mac. But it was the wrong play if I was trying to give him space. To give me a chance to hang on to some bit of my sanity. And heart.

I should have known he'd show up.

He stepped in, not giving me space. In fact, he took it all away by lifting me up, then kicking the door shut behind him.

"My dick has been hard all day because of you," he said.

"Oh?"

"You teased me at the photo shoot, then left me to have blue balls all fucking day."

Yeah, it had worked. He had no clue that I'd messed with his day. Yeah, I'd teased him, but he clearly didn't see that it had been a diversion tactic. Just like in the laundry room that night I was first invited to dinner.

"Do I drive you fucking crazy?" I asked, remembering his words from then.

He threw me onto the bed.

As if I wasn't a big girl. As if I weighed nothing.

"Yes."

He looked as cranky and grumpy as when we first met. But now, while it was all focused on me, I liked it.

He leaned over me, set his hands on either side of my head. His dark eyes met mine. In fact, they were all I could see.

How had I ever thought I could just stop wanting him? Andrew MacKenzie wasn't something a woman could give up cold turkey. Well, I would have to when I left on Friday.

But now? I knew the deal. Knew Mac wanted me, but only for now. Only to let off a little steam after having blue balls all day.

I'd take it. Because while I knew all too well I wasn't wanted with him for the long haul, he hadn't tricked me or lied to me or fucked someone else behind my back. Well, I couldn't be sure about that last, but he was so busy I didn't know when he'd find time to fuck someone else.

Mac was upfront. This was sex. Just sex.

When I got back to Georgia–or maybe Denver if Maverick James had a job for me there–I'd be back to my vibrators. Until then...

I'd enjoy myself and be lonely and alone later.

"This space works out well," he said, sounding triumphant. "You can make all the noise you want when I fuck you. Andy isn't down the hall."

"Where is he?" I asked.

"One of my dad's friends took them both out to dinner. It's fish fry and bingo at the Elks Lodge. We have two hours."

"Don't you want to eat? You must be hungry."

His brow winged up and the corner of his mustache twitched. Then he started walking his hands backwards until he got to my jeans, then started to open them.

"Yeah, I'm hungry and I know exactly what I want to eat."

With a few tugs, my jeans and panties were gone.

And Mac pushed my legs wide, settled on the bed and put his mouth on me. He ate his fill. And I didn't have to keep quiet while he did it.

59

GEORGIA

Turned out, only Maverick James and Mayor Mary were able to show for the last meeting for the fundraiser. This time we were in an office at City Hall and Mac and Patrick were both working. We'd waited five minutes and hadn't heard from either of them, so we assumed they were on an emergency call. Good thing I emailed everyone the final photos I was sharing this morning because to stay on track with the fundraiser schedule, we couldn't wait for either guy to be available for final approval.

All of the photos had been pared down to three per month. I liked all of them but to me, there was one clear winner for each. Maverick and Mayor Mary reviewed them all and agreed with me on ten out of the twelve, but for the other two they'd chosen great alternatives. I didn't have any reason to sway them.

"You can see the cover was done on the computer merging all of the firefighters into one image." I pointed toward my laptop that was between them.

Besides the posing with the puppies and kittens, we'd also stood each model along the side of the fire truck as part of their shoot and the graphic designer, using computer photo editing, was able to place all twelve of them into one image. They were side by side by side.

"This way there isn't one cover model, but all of them together."

Mayor Mary smiled as she looked it over. "It's so nice. I like the lettering you've used."

I preened, pleased she liked the almost-final product. Between me, the photographer and the graphic designer, we'd worked hard pulling it all together.

"The graphic designer will insert the selected images and then send the files to the printer once we have your approval. My role on the project is done, but know you'll have a final print proof to review with her for any last-second typos or oopsies, but then the orders can be fulfilled. There's enough time to have the few hundred printed and ready for the fundraiser event in a few weeks and extra batch orders can be made at any time."

"Impressive," Maverick said, his finger moving over the arrow on my laptop keyboard to continue to review the images. He looked to Mayor Mary. "You're pleased?"

She nodded and beamed at me. "I am. So much. Georgia, this has been an amazing project and based on the orders already put in, we've already earned more than the chili dinner. That doesn't include any upcoming sales during the event or those who wait until they see the real thing."

I was relieved and thrilled. Excited and a little sad. This had been a fun project. Hard work, but the people were amazing.

"I'm so glad. Several shops in town also said they'd sell copies, like Steaming Hotties and the mechanic shop."

"Excellent job." She stood, shook my hand. I smiled, pleased she was so satisfied. "I'll let you talk with your boss as I have another meeting. It was so nice meeting you and I hope you'll come back to Hunter Valley soon."

She stepped out of the room.

Maverick closed the lid on my laptop. "Please, sit."

I'd been standing like I always did for these meetings and settled into a chair across from him. I folded my hands in my lap, crossed my ankles. Back straight. The perfect seated pageant pose.

Maverick was a big man. Intimidating. But I'd seen him hold his new little niece the other night in the hospital and knew he was a big softie. And compared to Mac's grumpiness, Mav was easygoing.

But he was still my boss. My hope for a full-time job, not a short-term contractor, was in his hands.

"Your work has been impressive," he began. "The calendar idea itself was smart. The business side of it, estimating the profit/loss and other aspects shows an understanding of making a PR project successful. You found sponsors in a town where you have no connections and pulled in a secondary charity that will also benefit. That's remarkable."

I nodded, practically holding my breath. He could say *Thanks, you did great. Have a safe flight home.*

"You were also able to keep costs to a minimum with donations of time from various vendors. All in all, a success and it hasn't even launched yet."

I smiled like I always did. Big and megawatt. No matter what he said next, he was right. I'd done a good job. But was it enough? Would I head back to Calhan and my mother's house to pick up Sassy's second tier coaching jobs?

Or would I be able to work in Denver? Maybe be Bradley's roommate instead and carpool to the office together.

"Bradley was right in having you add your name to the candidate list. I never question anything that man suggests. He's too good at his job. But it wasn't Bradley who pulled this calendar together. You're James Corp material and I'd like to offer you a full-time job."

My smile grew the tiniest of bits, and it was one hundred percent real. My heart hammered and I was so happy. I did it!

"Thank you!" I gushed. I put a hand over my lips. "I'm very glad to hear that. Bradley, as you know, is my cousin and has already told me so much about the corporate office. I'm eager to live in Denver." *And not in Calhan.*

He shook his head. "No, not Denver. Because Silas and I are both based in Hunter Valley now, we've decided to grow the local office here. There are only a few employees currently and we are in need of a PR person at this location. Hopefully that will be you."

"Here?"

He nodded. "Yes, the job I'm offering is here in Hunter Valley."

60

MAC

I missed the meeting because of a multi-car pileup out on the highway. There had been several fatalities, a chemical spill and we'd called in a life flight helicopter out of Missoula. We'd been at the scene all day. After returning to the station and completing the paperwork, it was late before I saw Georgia's email. The one with the final proof of the calendar.

I hadn't seen my photos yet. I took in the cover and stared at it, confused. How was it done since I never stood beside any of the other eleven for the photo? I tried to figure it out, but gave up, then scrolled on to January.

To me.

Oh.

There was nothing to the picture. It was me sitting on the back running board of the engine. Roscoe was on my thigh. I was pretty much glaring at the camera. Somehow, Roscoe was, too. It was the whiskers on his chin that somehow mimicked the shape of my mustache. It was oddly cool and amazing that Georgia had the eye to see it.

While I knew my glare was all *I hate every second of this,* to everyone else, I just looked... intense. Powerful. Like I knew what I was doing and that was why I was the chief.

There was nothing inappropriate about it. Not one hint of porniness like I first pictured. I flipped through the other images. Some were funny. Some were light-hearted. Some were... just good.

The calendar was fucking good.

And I was going to have to eat every one of my grumpy words like I would a huge bowl of chili dinner.

This had been Georgia's idea. Her execution. Her delivery.

It looked and felt like her personality. Open. Bright. Upbeat–except for my January glare–and welcoming. It showed Hunter Valley Fire Department in the best possible light.

Everyone was going to love it.

I loved it.

And that made me an asshole, because deep down inside, I doubted her up until the very end. Until about five minutes earlier when I first opened the email.

I wanted to tell her how amazing she was. How the project was a hit and the community was going to love it. That it blew the chili dinner idea away. No one was going to even remember it was a possibility.

I wanted to tell her. To show her. To kiss her. To see her smile. To see her come one last time before she left. Because seeing the final product of the calendar meant that Georgia's job was done.

61

GEORGIA

MAC KNOCKED ON THE DOOR, then came in, not waiting for me to answer.

I was in the little apartment over his garage, packing. The fireplace was on because the temperature dropped since yesterday. So much for spring. I'd never used a fireplace before since they weren't found in many houses in Georgia. But I liked how cozy it made a space, even over-the-garage apartments and electric versions.

He took in the room as if assessing the scene of an emergency. My room did look like there had been an explosion since my clothes were everywhere. "What are you doing?"

I found one of the suede boots Mac despised behind

the reading chair and tossed it into the open suitcase. "Packing."

"You're leaving?" he asked. He looked surprised, as if that was even a possibility. Not that we hadn't talked about it ever since we first hooked up. My departure was always a constant reminder, even when we were naked.

I found a rogue sock and added it to the pile. And, shit, there was my vibrator peeking out from beneath a shirt. I covered it up. Then I looked to him. He was in his uniform, which fit him so perfectly. Snug button-up with his chief badge. Biceps bulged from beneath the short sleeves.

I knew that belt well, the one that circled his trim waist. And those sturdy legs. And what was between–

I swallowed, suddenly feeling overwarm. A constant condition around him.

"Yes, but don't worry. Your dad took Andy to his house for the night. Said Ralph would pick them both up and take Andy to school. There was something in there about pickleball, I think."

Maverick's job offer was the only thing I'd thought about since this morning. The whole Hunter Valley thing wasn't something I imagined. There wasn't much of a real office here yet, only a small staff. But if they wanted a PR person here, then they definitely planned to build it up. With me. ME! I'd be in a place where I knew my ideas were valid. In a job that could only grow. With people who were nice. Quirky. Fun.

I'd dreamed of working in Denver, getting based there, but this little town? With Mac and Andy and Drew? It would be perfect. But that whole *casual* thing made the decision tough. Should I move across town or back to Georgia? Mav said HR would email me the job details and I could take some time to consider. He knew all about moving to Hunter Valley and that the decision was bigger than taking the job alone. I still had to sell my house I shared with Art. I had furniture, clothing, belongings fifteen-hundred miles away. I'd need a place to live, one that wasn't over Mac's garage. A car that could tackle snow. Probably some winter driving lessons.

There was a lot.

But it all came down to one thing.

Mac.

Maverick didn't know my accepting his offer revolved around Mac. No sane person would tell the CEO of a billion-dollar company that she was debating a position because of a man.

I'd texted Keely as soon as I got back to get some advice, because I sure as hell needed it. The conversation went like this:

> I was offered the PR job. Here in Hunter Valley.

That's amazing! Right?

It is amazing.

But?

But I can't stay here if Mac doesn't
want me.

He wants you. How many times have
you two fucked?

I'm a fling. He's never once told me
otherwise.

Men are idiots.

We could've gone on like that forever and I hated
texting long conversations, so I called her.

"What am I going to do?" I asked when she picked up.

"Do? Take the job!"

God, it felt so good. So fulfilling. Wanted. Successful,
too. Except–

"It's not that simple."

The one thing I wanted came with strings. Big
strings. Which was ironic because I wasn't supposed to
have any strings.

Gah!

"Let me get this all straight. Your boss loved your
work. He's hiring you on full-time with James Corp, I

might add, in Hunter Valley with your dream job. The guy you want to be with and who gives you amazing orgasms is there. He's got a kid you love. What am I missing?"

I sighed, hoping the anxiousness and doubt would go away. "Yeah, I want Mac, but he doesn't want me."

"Are you sure about that because the other day you texted me with a lot of tongue and water droplet emojis. A few eggplants and–"

"I know, I know! But he doesn't want anything permanent. He said so."

"He said to you, *I don't want anything permanent*?"

I closed my eyes and remembered back. "He said, "*You're going to find a man.*" He even offered to kick the guy's ass if he treated me badly."

Yeah, that had been a great moment. Not. I was already overwhelmed and stunned by Lindy giving birth and then Mac had said that.

She was quiet for a moment. "Why would he say that?"

Why? "Because he's a man not interested in a relationship. He doesn't want me for more than sex. Oh, and a babysitter for his son."

"Oh."

I frowned, because recounting it made it sound even more obvious. "Yeah, oh."

"Then tell him how you feel!"

I sighed. "Again, it's not that simple."

"Yes, it is. Let's practice it together. 'Mac, I'm in love with you and I want to be with you and Andy and let your eggplant and my cat make lots of water droplets.'"

I rolled my eyes and began to pace. "I can't tell him I'm in love with him. One, because I'm not–"

"You are totally in love with him!"

I let my lids fall closed and I succumbed to the truth I'd been refusing to admit. That from the very first time I saw him at the airport, I was drawn to him. That what we felt, this chemistry, wasn't normal. It was special and crazy and– "You're right. I'm in love with him."

It was ridiculous. I'd only known the guy for about two weeks. In that time, we hadn't done a hell of a lot of talking. When we did talk, Mac was often obstinate and stubborn. Said I drove him crazy. But I saw through all of that. I thought I knew him. Knew his character, his honor. The depth of his love for his family. That was what drew me to him as much as that sexy mustache and his ability to handle chaos with a cool head.

He was so unlike Art or any man I'd ever met. I never expected to fall for someone so completely different. So temperamental. So basic. Simple. Someone who cared more about the people around him than things as superficial as appearances. Who... was insanely perfect.

She screeched. "Finally! I was fixin' to come up there and whoop your ass."

"It doesn't change a thing," I countered, frustrated now that I admitted my feelings aloud. Saying them didn't make anything easier. It actually hurt and I rubbed at my chest. I was stupid for falling for him when we'd clearly said it was just sex.

I swallowed hard, coming to terms with the truth. Of my mistake. I fell for another guy who doesn't love me in return.

I was an idiot. Weak. I had an impulsive heart. One that was attracted to things I wasn't supposed to have.

"He doesn't love me, K," I said. "He likes fucking me. He likes me babysitting for Andy. I'm replaceable. I'm temporary. No strings, remember?"

"Then you take the job of your dreams and steer clear of him."

She made it sound so simple. Why couldn't it be simple?

"Ha! This place is just like Calhan. Small. You think I can avoid Art and Pam?"

She laughed. "No."

"Well, I can't avoid the fire chief in Hunter Valley if I lived here. *Everyone* knows him. In the wintertime, I'd drive into a snowy ditch every day and he'd be the one to rescue me."

"Fine. Then ask him if he wants you to stay. Then you'll know."

Keely was right. I needed to know how he felt about

me. Because a job was a job. Love was something else entirely and I couldn't walk away from the chance of it. Not if Mac felt the way I did.

"Ask him, G," she pushed. "You have to. You spent years with Art not knowing he didn't feel for you what you thought. He's not Art and not every guy will let you down."

I bit my lip, worried. "What if he doesn't want me, just like Art?"

"Hon, then you'll come home knowing you took that dick for a ride and had some fun. That dick got you over Art once and for all and you'll be ready for the right guy when he comes along."

That had been the end of my call with Keely and when my nerves kicked in.

Mac was here, watching me.

Are you leaving? he'd asked.

Now was the time. The moment. My plane ticket back to Georgia was for the morning. I was so nervous my palms were sweating. I wiped them on my pants. Mac was everything I wanted. Moody, sure. But selfless and sexy. Bossy and an amazing father. An incredible lover.

I swallowed hard, licked my lips. God, I wanted to go to him, wrap my arms around him and hope he held me right back. I wanted him to kiss the top of my head, call me his good girl and then fuck me like I was very, very bad.

But more sex wasn't going to change anything except my orgasm count. I had to ask. I had to know if I belonged, and if it was here. With him. Do it. *Do it.* DO. IT!

"Do you... do you want me to stay?" I asked. *Do you love me? Do you want to be with me? Do you want* me?

There. I did it. My heart was pounding louder than Andy flying down the stairs. I smiled. Waited. Waited. Waited, just like when the emcee opened the envelope to announce the winner of a pageant.

MAC

DID I want her to stay?

Yes. But she was leaving. She was packing her bag. Her staying in Hunter Valley wasn't an option. If she wanted to be here, she'd have thrown out that broken zippered suitcase and jumped me when I came through her door.

Knowing this, seeing the proof of her departure strewn across the room, I needed her. To hold her, touch her. Fuck, I had to make her come.

With Andy at Dad's, we had the place to ourselves. Unfortunately, I was on call. I had the incident command truck so I could go directly to a scene, but I could get called out at any time. That meant I couldn't get naked.

But I could fuck her. I could be creative and quick. Because if she was leaving, I had to have her one last time. I had to feel her lush curves. Feel her clench my dick. Claw my back. Scream my name.

Fuck it.

I went to her. Kissed her. Grabbed her hair. Her ass. Cupped her tits. She was just as frantic, clawing at my clothes to get to my skin.

"Mac," she breathed, running her hands over me, too. "Yes."

I was in my fire uniform. All buttons, a heavy belt, sturdy shoes.

It didn't matter. I wanted her. Now.

"This is gonna be quick," I said, finally pulling my mouth from hers.

She nodded, her hair falling in her face. She wasn't calm and collected or poised like she told Andy. She was eager for my dick. "Yes. Quickly."

Her fingers worked my belt open, then my work pants. I hissed when she reached into my boxers and gripped me.

"Fuck."

I pulled her hand from me, gripped her hips and spun her so she faced the wall. Her hands were by her head, her face turned. She watched me as I got her pants and panties down around her knees.

Leaning in close, I spoke right into her ear. "You wet and ready, gorgeous?"

She bit her lip, nodded.

"Let me see." I slid my hand over her bare ass, smacked it. Fuck, my handprint bloomed on her creamy skin. Then I found her center, found her wet. With her legs trapped together, she was tight.

"Mac," she whispered. That wouldn't do. I wanted her shouting my name.

"Bend forward, stick that ass out."

As I pulled a condom from my wallet, I watched her get into position. I loved how she gave me sass one minute, then submitted the next. Her upturned ass with my handprint on it was a sign of that. How she held herself still, eagerly waiting for my dick.

Bending my knees, I lined myself up, slid the latex-covered head through her folds.

"Mac! Please." That was a little better.

Oh, she begged so good.

I lined up and thrust deep. Thank fuck she wasn't little. I didn't have to bend in half. Neither did she. We fit perfect. Tight. Snug.

"YES!" she cried, pushing back on me.

I hooked a hand about her waist, the other across her body to cup her tit through her top.

Then I began to move. Deep strokes.

"So tight. So wet." I nipped at her neck. "Perfect. You take me so good."

"So good," she repeated.

"Play with your clit, gorgeous, and come for me. Yes, just like that. Oh, you just got wetter."

It didn't take long and I could feel her clenching. Rippling. She looked over her shoulder at me. Those dark eyes met mine. They widened and then she came.

I followed, unable to resist getting lost in her. Fuck, she felt so good. I filled the condom and lost my mind. Got lost in Georgia.

I had no idea how long we stood there, her pressed into the wall, me still deep inside her, as we caught our breath.

The condom needed attention so I carefully pulled out, disposed of it in the bathroom. By the time I washed my hands, she'd righted her clothes, which was a shame. But I knew where my handprint was and she'd be feeling it, and the hard fucking, for a while.

Her cheeks were flushed, her gaze soft and she looked well fucked. At least to me.

I wanted to pull her into bed, to keep her there.

"You um... you never answered my question," she said. Her voice was soft, as if she were too tired to talk.

"I don't remember the question," I admitted, buckling my belt back up.

"Do you want me to stay?"

Oh. That question. Wasn't what we just did answer enough? It was sex. Amazing sex, but that was it.

Her life wasn't here. She had family in Georgia. A mother, a sister. A niece and nephew. I knew all along she wasn't permanent. Just like every other woman in my life. Mom left. Sure, she died, but she was gone. Tracy left. She didn't choose Andy or us. Teri didn't want my family.

I was used to being left behind. Expected it now.

Georgia, at least, had been up front about it. About what she wanted from me. Her screaming her pleasure just a minute ago proved I gave her exactly what she wanted.

But no matter how great the sex was, she'd never been permanent. She never was. I'd been smart. While getting close with her, I'd kept my distance emotionally. When I told her there was a man out there for her, she only smiled and nodded. She agreed.

I was just a Montana fuck.

Which meant I wasn't the one for her. If it wasn't now that she left, it would be later. This week, next week, she'd still go. She'd ultimately find something, or some-one, better and move on. This way, I was in control. This way, she could find the man who'd give her the life she wanted. And since my dick was happy and my balls drained because of her sweet pussy, I was suddenly a hell of a lot possessive and jealous of the man who'd finally get her.

She was watching me, smiling that big, perfect smile. I couldn't hold her back. Couldn't keep her in Hunter Valley if there was a man for her out there. She'd been so emotional about Lindy and Dex's baby. About not having one of her own. She'd get that, but Hunter Valley was temporary for her and so was I.

"They offered you a job?" I asked. "James Corp?"

She nodded.

I couldn't help but smile. She'd done it. Mav saw in her the same skills and traits as I had and I told her so. She was headed to Denver.

"That's great. I'm really proud of you. Mav knows a good thing when he sees it. You should take it, Georgia."

"But–"

I held up my hand. "No buts. We were just your hosts." I held up my hand and pointed toward the house. "The ones who make garlic bread for our special guests."

Her smile didn't falter. Not one bit. She didn't look saddened by my words. She got the job she wanted from James Corp. She was getting her life back on track. Denver was going to be perfect for her. Perfect. Especially now that she had good boots.

"Mac, I–"

My walkie talkie signaled a call. I closed my eyes for

a moment, wished for once someone didn't need me. "Fuck."

I looked at Georgia. She looked at me.

"I have to go."

She nodded. "Me, too. See ya, Mac."

I went to her, kissed her hard, then paused. Pulled the belt from my pants and handed it to her. "You'll need this."

And just like that, another woman was out of my life.

63

GEORGIA

Mac left. I wasn't sure if I should hate that an emergency call interrupted us. It kept the goodbye quick. If someone wasn't dying or a building wasn't burning down, he'd have lingered. I'd have surely cried. He'd have... well, I'd never know now.

He was gone. I felt him missing as much as I felt my pussy ache from his last bit of attention.

Even though he'd fucked me rough and hard up against the wall, that hadn't been the answer. With those kisses and that naughty sex, it wasn't him saying *yes, stay.* It had been, I need to fuck you one last time before you go.

I thought he'd been so consumed he couldn't hold

back, just like I'd wanted to go to him. So I had. But it hadn't been me being in love with him kissing him and him being in love with me kissing me right back.

Nope. It had been a dick sendoff.

He didn't pick me. He didn't want me. I wasn't permanent. Of making a family with me. I was only good for a fill-in position. A babysitter. What was the saying? Always a babysitter and never a baby of your own?

Now I knew. I wasn't worth keeping and making a life with. I'd put too much emotional stock into the past two weeks. I wouldn't cheapen it by saying I was only good for sex, but that was the value we were supposed to place on our time together.

Just sex. No strings. No feelings. Just fucking.

But I wanted more. I let my heart in. And so with an achy pussy and a broken heart, I cried.

64

MAC

GEORGIA WAS GONE before I got home from my shift the next morning. Her rental was gone out front. The garage apartment was empty. Clean. As if she'd never been there. Except her scent lingered. So did the memory of her standing in front of the door, baring herself to me for the first time. Of me pressing her against the wall and taking her hard and fast.

I slept all morning, but when I woke, it wasn't Georgia beside me.

It was Richard. He was curled up on her pillow.

I frowned. "You are not the pussy I want," I said, grumpy.

Richard eyed me in that asshole way only cats could

pull off, stood, then hopped off the bed and to... who the hell knew where he went.

I rolled onto my back, stared at the ceiling. My bed felt... lonely. It felt like something was missing. Something was. I shouldn't be surprised or disappointed. I knew this was coming.

It was back to life as usual. No woman to drive me fucking insane.

I showered. I got some groceries. I got in the carpool line and picked up Andy at school.

Normal shit on a normal day.

He climbed into the truck, settling into his booster, flinging his little backpack across the backseat.

"What's with the cool crown? You win something?" I asked.

He was quiet. And unsmiling. Completely unlike Andy. The school would have called if he were sick.

"It's from Miss GG," he said, sounding forlorn. "She made it for me."

"Oh?" The crown was clearly handmade, cut from cardboard and covered in shiny aluminum foil. It had zigzag peaks all the way around. I imagined her making it with the limited supplies she had in the garage apartment.

"She gave it to me this morning when she said goodbye."

Which had been before he went to school. Ralph

must've swung him and Dad by to see Georgia one last time.

"That was nice of her," I told him. It was. Just like her to give him something special.

"Yeah. She said I'm her favorite six-year-old. I won and there wasn't even a runner up. What's a runner up?"

"It means you didn't have any competition."

Well, shit. He wore the crown all day at school.

All. Fucking. Day.

"Should we go get Grumpy and go out to eat?" I asked, hoping to switch topics.

He shrugged his little shoulders in his winter coat.

"I miss her," he murmured, looking down in his lap.

Yeah, buddy, I missed her, too.

65

GEORGIA

"WINE. GIVE ME WINE."

I was on Keely's couch. Johnny was out with the kids. One look at me standing on his doorstep and he herded them out the door. Or it could've been the two bottles of wine I was carrying. And a family size bag of corn chips.

"I saw on the news that Dex James had his baby," she said, coming from her kitchen with one of the wine bottles and two glasses tucked under her arm. I'd already ripped open the chips. "He was even interviewed. Is he as handsome in person as he is on TV?"

I nodded, tucked my legs under me. "Yes. Taller, too. Super nice."

"I can't believe you were there and helped with the delivery."

Me neither.

"So have you heard from him?" She flopped down beside me and poured our drinks.

"Dex? No. I bet they're too sleep deprived to even–"

She held up a hand to stop me. "Not Dex. Mac."

Mac. Every time I heard his name, or saw a Big Mac commercial on TV, my heart gave a little lurch.

"Oh. No."

I'd been home for a week. Using Mac's belt, my suitcase had made it back to Calhan without exploding again. My life? Total explosion.

"How's it going living with your momma?"

I rolled my eyes. "The neighbors think I worked on a slutty firefighter calendar because that was the only option I had since I can't keep a man."

She laughed, then cut it off and frowned. "That's what she told everyone?"

I nodded.

Her fingers covered her lips. "Oh my Lord."

That had been pleasant, correcting everyone on the block. The only part that wasn't true was the word *slutty*. I did work on a firefighter calendar and I definitely couldn't keep a man. Hell, I couldn't keep two. It certainly didn't make it any more fun to be in her house again.

"Thankfully, the house with Art is under contract," I shared.

The Realtor called me a few days ago that they had a solid offer. I'd had to meet Art at their office to accept and sign paperwork. That had been fun, too. Seeing him again, seeing the wedding ring on his finger that was for a different relationship. As soon as I was done, I'd been out of there. While I no longer had any feelings for Art other than anger, he was a physical reminder of wasted time. Of wasted love.

It was almost May and it was hot in Calhan. I'd been sweaty and uncomfortable ever since I landed. The humidity was brutal and I forgot the amount of hair product needed to keep my long hair from frizzing. That had not been a problem in Montana. Lord, I missed the cold. I missed being bundled in thick sweaters, sturdy boots and a pink puffy coat.

Kelly had the air conditioning on and I was still sweating.

"I know! Amazing news." She leaned close and clinked our wine glasses together. "Goodbye, Art. Hello, half of the money!"

My meager bank account had made me nervous the past few months, but as soon as the house closed, I would have a little cushion. A little chance to consider what I wanted to do. "Right? Best news I've had in a while. Except I had to talk with Art while we signed the papers. But you know, I don't really give a shit any longer. Pam Buttermacher can have him."

"That's because you rocked the job and rocked all those orgasms." She said it simply as if the answer was obvious.

In the time I'd been back, I hadn't heard from Mac. I hadn't expected to.

"I can't believe you turned down the job," she said, biting her lip. Clearly, she thought I should have accepted. So had Maverick when I met with him at Steaming Hotties and shared the news. When he'd shook my hand and wished me well.

I shook my head. "I'm not going to watch Mac and Andy from afar. They're different than Art and Pam, but that baby's going to be tough." A baby was my kryptonite. "No. After all this, I learned a lot about myself. That I don't need to believe anything Momma or Art says about me. That I have a life outside of Calhan, outside of the expectations and limits they set on me. That I set on myself."

"You go, girl," she said, taking a swig of wine.

"I deserve it all and I'm going to get it," I said with confidence, then took a big gulp of wine. "Bradley's going to keep an eye out for other openings within the company. Maybe I'll end up in Denver after all. In the meantime, I've applied at other places and after seeing

Art, well, I don't give a shit any longer. He'll probably cheat on Pam next."

I remembered Mac had said something about that. Once a cheater, always a cheater.

Mac.

I had to wonder if he'd moved on. If a new tenant had taken over his garage apartment.

And his bed.

66

MAC

MAVERICK AND BRIDGET were having a get-together at their big house for baby Justine. We were invited. Me, Dad and Andy. Since I delivered the baby. Fortunately, I was officially off work. Unless catastrophe struck, I wasn't getting called out. I even planned to have a beer and finish it.

Bridget answered the door when Andy rang the bell. It'd been ten days and he was still wearing the crown Georgia made for him. Some of the points were a little wilted, but he refused to take it off. Even slept with it next to his action figure on his pillow.

"Hey, little man," Bridget said to him, holding her

knuckles out for him to bump. She stepped back and let us in.

"Here."

Andy held out a bottle of sparkling apple juice.

"What's this?" Bridget asked, taking it from him.

She studied the bottle as he answered. "You're supposed to bring a gift when you're invited to dinner. That's what Miss GG says, so this is for you."

When Andy heard we were coming to dinner, he made me stop at the store and pick up the gift. It was good manners and I couldn't fault him for being kind and thoughtful. But it definitely made me feel like an asshole because I hadn't even considered it.

If GG were here, then–

"Thank you, Andy. That's very thoughtful. Scout's around here somewhere and would love to hang out with you."

"Scout?" Andy asked as Bridget shut the door. He shrugged out of his coat and I took it.

"Our dog. He's–"

There was a woof and then a short-legged dog ran down the hall and practically ran into Andy. He dropped to his butt and stared up at Andy as if waiting for him to pet him, feed him or play.

"There he is," Bridget said, smiling. "Can you hang out with him? He's a little jealous of the baby getting all the attention."

Andy smiled–the first one I'd seen in a while–as he pet Scout. "Sure!"

"There are treats on the counter for him, too. But don't give him too many."

They ran off together.

"Thanks. I think he was afraid Mallory was going to give him some math work to do."

She grinned, then looked to Dad. "How's the foot, Mr. MacKenzie?"

"Getting there," he replied, picking up his foot and shaking it as if he were doing the Hokey Pokey. "Another ten days."

She turned to me. Smiled. "And Mac, you're the man of the hour."

"Me?"

"Yeah, Mr. Baby Deliverer. Come on in." She led us through her big house and into a huge great room. It was dark out, but I could only imagine the view out of the floor to ceiling windows. There was a roaring fire and everyone was spread out between the huge sectional and the food spread on the kitchen island.

"Everyone wants to hear the real story of Justine's birth," she told me. "Dex is saying some things that can't be true. Like he told you to stand back because if he could make a slapshot from the centerline, he could catch a baby."

I couldn't help but laugh because I remembered all

too well how Dex wanted me to avoid looking at his wife's pussy. As if I had any interest in that woman–baby being born or not–with Georgia in the same room.

"I did all the hard work, right, Mac?" Dex asked with a huge grin, coming over and shaking my hand.

"You did your part ten months ago," Lindy called from the couch. I hadn't seen her since the hospital, but she looked good, although maybe a little tired. Her blonde hair was pulled up in a bun and she had on a pale pink fleece top.

"Sugar, that's just mean. But true."

The four James brothers were here together with their significant others. Mav shook my hand, then Dad's. Silas and Theo followed.

Dex passed me a beer. "For your help. You earned it."

"All in a day's work," I said.

Eve, who owned Steaming Hotties and had tamed the billionaire CEO, Silas, pulled Dad into the kitchen with the lure of a barista-made cup of coffee. I was steered in the opposite direction to see the baby. Dex's hand on my shoulder. He beamed like an idiot, but it looked good on new fathers.

I leaned over the back of the couch to study the newest James in Lindy's arms. "Hold her," she prompted, passing her over.

I took her and pulled her into a snug football hold. She was so light. So little. Even though I saw her when she just came out, literally brand new, she seemed extra tiny now.

"Hey! I thought I was next," Silas muttered.

"He delivered her," Lindy reminded her brother-in-law.

Justine was asleep, swaddled in a pale pink blanket. Her fair hair was wispy and almost invisible. Her little nose was like a button and her lips moved as if she was nursing.

So sweet. Had Andy ever been this small or this calm and quiet?

I smiled at Justine, then down at Lindy. "You did a good job."

She grinned at me. Motherhood suited her. "Thank you for your help, and for putting up with this guy." Her blue eyes shifted to Dex beside me. He leaned down and kissed her.

"We're back to Denver tomorrow," he said. "We didn't want to miss saying thank you. If you weren't there, well, I'd be getting a new car right now. I don't think detailers would be able to get childbirth out."

"I didn't do it all myself," I told him. "You helped."

"Don't build up his ego," Lindy warned.

Andy tossed a ball for Scout and the dog ran across the room right behind us.

"Georgia helped, too," I added. "You can thank her personally when you get back."

They glanced at each other, then back at me. I couldn't miss the confusion.

"In Denver? How can we thank Georgia?" Dex asked.

"She took a job with James Corp."

"Hey, Mav!" Dex called, scratching his head. The baby didn't even stir when her daddy shouted. Silas came over and I passed Justine off.

I turned to look at Mav, who was with Bridget making plates of food from the buffet.

Mav looked up.

"I thought you said Georgia turned down the job offer," Dex said.

Mav held a chicken wing in one hand, a loaded plate in the other. "She did."

WHAT?

I stalked across the room to stand on the far side of the huge island from Mav and Bridget. "What do you mean she turned down the job?"

He shrugged. He had on a Steaming Hotties t-shirt that was small enough to make him look like he was the Incredible Hulk. Eve didn't need a billboard for advertisement when she had him. I had no idea what the deal was with him and that shirt. "She said she had to pass, that Hunter Valley wasn't the right place for her. She's–"

"Hunter Valley?" I snapped back as if he punched me.

Dad and Eve turned at my tone.

My head was exploding. I hadn't heard a thing about

Georgia all week and now, *now,* I was finding out she didn't take the job she'd been hoping for.

Mav nodded. "You okay? Don't worry, she had the event night all organized before she left. You won't have to buy kidney beans in bulk ever again."

"What do you mean Hunter Valley?" I repeated, ignoring the part about the chili dinner.

"I offered her a job here as the PR director. Since Silas and I are up here full time, we're growing the local office. I wanted her a part of it."

"She turned you down?" I repeated, trying to understand. I ran a hand over my mouth, my mustache rasping my palm. Why would Georgia give up her dream job and move back to a town with her seemingly crazy mother and asshole ex? "What the hell?"

67

MAC

"WHY ARE you so upset about this?" Dad asked.

After the party, we went back to the house. We were in the kitchen and I was pulling out chicken nuggets from the freezer for Andy, slammed the door shut. While there'd been tons of food at Mav's place, Andy'd been too busy playing with their dog to eat. Now he was hungry and searching for Richard while he waited. Why, I had no idea. I hadn't seen the cat in three days, but the food bowl was empty every morning so I knew he was alive.

Dad was at the kitchen table, his booted foot propped up on a chair.

"About Georgia?" I asked, pulling the cookie sheet

from the lower cabinet. I dropped it onto the counter with a loud clang.

"Yes. Clearly, she didn't want the job after all."

I huffed and glared at the cookware. "She wanted it."

"You're really worked up over a woman you don't care about."

I eyed him. Frowned. "She *wanted* that job, Dad. It makes no sense."

He was quiet for a moment. "Did you know she stayed at the James Inn?"

I shook a few chicken nuggets from the bag and onto the tray, then glanced at Dad. "What? When?"

"A few nights when she was here."

I shook my head. I straightened the frozen shapes on the tray. "She had the apartment," I said, pointing out the back window. "I know it's not fancy, but–"

"Son, while the little garage apartment isn't the James Inn, the woman didn't relocate there for the amenities."

"Then why?"

He sighed. "You can assess a fire from the glow it gives at night from a mile away. You can tell when to send your crew into a burning building and when to maintain from the street. You can tell if someone's having a diabetic emergency and now help deliver a baby. But you can't see this."

I leaned on the counter and stared at him. "Dad, what the hell are you talking about?"

"That woman is in love with you."

I blinked. Then again. I shook my head. Georgia? I love with *me*? "No. No way."

"Georgia went to the inn to get away from here. From you. She was protecting her heart."

I shook my head.

"How the hell do you know this and not me?"

"Because you seem to have your head up your ass." He crossed his arms over his chest.

"Not about this," I countered. I'd have known. I'd have *seen*.

The oven beeped letting me know it was up to temperature. I opened the door and slid the cookie sheet in. "If she went to the inn, it was because she wanted never-ending hot water."

Right?

68

MAC

THE NEXT DAY, I picked up Dad to take him to his doctor's appointment. I asked him what had been on my mind since the night before. All night.

Georgia was in love with me? She never said. Never let on. Were women crazy? It seemed so because why would she go to the James Inn if she wanted to be with me?

"About Georgia. She went to the inn, which means she didn't want to be with me. Then why did she say yes to helping out with Andy? Plus, taking care of you and staying in my bedroom if it wasn't what she wanted?"

He glanced my way. "Who says it wasn't what she wanted?"

I flicked my gaze at him, then back on the road. The sun was shining. It was bright. Too bright. Reaching up, I pulled my sunglasses from the little holder and put them on.

"Maybe it was *exactly* what she wanted but you told her it was only casual. Turn in here. I want to get a donut. Maybe I'll get an extra for the doctor and she'll get me out of this boot faster."

I blinkered and turned into the local donut shop.

"She'd have told me if she felt more," I said, sticking with Georgia and not donuts.

I pulled into the drive-thru line.

"Really?" he asked. "And what would you have done? Deny how you feel like you are right now? Deny how *she* feels about *you*? She'd be mortified and hurt if it wasn't reciprocated. Just like with her ex. From what I understand, he took her love and tossed it aside for another woman. He even married her."

I huffed because I didn't like being compared to Georgia's ex. I asked the question and now I wasn't liking the answers. The drive thru line moved and I pulled forward.

"And got her pregnant," I added.

"What? Her ex is having a baby?" Dad asked, clearly surprised.

I nodded. "Yeah, he strung her along about a baby during their marriage, obviously not giving her one.

Then he cheated on her as you know and now, he's having a baby with someone else. Georgia doesn't want to have to see them, to know what she was missing because–"

Oh shit.

I couldn't finish, so Dad did it for me. "Because she didn't want to stay in Hunter Valley where she'd see you and Andy when she wasn't wanted. When her feelings weren't reciprocated."

We pulled one car closer to the order window.

"Son, all she wanted was to be picked. To be chosen. To be someone's top choice, not runner up."

69

GEORGIA

"Good morning, Momma," I said, going to the coffee pot. It'd been tucked in the corner by the stove all my life.

I had on my satin sleep shorts and top. My hair was up in a sloppy bun. I'd brushed my teeth but needed coffee to do anything else. I wasn't sleeping well. Imagine that.

She was switching purses on the counter, moving everything from the blue one from yesterday to the pink one that matched today's outfit.

"Sassy has an extra pageant girl this morning. I told her you'd take her. You'll meet at the mall because the dear thing needs help choosing the right support wear and I know you know just the right thing."

I closed my eyes for a moment. I didn't need this. Not before caffeine. I grabbed a mug and filled it, then turned to face her. She was fully dressed and ready for the day, meaning she had on a dress, shoes, jewelry, makeup and her hair was styled. At eight. She was ready for anything, even a religious cult that might knock on the door.

"Momma, I am not taking Sassy's extra pageant girl," I said. "She shouldn't have double booked."

She looked up from her task.

"Of course, you will," she countered, waving her hand as if my words meant nothing. "You have nothing else going on. It's not like you have a–"

I held up my hand. I'd had enough. I was done. I wasn't fixin' for a fight, but I'd been used and walked on enough. I put the blame squarely on myself. For years... decades, hell, my entire life I sat by and let others dictate what I wanted and what I did. I smiled and made nice and didn't ruffle feathers.

I took a sip of fortifying brew, then set it down. Crossed my arms over my chest like someone formidable and brave I knew.

"That's right," I began. "I don't have a job. I had one and it went well, but it finished. I was offered a full-time position, but I declined."

The ache was still there. The double loss of the MacKenzie family and the job with James Corp. I'd walked away from everything I ever wanted because it was just too painful.

Every night since I flew home–without a cute little boy sitting next to me to share my peanuts–I'd cried myself to sleep. I was surprised Momma hadn't mentioned my blotchy face or swollen eyes. I needed cucumber slices and hemorrhoid cream to calm the bags under my eyes.

"Which was silly of you." She pursed her lips. Today, the lipstick choice was a mauve. It was a good color for her.

"Momma, y'all can't have it both ways. Y'all can't say it's silly for me to turn it down and then point out it was in such a backwater, dangerous place."

She remained quiet because she knew I was correct. Then she went back to her purse shift and moved her cosmetics bag and compact. "You could get a job here."

I nodded. "Yes, ma'am, and I have resumes out for positions that are best suited for me. That does not mean I'm to be used as an assistant to Sassy. My time is my own. My choices are my own."

Her eyes widened. "Where is this bold streak coming from?"

I thought of Mac, of standing in front of him that first time in the little apartment, of me being nervous in showing him my body in just my bra and panties and he told me to rule his world. And it seemed I did. For a while.

"I've always been this way, Momma. I just found it easier to go along. To paste on that pageant smile and pretend everything was perfect. With you and Sassy. With Art. I thought he might love me more if I bent over backwards for him."

"He–"

I shook my head and held up my hand once more. "Your opinions on my marriage are just that. Your opinions. He cheated on me and regardless of the reasons for him doing so, he broke our wedding vows. I take those seriously and I know honor is important to you as well. If you continue to take Art's side, then you're hurting me and only shaming yourself."

"I don't take Art's side," she countered, grabbing the small pack of tissues and stuffing it into the new purse. "You had a solid marriage and you let it go."

"Of course, I let it go. And it wasn't solid. Not for years. Do you truly want me to stay with a man who cheated? Who flaunted it in my face at home and at work?"

"Well, of course not."

"Then enough. I'm fixin' to put him in my past and so should you."

"I only want you to be happy."

"No, you want me to be happy with what you want

me to be. I'm thirty-five years old, Momma. I'm never going to win a pageant. I'm never going to be skinny or Miss Georgia like Sassy."

"Not everyone has her genes and talent."

"You're right. I have my own genes and there are people who like me exactly as I am. I have talent and skills that I shared with an entire town. No one cared I could sing or twirl a baton. I was wanted for being smart, not beautiful. The job was mine."

"Then why did you turn it down?"

"Because I wanted more." I wasn't going to tell her about Mac and Andy. About Drew and the mysterious Richard, the cat. I was too raw to talk about them. I missed them all so much, but they weren't mine. And I deserved to have a man tell me to stay. To be his. To get on my knees. "And from now on, that's all I'm going to take."

She looked at me wide eyed, as if I'd been possessed by aliens while I slept.

"No more shaming me," I warned. "No more comparing me to Sassy. No more. You accept me and love me as I am or I will walk right on outta here. Head high, pageant smile in place."

She swallowed hard but clearly I'd made her speechless.

I'd said my fill. I told her what I should have years before. Now time would tell. And many reminders.

I looked at my coffee, thought it was good but much too hot for the weather. It needed to be snowy and crisp for a hot drink and Georgia in April was neither. "I think I want to go get an iced coffee. Would you like to join me? We could make it a girl's day and get our nails done." I looked down at my hand. "I will admit, Montana air is hard on my cuticles."

She looked surprised, then pleased. She nodded. "That sounds lovely. Before you walk anywhere though, including the coffee shop, you better put on your face."

MAC

"YOUR DAD TOLD me you're still being a dumbass," Theo said, the second I opened the front door for him. He shrugged out of his coat and handed it to me.

"Is that why you're here because I didn't invite you."

He went into my kitchen and I followed after hanging up his coat. "Got any coffee? Mallory has me cutting out baby chicks and spring flowers for a bulletin board in her classroom. Brain surgery was less labor intensive."

"In the pot. Dad made it just a little while ago."

The weather had improved enough that the snow was gone from the back yard. Dad and Andy were on the deck building a bat house. The sun was bright and they'd shed their heavy coats.

Their project looked like a flat bird house and it was going to be hung on the side of the garage. It was their hope the bats would eat mosquitos and keep our deck free from those pests this summer. I didn't think we would see them–mosquitos or bats–for another few weeks, spring was starting to creep in.

There were also new guests in the garage apartment. A couple from Utah in town looking to buy a house. They left first thing this morning with their Realtor and I hadn't seen them since.

Theo started opening and closing cabinets until he found where the mugs were kept. He filled one with hot coffee. Then he leaned against the counter and faced me.

"This is an intervention," he said.

I sighed, ran a hand over my face. I hadn't slept well since Georgia had been in my bed. I didn't want to wash my sheets because they still smelled like her, but I had to soon.

"Seriously? Only you showed up? I figured at least Smutters and Mav would be here."

He took a sip of coffee. Somehow, he didn't seem to be in a rush. Clearly cutting out paper flowers was worse than an intervention with me. "Your dad tried to talk sense, but he gave up. I think it's because he's too nice. I'm not."

He gave me the patented Theo the Doctor look.

I crossed my arms over my chest. "Okay, asshole. Intervene. On what exactly?"

"On you being an idiot about Georgia. Why hasn't anything he's said sunk in? Or Andy. He's six and know's she's a keeper. Mav wanted her."

I glared.

He rolled his eyes. "For work. Jesus."

"Fine. How am I an idiot?"

"Because you love her and you haven't told her and she's not here."

"And you're an expert on love?"

"No, I'm an expert on being a dumbass. Ask Mallory. It takes one to know one. That's why I got called for this. You're a lot like me."

"Oh?"

"The reason I walked away from being a surgeon and moving here for the quiet life of a small town doctor was because I had a kid on my table who died. I should've felt something. Sadness at the loss of someone so young. Anger for the kid missing out on so much just because he got in a car accident. I compartmentalized all too well."

"That sucks." I never heard the exact reason before.

"You, as a first responder, see sad and horrible shit all the time. Before patients even got to the hospital and someone like me. You have to put those feelings aside."

"Yeah," I agreed.

"Georgia may have worked on the fire department fundraiser, but what you two shared wasn't part of the job. It's okay to feel something for someone."

I leaned a hip on the counter, facing him. "Look, I told Dad and I'll tell you, it was casual between me and Georgia. Nothing more. Remember at Kincaids? You were the one who told me to think with my dick."

"Dick, not heart. You're the one who got his heart involved."

I frowned. "How so?"

"If it was casual, you wouldn't have had her watch Andy. And help your dad. That takes trust."

"I trust her. Why shouldn't I?"

He shook his head. "Of course you should! It's one thing to share your body with her, that's easy. A quick lay is quick for a reason. It's another to share your life. You did, but with conditions."

I scratched my head. "What are you talking about?"

"She was literally part of the family. She loves you. She loves your dad. She loves Andy. She doesn't give a shit that you're a grumpy fuck and that you work ridiculous hours. That you have to get up and leave at any time for an emergency."

What was he getting at? "Okay."

"You gave her everything except the one thing she needed to stay."

"I got the hot water heater fixed."

He rolled his eyes. "Jesus, you're worse than I ever was. It's not fucking hot water."

I tossed my hands up. "Fine, what is it?"

"*Your* love."

"I don't–"

He held up a hand. "Don't lie. If you didn't care for her, you wouldn't be moping and be a grumpy fuck. If you didn't give a shit about her, you wouldn't remember her name. Or need your dad *and* me to help you get your head out of your ass."

I sighed.

"Did you tell her how you feel? Did you tell her and she turned you down?"

I thought back. "I told her... I told her I hadn't met the right woman yet."

He stared at me like I just told him I drank bleach because I wanted to clean out my insides.

He set his mug down and put his hands on his hips. "To her face. You told Georgia TO HER FACE you hadn't met the right woman yet?"

"Yes. We were in bed and–"

I'd been in bed with her. She'd been naked, a pink flush on her skin because I'd fucked a few orgasms out of her.

"And?"

I thought for a second. "And then I added that Hunter Valley had everything I could ever want."

"Then what did she do? Kick you in the nuts? You were in bed with a woman and told her you hadn't met the right one yet and the only one you'd find would be in Hunter Valley, where she wasn't going to be. As if *she* wasn't The Woman. Do you see what you did there?"

I frowned. Nodded.

"Of course she left town. She left because you told her the right woman for you is out there and it's not her." He closed his eyes and shook his head. "Jesus, you're the king of dumbasses. Seriously, you get the crown."

Crown.

"Oh fuck," I said, running a hand down my face again. My whiskers rasped against my palm and I didn't remember the last time I shaved. "Her smile. It's a pageant smile."

"What's a pageant smile?"

She gave me a clue that night we had spaghetti and meatballs. "It's a smile you paste on when you're in a pageant. She said you smile even when you're nervous. It's fake, hiding everything you don't want people to see."

I laughed, but it wasn't fucking funny.

"How many times had she pasted that gorgeous fucking smile on for me when she felt anything but happy?"

All those times—including in bed when I told her

unintentionally that she wasn't the woman for me–she'd smiled brilliantly. She'd dazzled me into thinking everything was fine with her.

"Did you ever even ask her to stay?"

I shook my head and now I was starting feel a little sick. I ran a hand over the back of my neck. "She asked me. She asked me if I wanted her to stay."

He winced. "Fuck, I'm scared to find out what you said. It can't be good."

"She told me she got the job. I thought she meant in Denver, so I told her she should take it." I tossed my hands up. "That's what she wanted!"

Now that he was analyzing the hell out of everything I said to Georgia, I should have kept my trap shut.

"She's career driven?" he asked. "Got her eye on the top of the corporate ladder at James Corp?"

I shook my head. "No. She worked as an assistant at the same PR firm as her ex so they could work together. She wanted a baby."

"She wanted a *family*, but never got it with her ex. So she comes here, meets you and your family and surprise! She meshes right in. You three are everything she wants. And she helped you deliver Lindy's baby."

No wonder she'd been crying after. It'd been fucking cruel. All of this had.

"Fuck," I muttered, looking down at my work boots.

"Yeah, fuck. So do you think she really wants the job?"

I nodded. "I do. I mean, she needs one since she's divorced. Mav wants her and based on her work on the calendar, it's a good fit."

"But her dream is a family. She asked if you wanted her to be a part of it and you told her no. You told her to take the job."

"Yeah. I thought... I thought it was in Denver at the corporate office, so you have to lay off me a little bit. She never said it was here. The first time I learned it was in Hunter Valley was at Mav's the other night. I didn't want to hold her back so I said I was only her host because she was in the garage apartment and made garlic bread for all my guests."

He frowned. "I don't know what the hell the garlic bread thing means. But if a woman asks if you want her to stay, it means she wants to stay and wants you to tell her you want her to stay." He ran a hand over his face. "Fuck, I don't think that made any sense. How about this? Did you want her to stay? Do you want her to be here with you *not* in the garage apartment?"

"Yes."

Yes. I did. I'd wanted her to stay. I'd wanted her to want me. Us. I'd wanted her to choose me, choose Andy. To love us all. And I fucked it all up.

She'd stood there and asked me if I wanted her and I said no. Like a dumbass.

"I haven't seen you afraid of anything. Why are you so afraid of Georgia?"

I sighed. "People leave, Theo. My mom. Even though I know it's stupid because she died but missing her hurts. Tracy, my sister, she didn't choose us. Man, when she took off and left us, left Andy, that cut deep. I know Dad puts on a good face, but it's tough for him. Then Teri, she was an ex. She didn't want Andy. Georgia walked through the security area in all her high-maintenance perfection, pulling a pink suitcase and wearing high heels. I swear, that lipstick color she wears works like Viagra."

"So you thought it was better to keep her away than let her in since you knew she was leaving."

I nodded.

I was so afraid of people leaving me that I never gave Georgia a chance to stick. That it was easier to recognize that they probably wouldn't. Georgia had said she wasn't staying. That was her plan. But if what Dad and Theo said was true, she fell in love with me. With us.

In the time she was here, she became one of us. She blended into our lives seamlessly in no time at all. Unlike what Andy said about pooping, sometimes it *didn't* take a while. Sometimes it was fast, too fast.

She gave us—me—everything and in return, I didn't.

She would've stayed. Yet, I let her go. My fear sent her away.

"So, do you want her here in Hunter Valley? With you?"

"Yes."

"Did you tell her that?"

FUCK! "No."

"Then there you have it. It's official. You wear the dumbass crown."

71

MAC

KING OF THE DUMBASSES. That was me. I could run into a burning building, but I couldn't open up my heart.

While Theo drank his coffee, I went to the window and stared out at Dad and Andy working on the bat box. The crown GG made him looked really sad after over a week, but Andy still wore it.

The crown meant love. Georgia's love for Andy and him not taking it off showed me he loved her in return. Missed her. I was jealous of a six-year-old on how he could give his love so freely, so unconditionally. It had literally been love at first sight for him.

Maybe it had been with me as well. Seeing her at the airport and fucking BAM! I wanted her in my life. And she kept popping into it. Being the renter of the garage apartment. The organizer of the fire department fundraiser. Even Dad's broken foot. Over and over again, she was put in my path. Yet, I fucked up every chance. Every single one.

Because what I gave to Georgia had been conditional. I put boundaries on it and I could see now that love couldn't be confined. It couldn't be controlled. Just like Georgia herself.

Did I want to stay in my safe, controlled, in charge life and be alone, or did I want to let Georgia rule my world again?

It was time to find out.

I opened the back door. Andy and Dad looked up from their hammering.

"You want Georgia to be your new mom?"

For the first time in over a week, Andy's face brightened and he smiled. He dazzled with the joy that came from loving someone else.

Fuck, Andy was the smart one. And he was six.

"Yes!" he said, jumping up and down.

"Then let's go get her."

"It's about damned time," Dad muttered, but he was smiling.

Andy ran up to me and hugged my legs. "I told you she was the one."

"Now we just have to get to Georgia. In Georgia."

Theo came over and slapped me on the shoulder. "Good thing you know someone with a plane."

72

GEORGIA

Sassy was over for dinner. Since the weather was nice, we were eating on the patio. Momma's house was a large old house in the original part of Calhan. The houses were stately, set back from the road that was lined with live oaks, Spanish moss dangling from the branches. Thick lilac bushes separated back yards, although it was typical southern nature to be in everyone else's business.

Tommy and Sally Ann were in their bathing suits, running through the sprinkler. Joining them were Keely's boys, hooting and hollering and having a grand time. When I found out Sassy was coming, I'd texted Keely for some BFF support. Her husband, Johnny, was at the bowling alley for league night and Troy, Sassy's husband, was at work still.

Dinner was over but we hadn't yet brought out the sliced fruit and sherbet.

Ever since my little chat with Momma the day before, she'd been quieter. Perhaps that was because she was practicing the *if you don't have anything nice to say, don't say anything at all.* Which only proved she never said much that was nice.

But she was trying and I appreciated that. But it was stifling–and not just because of the heat–staying with her. I was too old to live at home. I was eager to get my half of the money from the house sale and move out. I felt as if I was stuck waiting.

For what, I didn't know. I'd gone to Montana to move on, to escape my life, but it only got me right back where I started.

The doorbell rang.

"I'll get it," Momma said. "I saw the marching band going door to door earlier and I'll give them a donation. Then we'll have dessert."

"Is that a new lipstick color?" Sassy asked when Momma had gone inside. Her blonde hair was in perfect curls over her shoulders. Her Lily Pulitzer outfit was a striking pink and green and the pearls at her ears matched the choker around her neck.

I licked my top lip as if that helped me remember. "Oh, um. No. It's clear lip gloss."

"Clear?" she asked. She looked so stunned by the concept. This, to her, was one step up from lip balm.

I nodded. "Yes, I think the shine is nice, don't you?"

Keely, sitting next to me, grabbed my chin and turned my face toward her. Studied my lips. "You'll have to tell me the brand. It looks good."

"Um, Georgia," Momma said from the doorway. She, too, looked picture perfect, also wearing a dress, although she skipped the green. It wasn't a good color on her and she knew it. "There's someone here to see you."

I looked to Keely and being best friends since we were six, we didn't have to say out loud that we both thought it might be Art.

I stood. If I was going to confront him, I'd do it out front, although Momma probably wouldn't want me to air my dirty laundry on the walkway for the neighbors to witness.

But it wasn't Art and he wasn't on the front porch.

It was Mac. And he was here.

"Miss GG!"

With Andy.

Oh my sweet Lord.

73

MAC

GEORGIA STOOD AND STARED. I stared right back.

Besides naked, I hadn't seen her in anything but thick winter clothes. Now she was in a pretty sundress. Her shoulders were bare and it had pretty flowers all over it. Her hair was in the usual lush curls past her shoulders and her lips were shiny as fuck.

She looked beautiful.

And stunned.

Andy ran to her and wrapped her in a hug. He wore the crown she made him, although the foil was ripped in a spot and one of the points was bent down. The two short flights to and from Disney in California were nothing in comparison to the trip to Georgia, but I sure as hell appreciated the James Corp jet.

Holy fuck, was that handy.

She squatted down and hugged him right back. Good and fierce.

"Miss GG, you're gonna be my new mom! I told you!"

The woman who'd answered the door–clearly Georgia's mother–gasped. "Georgia Lee Gantry, please introduce us to your friends."

Georgia stood and looked down at Andy with a smile. This wasn't one of those pageant fake jobs, but a real one. Now that I was onto her, it was really fucking obvious. She was really glad to see Andy. Me? I wasn't so sure. Not yet.

"Momma, this is Andrew MacKenzie and his son, Andy. Mac, this is my mother, June, my sister, Sassy, and my good friend, Keely. Over in the sprinkler are my niece and nephew and Keely's three sons."

"Sprinkler?" Andy asked, whipping around so fast I'd have a crick in my neck. "Can I play?"

Keely stood and went to Andy. "You sure can!" she said with a thick southern accent. "Just go right over there and leave those shoes and socks. You can take off your shirt, too. We're fixin' to have some dessert soon, but y'all keep right on playing."

Andy dashed over to where Keely pointed, a patio

chair with a pile of towels and stripped down to his shorts, carefully setting his crown down. Off he ran to the sprinklers where the kids made swift introductions and were running and playing like best friends in all of five seconds.

Keely went to stand beside Georgia. She was still staring at me. "Is this the guy?" she asked, her voice low, but not low enough.

Georgia nodded.

"Well, I'll be dipped and rolled in cracker crumbs," Keely murmured.

That was a phrase I'd never heard before. Georgia had tossed a y'all out there a time or two, but she didn't have the strong accent or phrases like her best friend.

"Yeah, G, what's going on?" Sassy asked. Now I could see why Georgia thought she was inferior to her older sister.

The woman was insanely pretty. Every hair was in place. Every long curl was perfect. I'd never seen eyebrows arched like two perfect rainbows. I didn't see a pore on her face. Her pink and green outfit was blinding, but a dead man couldn't miss how skinny she was. She looked like... a mannequin.

"What is this about the little boy saying you're his new mom?" June asked, clearly flustered. I probably couldn't blame her. Andy was the least subtle person in the world.

"Ma'am, I'm from Hunter Valley and I've had the

pleasure of getting to know your daughter." I couldn't take my eyes off of Georgia.

I could have sworn Keely say *the pleasure's G's,* but she covered it with a cough.

Keely came over to me, not Georgia. "Mac, you must sit. You've come a long way and we want to hear *all* about you, so don't leave anything out."

"I thought I might talk to Georgia alone."

Keely shook her head. "Nope, not happening."

I let Keely lead me to a chair, thankfully right beside Georgia. We were only a foot apart. I looked to her. She looked to me.

"Hi," I whispered.

"Sit," Keely said, practically kicking me behind the knees so I would drop into the chair.

Georgia settled beside me.

While the kids screamed and played in the sprinkler, the grilling from three southern women began. But all I had interest in was the fourth.

GEORGIA

MAC WAS HERE. Here. In Calhan.

Andy, too. And he said I was to be his new mom now. *And* he was wearing the crown I made him.

It wasn't like at the airport when Mac hadn't been in on it. But now he was.

My heart was racing and I was thankful for my pageant times now. Every single second of practice because I sat calm and collected, not shaking and sweating and climbing in his lap.

The one thing about southern women is that they wanted to know more about any situation than the people in it. We were nosy and the biggest bunch of busybodies.

When a man as handsome as Mac showed up on Momma's doorstep with a son telling everyone I was his new mom, the vultures circled, then settled around their prey.

Mac.

The questions came out, rapid fire, with expert precision. For once, Keely was on the same side as Sassy and Momma. They all wanted to know about Mac. Of course, Keely knew everything and Sassy and Momma knew nothing. I hadn't mentioned him to them at all.

For obvious reasons, because I was the one who would have been circled and questioned if they knew I'd had a fling with a Montana fireman.

"What do you do in Hunter Valley?" Keely began, even though she knew the answer. It was a warmup question.

"Fire chief."

"How old is your son?" Momma asked.

"Six."

"Where is your wife?" Sassy asked.

"Not married."

Mac shifted a little in his chair, but he didn't squirm.

"Divorced?"

"No."

Sassy and Momma gasped at the same time.

"Widowed?" Their sympathy for those who lost a spouse went deep.

"No."

"Then you don't know how to use birth control?"

It was my turn to gasp. "Momma!"

"Andy is my nephew. My sister chose drugs over him and now he's mine."

That shut Sassy and Momma up for a few seconds.

"And the rest of your family?"

"I have my father who lives around the corner."

"Is he married?" Keely asked.

"Widowed."

"Oh, Mrs. Gantry, he might be just the thing," Keely added.

Momma blushed furiously for a moment, then got the serious look back. She wouldn't be deterred and had no interest in a man who wasn't in Georgia.

"What size shoe do you wear?" Sassy prodded.

Mac frowned but answered. "Twelve."

Sassy looked to Keely. Keely looked to Momma. Momma looked to Sassy. I knew what they were thinking. Big shoe size, big–

"Do you rent or own?"

"Own."

"Did you play football?"

"High school."

That was Momma's question. She and Sassy took turns, one right after the other, not giving Mac time to think.

"Baseball?"

"T-ball only."

"Do you eat meat?"

"Yes."

"401k?"

"Yes, and pension, too."

This line of questioning was getting a little ridiculous. I wanted to interrupt, but a strange man showed up on the doorstep and they needed to vet him how they felt best. Even if it was batshit crazy.

"How do you know Georgia?"

"From the fundraiser project and her being the tenant in my garage apartment."

"Do you work out?"

"Yes."

"Are you a Baptist?"

What in the world?

"No."

"Why aren't you married?"

"I was an idiot when I found the right woman."

"I'm sorry, what?" That was me. I asked that.

He turned to me, looked me straight in the eye and said, "I was an idiot."

"Why?" Keely asked, smiling. I saw it out of the corner of my eye.

If she had popcorn, she'd be eating it right now. She was pushing him when she knew I wasn't going to.

Because I was stunned. Mac was here. And he *was* an idiot.

"Because when you asked me if I wanted you to stay, I should have said yes. When I said I wanted you to take the job, I should have said you already had one with me. As... hopefully, my woman and Andy's mom."

Momma gasped.

Sassy didn't say a word.

Keely was squealing.

I smiled. Big. Bright. Dazzling.

75

MAC

I TOOK Georgia's hand and pulled her to her feet. "Oh no, you don't. Not that pageant smile. Not this time." I looked around the table. "If you'll excuse us."

I glanced toward the grass where Andy was happy playing with the other kids.

"I'll watch him," Keely offered, reading my mind. He seemed fine, but we were someplace new and with strangers.

And then I pulled Georgia inside.

The air conditioning was on and the house was at least ten degrees colder than outside. No one I knew in Hunter Valley had it. It didn't get hot enough to need it. If it did, it cooled off at night, which was exactly how I liked it. This? This pea soup of weather in April? I couldn't handle it.

The sooner I got Georgia back to Hunter Valley with me, the faster I could be out of the crazy weather.

First, I had to grovel.

Once the door was closed behind us, I dropped Georgia's hand. I didn't think she'd run. At least not out the back door. Maybe the front, but I didn't think she'd get far without breaking an ankle in those heeled sandals.

"You came all this way to–"

"To tell you I don't want you to smile at me when you're angry with me," I said. "I don't want you to smile at me when you're sad. Or unhappy. Or nervous. I don't want you to smile at me unless you mean it."

I pointed at her.

"See? Right now. You're so fucking unhappy and yet you've got that gorgeous smile."

I hadn't even realized I was doing it. That I had a pageant smile pretty much frozen on my face. I let it slip, then fall away.

He nodded. "Yes. That. I want that from you. The real Georgia. I want you to fight with me while I fight for you, okay?"

"What?" I whispered.

Fight for me?

"I'm here to tell you I'm sorry. To say I'm an idiot. To tell you Dad and Theo and everyone else think I'm one, too. To tell you I love you."

76

GEORGIA

HE LOVED ME.

Tears filled my eyes. I hadn't been crazy falling for him so quickly because he'd been falling right along with me.

The back door opened and Momma came in, looked at us and didn't look the least bit contrite when she said, "I came to get some... some napkins."

No, she came to snoop.

I frowned through my tears. Mac said he loved me and she wanted to interrupt?

It was my turn to take Mac's hand. I tugged him across the first floor to the staircase and up to my room. I shut the door behind us.

"Sorry... um, you were saying?"

Mac looked around at the large floral wallpaper, pink bedspread, standing mirror, taking it all in. But not for long. His gaze landed on mine and it was searing.

"I love you."

He gave me a soft smile, unlike the first time he said it, when he seemed to be focused, as if he'd practiced what he'd say the entire flight here.

Maybe he had.

I was used to practicing speeches and what he said would've won over the judges. It was winning over me.

What was better to hear than *I love you?*

His eyes widened as if he remembered something and he held up a hand. "Stay here. Don't move."

I nodded.

He raised a brow as if doubting me.

"Okay."

He spun around and ran out of my room, stomped down the stairs, then ran right back up. He shut the door again, then dropped a travel bag.

He grabbed something from it and brought it back to me. "Here," he said, a little out of breath.

I blinked. In his hands was a–

I started crying. Real tears. Real ugly tears.

"It's a crown," he said, as if I couldn't tell. "For you. You're the winner, Georgia Lee Gantry. You win my heart. There's no runner up. No competition at all."

"But–" I said, holding my hand over my mouth to try to stop crying.

"You were it for me the minute you came into the baggage area at the airport. Andy knew it then. I think I did, too, but I fought how I felt for you the entire time you were in Hunter Valley."

"You... you didn't want strings."

He shook his head. "It seems I like to use being a grumpy asshole as a way to protect myself. I'm also used to women leaving so since I knew you weren't sticking, so I tried to keep it casual. I thought it would be safest. Dumb, huh?"

I bit my lip and nodded, trying to will my tears away. "Yeah, dumb."

"That night you were packing, why didn't you tell me the job was in Hunter Valley?" he asked, his voice deep but soft. No Mr. Grumpy now.

I swallowed, wiped my face. Sniffed. "Because I couldn't be in the same town with you and not have you. I couldn't do that again, especially since I love you and I–"

He stepped close, setting his hands on my waist, looked at me in a way I'd never seen before. Awe. "You love me?"

I sniffed again, looked up at him through watery eyes. "Do I need to drag you into the laundry room to prove it?"

"You can just wear this." He held up the crown, clearly made by hand and a little crushed from being in a bag. It was just like the one I made for Andy, but there were little plastic jewels glued to each point. On the front, in black marker and in a six-year-old's neat penmanship: GG.

I tipped my head down and Mac set it in place. It was the first crown I ever got and now, looking back, the one I'd always been waiting for.

And this time, it was Mac who smiled. Dazzling and perfect. Because he knew, with me accepting the crown, that I was his.

Then, he leaned down and kissed me.

77

MAC

S<small>HE WASN'T KNEEING</small> me in the nuts! No! She was kissing me back. Sure, I'd kissed the hell out of her in the past, but this was different. This time, Georgia was mine. I felt it in the kiss, and I showed her how I felt for her with my mouth. With my hands around her.

Fuck, I'd missed her. This. Holding her. Knowing she was safe, that she was with me and that she was mine.

I now could see what Theo meant. What Dad meant. What every single person who gave me a weird look in the past week about Georgia being gone probably thought.

How the hell had I ever thought I could let her go?

My hands began to roam, sliding beneath the hem of

her sundress to cup her ass. I felt the cool satin of her panties and I squeezed.

I couldn't get enough. Couldn't get close enough.

Her hands were on my chest and drifting lower, too. In a second, she'd find out how hard I was for her. How I wanted to bend her over her childhood bed and make her shout Hallelujah like a good Southern Baptist would.

I'd make her see God, too.

My very dirty thoughts were going to have me smote dead or whatever the Biblical term was for wanting to defile her in her mother's house, but I was willing to take the risk.

"Mac, I need—"

"Yes," I breathed, my dick hard and aching to get in her.

A stampede of wildebeests, or a group of kids, stomped up the steps. Georgia's mother's place was an old sprawling house that hadn't seen much updating in the past fifty years. The wood staircase was solid and could stand the test of time, and a bunch of children.

We stepped apart a second before the door burst open. I shifted Georgia in front of me so the kids wouldn't get an eyeful of the hard dick outlined in my jeans.

"Ew, gross."

"Gag, they were kissing."

"Yuck."

"Just wait!" Andy said to them. "Their love's going to overflow any second and they're going to make a baby!"

I looked down at the six little faces, then up at Georgia.

Next, Keely stuck her head in and caught on that Georgia was standing strategically in front of me. Her gaze drifted to the hem of Georgia's dress and she hastily smoothed it down, not realizing it had been folded up on the side. She grinned. "Kids, c'mon out of there. That man's got a size twelve shoe and your Aunt Georgia's gonna see if it fits."

They turned right on around and ran out the door beneath her arm, all except for Andy. He stayed and stared up at us with all the hope and eagerness I saw on his face at the airport.

"She's wearing the crown!" he said excitedly.

"I guess I never asked... come back to Hunter Valley?" I asked, then held my breath.

"Do you want me to stay?"

This was the question she asked me that night in the garage apartment. The one I fucked up. "YES!" I shouted. "The answer I should've said the last time was yes."

She nodded and grinned, then pointed at her mouth. "A real smile and my answer is yes."

I smiled too and felt the relief course through me like adrenaline on a fire scene. "Take the job with James Corp?"

"Yes."

I turned her to face me, so she could see the intent in my eyes. The truth that was there. "Be mine. And Andy's. And Dad's? Georgia Lee Gantry, will you be ours?"

She glanced down at Andy, who was eagerly waiting.

"Is that okay with you?" she asked him.

He nodded and hopped from foot to foot with his excitement.

She looked back to me, happiness lighting her eyes and giving me a real fucking smile. "Then yes. I will be you yours."

Andy jumped up and down and whooped while he dripped water from the sprinkler all over the floor.

"I knew it would work," Andy said, fist pumping the air. "They said the whole makematching thing would work!"

I stared at Andy and tried to understand what he was saying. With a glance to Georgia, I wanted to see if she did. We were both clueless.

"Bud, *makematching*?"

He nodded at my question, his hair dripping water down the sides of his face. "Yes, when grownups play a game to make two people fall in love."

Now Georgia and I looked at each other, trying to figure out what he meant.

Then her eyes widened in surprise. "*Matchmaking*?" she asked.

What? Someone tried to put us together? That made no sense.

"Yes!" Andy said, pointing at Georgia. "That! It worked!"

I ran a hand over my face, then leaned down and set a hand on Andy's bare shoulder. "Andy, who was playing this game? Which grownups?"

Andy beamed, clearly not realizing that he'd shared a very big secret.

"Grumpy said Mr. Maverick, the big guy with the dog and a man named badly were playing the game and we were going to help."

"A man named badly?" I asked, looking to Georgia. What the hell?

She blinked. "*BRADLEY?*" she said, a little too loudly.

"Yes!" Andy confirmed.

"Is that–" I began.

Georgia's eyes narrowed and she set her hands on her hips. I didn't remember seeing her angry before, but the look was a little scary, maybe because it was coming from someone so damned nice all the time. "Bradley and Maverick played matchmaker?" She huffed. "My cousin is in serious trouble."

78

GEORGIA

FIFTEEN MINUTES LATER, Sassy left with Tommy and Sally Ann. Keely took her brood home but gave me a thumbs up on the way out the door. Momma was downstairs with Andy. Together, they were making cookies, even though Momma had prepared a different dessert which we didn't get to eat. Andy had taken to her like a bee to a flower, even though she was a little prickly. But having a grumpy father must've given Andy coping skills because he was handling her like a pro. He could man handle anyone, that kid never knowing a stranger. Plus, he loved cookies.

Mac and I were in my room. Officially, we were alone. Sorta. We had two chaperones downstairs, but I doubted they'd disturb us, especially since I caught Mac locking the door. The kiss earlier, and the time apart, made me eager to try on his size twelve shoe.

But we had something to tackle first. Like finding out what some people had been up to.

I had a video call pulled up on my laptop and I'd gotten Bradley, Maverick and Drew in a meeting room. Mac and I were in a little box on the screen. We were side by side on my bed leaning against the white Sears headboard. The pink pillow shams and floral wallpaper couldn't be missed in the background.

Thank the Lord this wasn't a business call.

The others were in their own little video windows. They had to know why we'd texted and told them to get on this group call. Therefore, there was to be no southern chitchat that was a polite start to a conversation. I was going straight to the point.

"Did y'all play matchmaker?" I asked.

"Yes," they said at the same time.

There wasn't any lying or waffling. They admitted it outright.

"I told you she'd find out!" a woman called. It sounded like Bridget and it was coming from off screen. So she knew, too.

I glanced at Mac out of the corner of my eye.

"Explain," he said, staring at the laptop screen.

Bradley started. "A while ago, Theo told me about

Mac, how they worked together on the fire trainings. Then I met him back in the fall when I was in Hunter Valley."

"At the party for Theo and Mallory," Mac said, confirming Bradley's statement.

Bradley nodded.

I didn't know when that was, but the details of the event were probably irrelevant. But they met.

"I thought you two would be perfect for each other. Coincidentally, you just found out about Art and you needed a man who wasn't an asshole in your life. I confirmed personally that Mac is not an asshole."

"Thanks," Mac said at the odd compliment.

"An idiot, or at least dense since it seems you're *finally* together, but not an asshole," he corrected.

"Yeah, um, true, and thanks," Mac said again, rubbing the back of his neck.

"That was months ago," I reminded.

Bradley nodded. "I know. Bridget is tackling the philanthropic arm of James Corp and has been working on a list of ways to support and grow Hunter Valley. Like the small business grants. It was Theo, though, who mentioned the fire department fundraiser. He knows about it because of the trainings."

"This is where I come in," Maverick said. "Bradley told me about you, Georgia. The situation you were in. He thought, instead of a lower earning fundraiser, he suggested it as a way to grow income for the kids' club, merging the James Corp community donations with it."

"You brought the idea of switching the charity to me," Mac said.

Maverick nodded. "Yes, but the fundraiser resource was added on."

"You made the job for me to go to Montana to meet Mac?" I asked. That seemed a little far-fetched, but it seemed exactly what they did.

"In one sentence, yes," Bradley said.

"This is insane!" I was indignant. Hurt. "Did I get the job because of my abilities or because I was the only applicant?"

"Both," Maverick and Bradley said at the same time.

"I... I wanted a job because I'm good," I said. Mac wrapped his arm around me and pulled me close.

"You are good, G," Bradley said, emphatically. He looked me square in the eye. "There was no way I would have suggested this avenue to get you both together if I didn't think it would work. I'd never set you up for failure. In fact, based on the way Mac wants to kill me with his eyes and has his arm around you, it seems we were successful."

Mac wanted to beat Bradley up because I was feeling upset and he wanted to hold me and know I wasn't alone. So yeah, they were successful. Still...

I waved my hand in the air. "Irrelevant."

"Georgia, do you think I would hire someone unqualified to represent James Corp? You were my resource, my representative on this project with the town. Your work attitude, effort and abilities reflected on me."

When he put it that way...

"So I got the job and came to Hunter Valley," I said, moving the story along.

"And got on the same plane as Dad and Andy," Mac added.

"That was me," Bradley admitted.

"I knew it!" I said, sitting up and pointing at the screen.

"And he put you up in my garage rental," Mac added.

"Again, me."

"I told you, Bradley. I figured you were up to something that first day when I called you. You denied it."

"I did and I'm not sorry," he said in his usual, precise way. "You hadn't fallen in love yet. Or you had and definitely weren't admitting it."

"The flight, the rental, the job, it was all to put me with Mac?" I was amazed. This was more coordinated than the pulling the calendar together.

"The calendar idea was unexpected," Bradley admitted, the corner of his mouth tipping up. "So was both of you being so stubborn."

"So was Lindy having Justine while you were over their house for dinner," Maverick added.

"And Dad?" Mac asked. "You didn't break his foot on purpose."

Drew had been quiet until now.

"Of course not," he said. "I will say it helped and that was the only perk of this stupid boot."

"How did you get Andy to keep the secret all this time?" Mac asked.

That was a good question. That little guy had zero filter talking about nipples and toy submarines without a bit of embarrassment.

"Oh, he didn't know anything about it," Drew said. "Not until he was in the car with me and Ralph. Ralph asked how it was going and Andy asked after what *make-matching* was. Out of everyone, he was the most genuine in his feelings for you, Georgia. I hope you know you had more than one man fall in love with you." He cleared his throat.

Tears filled my eyes because he wasn't only talking about Andy.

"I fell in love with three Andrew MacKenzies," I admitted.

He smiled. I smiled. A real one.

If I started crying again, I wasn't sure if I could stop, so I stayed on topic. "Back to the fundraiser. With your talent for organization and planning us getting together,

I don't know why I was needed for the fundraiser. Y'all could do it by yourselves."

"Because Bradley said I needed you at James Corp," Maverick explained. "He was right. I wouldn't have my new Hunter Valley-based PR director otherwise, now would I?"

"Oh dear Lord," I said, putting a hand on my cheek, then glanced at Mac. He'd been quiet for most of this, most likely trying to come to terms with several people conspiring behind our backs.

We'd been set up in secret in a very big, very planned way.

"They put us together," I said. If it wasn't for them, we never would have met. I sure as hell wouldn't have taken a job in far off Montana.

I wasn't sure if he was angry or not.

For a second.

Then Mac smiled. "Yeah, they sure did."

Then he shut the lid on the laptop, ending the call, and kissed me.

79

MAC

HOLY HELL, we'd been fixed up. Not a simple blind date, but serious planning had gone into it. The plane, the apartment, the fundraiser. All of it.

I wasn't mad at the guys. In fact, I owed them a beer or two.

Because without their meddling, I wouldn't have met Georgia. And that would have been a fucking shame.

I moved the laptop out of the way, then pulled her onto my lap so she straddled me. The bottom of her pretty dress billowed around us and I took advantage and slid my hands up her bare thighs to cup her ass cheeks again. I liked summer clothing on her, and the easy access.

"You're not upset?" she asked as I kissed along her jaw, tilting her head for me to have better access.

"No. Not at all," I said, making my way to her neck. "I'm taking you home. Back to Hunter Valley and my bed. Andy was right. I tried it and liked it."

I found the little tie at the back of her neck and–yes! The entire top of her dress dropped to her waist. I was sure there was some name for it, but it was definitely invented by a man who loved his woman's tits and wanted to get to them as easily as possible.

"Are you upset?" I asked. They had organized a job specifically to get her to Montana and me and I worried she'd feel devalued for that. I wouldn't blame her.

She shook her head as I cupped her tits in her strapless bra. "No," she whispered. "God, no. Amazed. The only thing I would change..." she began, but stopped when I undid the bra and flung it aside.

"Is?" I asked as I played with her nipples, watching them harden. Fuck, I loved her tits. Big. Heavy. Full. *Mine.*

Whatever her worry, I'd take care of it. It was my job now to keep her happy and I wasn't stopping. Ever.

"Is my thoughts earlier about fucking in my childhood bedroom."

My hands stilled and I looked in her dark eyes. "You don't want to?"

We were in her mother's house and she and Andy were downstairs.

She set her hands on top of mine and licked her lips. "Oh, I do. I so do. I've never done anything in here like this."

"You didn't play with your toy submarine?" I asked, lifting my head and meeting her eyes.

She smiled, taking one of my hands and sliding it beneath her dress and over her pussy. I could feel how wet she was through her panties.

"Oh, I played with that, but not a man."

"I'm your first?" Hooking her panties to the side, I slid two fingers into her. She clenched around them and my dick was telling me to let him in on the fun. "Fuck."

She began to ride my fingers, her hands going to my shoulders for balance. "Have you... have you ever fooled around in someone's bedroom with their mother downstairs?"

"I did it with you in the laundry room, with Dad and Andy." I watched her closely, seeing how her lids slid lower, her mouth opened and her tits jiggled with every little pant.

"You know what I mean," she whispered, then moaned softly.

Leaning close, I nipped at her neck, then whispered in her ear. "Did I make out in a girlfriend's bedroom in high school? No."

Sure, I fooled around, but with Georgia dripping on my hand, I didn't remember anyone who came before.

"I hope we're not just making out," she whimpered. "Mac, please."

"Oh, hell no," I growled. She was topless, sitting in my lap. Her pussy was pressed against my hard dick and the only thing keeping me from sliding into her were our clothes.

"Good. Don't stop."

"I won't stop if you say it again," I said, leaning down and peppering kisses across the tops of her perfect swells.

"Say what?"

"You love me." I kissed her jaw, slipped my fingers from her and replaced it with my dick at her entrance.

"I love you," she breathed.

"You need me." I kissed her nose, then lowered her onto me.

"Oh, Mac," she said, her eyes falling closed. "I need you."

Fuck, she was tight. Perfect.

"Tell me that, someday, we'll do this and make a baby."

Her eyes flew open, then filled with tears. I wasn't having her cry on my dick. I swiped them away immediately.

"I'm bare, gorgeous. Say you're on birth control, or we could be making that baby right now."

She clenched around me. "I've got an IUD."

For the first time ever, I had a twinge of disappointment and caveman possessiveness, that the first time I took her bare that my boys wouldn't get the job done.

"Then this'll be practice." My hips rocked up, my dick needing to move in her. Fuck, she was so warm and wet and tight and fucking perfect.

"Practice," she agreed, smiling brilliantly. Yeah, that was a real smile.

"Now fuck me." I kissed her mouth, lifting her up and pressing her down on my lap.

"Yes, fuck me," she repeated, looking me in the eye. Yeah. She was mine. "Quietly."

———

The On A Manhunt series isn't done yet!
Get Man Spread next!

BONUS CONTENT

Guess what? I've got some bonus content for you! Sign up for my mailing list. There will be special bonus content for some of my books, just for my subscribers. Signing up will let you hear about my next release as soon as it is out, too (and you get a free book...wow!)

As always...thanks for loving my books and the wild ride!

JOIN THE WAGON TRAIN!

If you're on Facebook, please join my closed group, the Wagon Train! Don't miss out!

https://www.facebook.com/groups/ vanessavalewagontrain/

GET A FREE BOOK!

Join my mailing list to be the first to know of new releases, free books, special prices and other author giveaways.

http://freeromanceread.com

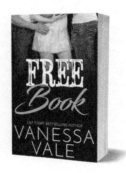

ALSO BY VANESSA VALE

For the most up-to-date listing of my books:

vanessavalebooks.com

On A Manhunt

Man Hunt

Man Candy

Man Cave

Man Splain

Man Scape

Man Handle

Man Spread

The Billion Heirs

Scarred

Flawed

Broken

Alpha Mountain

Hero

Rebel

Warrior

Billionaire Ranch

North

South

East

West

Bachelor Auction

Teach Me The Ropes

Hand Me The Reins

Back In The Saddle

Wolf Ranch

Rough

Wild

Feral

Savage

Fierce

Ruthless

Two Marks

Untamed

Tempted

Desired

Enticed

More Than A Cowboy

Strong & Steady

Rough & Ready

Wild Mountain Men

Mountain Darkness

Mountain Delights

Mountain Desire

Mountain Danger

Grade-A Beefcakes

Sir Loin of Beef

T-Bone

Tri-Tip

Porterhouse

Skirt Steak

Small Town Romance

Montana Fire

Montana Ice

Montana Heat

Montana Wild

Montana Mine

Steele Ranch

Spurred

Wrangled

Tangled

Hitched

Lassoed

Bridgewater County

Ride Me Dirty

Claim Me Hard

Take Me Fast

Hold Me Close

Make Me Yours

Kiss Me Crazy

Mail Order Bride of Slate Springs

A Wanton Woman

A Wild Woman

A Wicked Woman

Bridgewater Ménage

Their Runaway Bride

Their Kidnapped Bride

Their Wayward Bride

Their Captivated Bride

Their Treasured Bride

Their Christmas Bride

Their Reluctant Bride

Their Stolen Bride

Their Brazen Bride

Their Rebellious Bride

Their Reckless Bride

Bridgewater Brides World

Lenox Ranch Cowboys

Cowboys & Kisses

Spurs & Satin

Reins & Ribbons

Brands & Bows

Lassos & Lace

Montana Men

The Lawman

The Cowboy

The Outlaw

Standalones

Relentless

All Mine & Mine To Take

Bride Pact

Rough Love

Twice As Delicious

Flirting With The Law

Mistletoe Marriage

Man Candy - A Coloring Book

ABOUT VANESSA VALE

A USA Today bestseller, Vanessa Vale writes tempting romance with unapologetic bad boys who don't just fall in love, they fall hard. Her books have sold over one million copies. She lives in the American West where she's always finding inspiration for her next story.

vanessavaleauthor.com

- facebook.com/vanessavaleauthor
- instagram.com/vanessa_vale_author
- amazon.com/author/vanessavale
- bookbub.com/profile/vanessa-vale
- tiktok.com/@vanessavaleauthor